CIRCLES IN HELL SERIES

Hell's Super
A Cold Day In Hell
Deal With The Devil
The Reluctant Demon

The Reluctant Demon
(Circles in Hell, Book Four)

by

Mark Cain

ISBN-13: 978-1518769948

ISBN-10: 1518769942

'The Reluctant Demon' is published by Perdition Press, which can be contacted at:

hellssuper@hotmail.com

Cover design by Dan Wolfe (www.doodledojo.co.uk)

To Matt

Chapter 1

The constant, rapid trudge, trudge, trudge as the platoon trekked across the desert landscape was beginning to get to me – mainly because it was boring. To call our hike a trudge was complimenting the activity. It was more a series of plunges into the sand, as a foot would hit the surface, disappear beneath, then be pulled up by its owner, creating a slurp-pop sound more akin to plunging a clogged toilet. Then the next step would be taken, the second foot would sink in similar fashion and have to be slurp-popped out.

There was no sun in the sky – there is no sun in Hell, even in the arid wasteland of the Eighth Circle – but it sure felt like one was baking down on us, and from above there was a glare, enough to make me squint and point my face back toward my feet.

We were all in full pack, which for a demon meant five hundred pounds of dead weight, and this was a two hundred mile hike, at double time. If I hadn't been so intent on keeping my forward momentum, I might have reflected on the absurdity of it. Twenty recruits in a row, forty legs slipping beneath the sand, being popped back out hurriedly, so we could maintain our forty mile an hour pace, a brisk though not impossible speed that demons could maintain indefinitely. The pop-pop-pop sounded like a bubble wrap popping competition.

Things could be worse, I reflected, trying to keep up my spirits, which had been as low as Death Valley – an apt simile considering the circumstances – since I'd been tricked into becoming a demon. My horns and tail had begun to grow in – the tail was almost full size – which meant I had been allowed to abandon my plush demon costume, with its clip-on horns and fabric tush brush, the latter shaking formlessly as I walked. Now I wore what the other recruits had on, a dark blue tunic and red loose-fitting trousers, though no boots, since the drill sergeants were trying to toughen up our soles – if not our souls, which were pretty threadbare at this point – by exposing them to the blistering hot sand. I also had on a fairly smart looking red cap, with a two-inch visor and a piece of fabric hanging from the back of the hat, presumably to protect my neck from the sun. Since there was no sun, though, it was mere affectation. My new pitchfork was resting on my shoulder, like a rifle might have if I were in the French Foreign Legion instead of the Demon Corps.

I, Steve Minion, formerly Hell's Superintendent of Plant Maintenance, was the Underworld's newest recruit to the Corps. A cohort had started at Beast Barracks a week before I'd become a demon, but Satan, not wanting to delay my training, let me join the group late, forcing me to play catch-up. That said, I was holding my own, and then some, with the other, more experienced cadets. In fact, when the sergeants weren't performing their primary function, which was chewing us out, calling us the most miserable excuses for demons they'd ever seen, they'd privately told me I was the most promising new recruit they'd seen in centuries. I was already as strong as a demon, first class, and my strength was increasingly daily. I was also faster than even the most experienced members of the Corps. This last bit didn't surprise me as much as the strength thing; years of slinging duct tape at preternatural speed had me halfway there already.

Still, my natural aptitude in these areas was a bit of a mystery to me. The staff at Beast Barracks was as perplexed by my talents as I was.

And then there was my ability to teleport. The other recruits looked on me with envy, because I was the only one who had signed up during the "limited time offer" and gotten this special ability – very special, since apparently fewer than two dozen creatures in all of the Underworld possessed it. Of course, I wasn't very accomplished with teleportation yet. For example, I couldn't just do it at will. Yet sometimes, when I ate something that disagreed and belched, or when I got a case of the hiccups, I would transport ten or twenty feet. The end result usually left me slammed against a wall or boulder, tripped by an inconveniently placed cot, that sort of thing, but Sarge, the tall demon with primary responsibility for my training, said I'd get control over the ability soon enough. The power would be limited – it was unlikely I'd be able to instantaneously travel more than a mile at a pop – but that was more than almost any demon and even some devils could manage, so that made me something special.

Yep, I was going to make a great demon, just like Satan always said I would. That might have been a point of pride for me, if the consequence of my joining the Corps hadn't severed every relationship I'd built and cherished with a handful of other damned humans down here.

And one, undamned one. Flo, Florence Nightingale, who was in Hell trying to make the Underworld a little bit better place, would no longer have anything to do with me. Well, I didn't know that for a fact, since I hadn't seen her since agreeing to become a demon and being swept up into Beast Barracks for my basic training. Yet Flo loathed demons, perhaps even more than devils. Devils had had no choice in becoming what they were. They were intended to rebel in Heaven and fall to Hell. Demons, though, were generally former humans who elected to become demons of their own free will. Flo found this particularly despicable, that a human would choose to become a demi-devil – which, by the way, may be where the word "demon" came from in the first place, though some people think the word is shorthand for "devil-man" – a stand-in for Satan and the rest of senior management.

In my own defense, I had good reason for agreeing to be a demon. Well. That's not exactly true. It wasn't a good reason, but a stupid if well-intentioned one. I had been a dupe, a patsy. Satan had tricked me into thinking Flo's eternal soul would at best be tortured for all eternity and at worst be destroyed completely if I didn't volunteer for the Corps. To protect my one true love, I joined, not thinking things through carefully. If I had, I would have known that Satan had no power over Flo. He could bury her in as many slings and arrows as he'd like, and she would emerge unscathed.

I should have known that, but like I said, I was conned. My motives were good, but this was a time when letting my heart overrule my head didn't work out very well. Sourly, I reflected that I probably didn't even have a heart anymore. Now that my body was changing to the anatomy of a demon, there was likely some other organ that pumped the yellow ichor that served as demon blood through my veins.

Probably the spleen handles that.

"Pick up the pace, you goldbricks!" yelled one of the sergeants. The overseers of today's hike were traveling quite comfortably in a jeep. "I want to see you hit eighty miles an hour before we crest the next sand dune." He floored the accelerator and took off.

You want us to go fast? I'll show you fast. I kicked up my pace and practically flew across the sand. Shit, maybe I *was* flying. I could do all sort of things that used to be impossible for me.

Soon I was running faster than the jeep. I sped past them at what must have been a hundred miles an hour. My tail, which had been slapping limply against my butt all day with each step I took, was now stretched out behind me. I imagined it looked like an arrow, traveling at high speed but in reverse.

One of the sergeants looked at me in wide-eyed wonder, and I gave him a saucy little salute before leaving the jeep in my dust. I reached the top of the sand dune fifteen seconds before they did. That's when I saw the rock outcropping fifty feet ahead of me. At that moment, a mote of sand got lodged in a nostril, and I sneezed, teleporting the extra distance and plastering myself against the stone.

"Ooh … " I felt a little woozy.

"Break's over!" yelled Sarge, my sarge, who was in the passenger seat of the jeep. "Get back in formation!" The vehicle zipped past me, followed in close order by the line of cadets.

"Show off," said the guy on the end, kicking sand in my face.

Well, I deserved that. Painfully I got to my feet and started running again. In a few seconds, I reached the back of the line, matching my pace with the rest of the crew.

The remainder of the day was spent in pitchfork practice. We started with one-on-one sparring, each trying to pierce the skin of his or her opponent first. I was coming along with the demon weapon-of-choice, but I had a long way to go. I quickly defeated my first partner, a buck-toothed fellow who reminded me of Gomer Pyle. He was probably too dim to realize he'd signed up for an eternity of being the guy in the black hat. I think he just liked the pitchfork. My second opponent, though, was a demon named Maximus. He was a natural fencer, not to mention being near to graduation – due to some pressing need for an additional demon in one of Hell's other circles – and he handled his weapon with a skill that I could only admire if not

11

yet emulate. He also had a longer reach than I had, if not my speed. I tried to use my main advantage to get behind him, but as I swung by his right, he snagged the tines of my pitchfork with those of his own. With a deft flick of his wrist, he twisted the weapon out of my grasp. "Tag!" he said, snickering, as he poked me in my now-exposed side.

"Minion, you miserable maggot!" yelled Sarge. "That's the fourth time you've fallen for that maneuver. You're out of the game. Tomorrow morning, oh four hundred hours, you'll train with me, and I promise that when I'm done with you, you'll never fall for that sucker ploy again." He grinned evilly at me.

Oh, shit. And that's two hours before reveille.

"Go practice transmutation, while the real fencers continue the game."

Discouraged, I walked over to a low wall and sat down. Then I began the transmutation forms I'd been taught. First, my pitchfork became a sword, then a tommy gun, like what Capone or one of his men might have used. After I'd practiced all the mandatory transformations, I was allowed to use my own imagination to come up with new forms. I turned the fork into an umbrella, a belt, which I thought would be a good way to carry it if I wanted to be incognito. I transformed it into a pink feather boa, draping it around my neck and doing a Carmen Miranda impression before a dirty look from Sarge cold-cocked me. Quickly I transformed my pitchfork into something more threatening, a spear.

"Better, maggot!" he said, walking over to me. "But it's easy to change a pitchfork into something with a similar shape. Try one that's completely different."

I nodded and concentrated. The spear collapsed in on itself, becoming a small, plastic container the size of canned peaches. Except it wasn't a can, it was …

12

"A jar of Vaseline? Why the hell did you do that?"

I picked up the jar and opened it, smearing some of the petroleum jelly on my lips. "I really hate chapped lips," I said, mildly embarrassed.

"Wha … ?" Sarge broke out laughing. "You know, maggot, you're all right. For a maggot, that is."

"Thanks, Sarge," I said, blushing slightly, as I returned my jar of Vaseline to its original form.

He wiped a tear from his eye, still chuckling. "Tell me, maggot, do demons always carry their pitchforks?"

"No," I said, thinking back on all the demons I'd ever known, which in over sixty years of being in Hell, had been quite a few. Uphir, the demon physician and chief administrator of Hell's Hospital, for example, never carried his. "Well, some do, I guess, though they look pretty junior. Don't know what the more experienced demon does, but that's why I practiced the belt just now."

He shook his head. "That's not how it's done. Put it someplace else, where no one but you can get at it."

"Where would that be?"

"Figure it out for yourself."

I frowned. I'd seen some demons make their pitchforks appear out of thin air. That seemed to be a clue. I closed my eyes and imagined a little pocket universe that floated around with me, a place I could reach at any time, but that no one else could. Then I took my pitchfork, put it there, and closed up an invisible seam.

There was the sound of applause, and I opened my eyes. "Bravo!" said Sarge. "It takes some demons years to master that little trick."

"Can I put other things in there? Besides my pitchfork?"

"Yeah, a change of clothes, for example. I know one demon who plays the bassoon. He keeps his in his secret place and practices when he's off duty."

A demon bassoonist. Oh boy.

"You're a natural, Minion. I mean, maggot! You're the most talented new demon I've seen in almost two millennia of training you scum."

"Two millennia?" I said, appropriately impressed. "That would make you a pretty early Christian."

"You have no idea," he grumbled. "Oh well, forget about that. What I'm trying to say is, you're talented … but don't let it go to your head!" he said abruptly, realizing he wasn't doing a sergeant's proper job of treating me like shit. "You still have a lot to learn. Now, get back out there and spar some more with your squad."

My pleasure at being praised for being a good little demon wasn't exactly rational. The last thing I'd ever wanted to become was a devil wannabe, yet, here I was, a new recruit. But Sarge's praise had its intended effect; I did a little better afterward, winning two out of three bouts.

Around eighteen hundred hours – or at least what the drill sergeants called eighteen hundred hours, since time really means nothing in Hell, and any reference to days, weeks or hours and minutes for that matter, were all pretty random – we headed to the mess hall. Standing near the back of the line, I grabbed a metal tray and an oversized spoon. Cookie took a large ladle out of a simmering vat and dumped its contents in one of the compartments of my tray. It spread out on the metal, filling the space and nearly overflowing into the next compartment.

I looked with distaste at the thin yellow gruel, punctuated with slightly more yellow larvae moving sluggishly through the boiled oats. Maggot stew for the maggots. I had long since gotten used to it, though. Besides, the stew was filling and nutritious, a good source of protein. It stuck to the ribs, when it wasn't slithering around in my stomach.

Added to my tray was a biscuit filled with nails that, surprisingly, my demon teeth had no trouble chewing, and a quivering mass of green Jello. In some ways, the gelatinous mass was the least appetizing item on my tray. I'd always hated lime Jello.

The food at Beast Barracks didn't fit the promotional brochures. For that matter, our accommodations in general were a far cry from the sun-drenched sandy beach prominently featured in all the PR. Not exactly Club Med. More like Club Dead, I suppose. About the only thing they got right, I thought ruefully, was the sand. Sarge told me the scene I'd experienced in Satan's office, the one with the beach babes and the umbrella drinks, was just a demo, a demon-stration if you will, although he promised that after Beast Barracks, frolicking by the ocean with someone of the nubile persuasion was entirely possible for a demon.

After having my tray loaded for me by Cookie, I went over to the large drum in the corner. I picked up a tin cup and filled it from the spigot sticking out of the barrel. This was my favorite part of the meal: demon rum. It was dark and rich and slightly sweet. It also packed a wallop. One of the things I was enjoying about being a demon was that I could now drink booze and get a little buzz from it, not enough to impair my job performance, from what I'd been told, but enough to mellow me out a little. The thought of a mellow demon seemed oxymoronic, but there you go.

I looked for a place to sit. Most of the tables were full, so I plopped down next to Gomer. In a few seconds, Maximus joined us.

I wasn't the most popular demon at Beast Barracks. My talents had manifested themselves too early, too forcefully also, and most of the others were either envious of or intimidated by me. That suited me fine. I really wasn't looking for friends in the ranks of the demons; I was still mourning the human ones lost upon joining the Corps. That said, I didn't have any particular aversion to my new colleagues. They weren't much different from me, except they'd willingly volunteered, while I'd been tricked into enlisting.

Most people ignored Gomer; as I said earlier, he was a little short on mental wattage, and so not exactly the best conversationalist. He was a simple soul, and my heart, or what would have been my heart, if I'd still had one, went out to him. He smiled at me when I sat down, then went back to consuming his gruel with unusual relish.

Maximus was another matter. Other than me, he was the most talented demon at Beast Barracks, and since he was getting ready to get his orders, he felt himself senior to and at least as good a demon as me. Certainly with a pitchfork, he was better, and that one advantage seemed to be enough for him. We actually got along pretty well.

"Hey, Steve," he said, sitting down next to me. "I loved that little maneuver you did on our hike today, the way you blasted past the jeep."

I smiled wryly. "Thanks, Max. Did you like the part where I slammed into the rock?"

"Yeah!" he said chortling. "That was hysterical."

"Have you gotten your orders yet?" I said, biting a chunk off my hardtack. One of the tacks got stuck between my teeth, and I used one of my carefully cultivated claws to pry it out.

Demons, unlike devils, don't really have claws, but grow their nails out and file them to sharp points to emulate the claws of their superiors.

"Yep. They were waiting for me when we came back from our hike. I'm going up to Four to work for Mammon."

Mammon's domain was a golden reproduction of ancient Rome. It was one of the best assignments in Hell. "Oh, that's fantastic! You'll like it there. Pretty spiffy setup up on Four, and with your pitchfork skills, they'll make you a demon centurion in no time."

He grinned. "Hope so."

I lifted my cup. "A toast to your new assignment. Best of luck with it!"

"Thanks. Hey, Gomer, you want to get in on this?" Apparently my nickname for the goofy little demon had stuck. Still, asking him to join in the toast was a magnanimous gesture on Max's part that was not lost on me.

The other demon looked up from his plate, startled, then seeing what was going on, he raised his drink as well. The three tin cups clanked together, then we all drank down the rest of our rum. Gomer made himself useful and took the empty containers back to the drum and refilled them. Max and I thanked him, and we all settled down to finish our meals in companionable silence.

The movie that evening was 'Sahara,' starring the incomparable Humphrey Bogart and the comparable Lloyd Bridges. I'd seen it many times, and it had never been one of my favorite Bogie films anyway, so I excused myself and headed for my bunk.

I wasn't really tired – it's hard to tire out a demon – but I wanted to be alone. I stretched out on the cot, which was surprisingly comfortable for a piece of canvas supported by a few slats of wood, much more comfortable than the old Murphy bed in my former apartment. Yes, even in the worst demon circumstances, which everyone assured me was Beast Barracks, my afterlife as a demon was much more pleasant than what I'd experienced as a damned human. I could even sleep, if I wanted to, not that demons needed sleep, but I could do it if I was of a mind. Humans never really slept in Hell, but tossed and turned in insomniac misery the whole night through.

Right now, though, I wasn't in the mood for sleeping. I was thinking of all the friends I'd lost by becoming a demon, of Louis Braille, Nikola Tesla and Allan Pinkerton, even of Shemp Howard, Thomas Edison and Henry Ford. The last two were not friends by any means, but they had played a part in my damned afterlife, and I missed them. Of course, Orson was frequently on my mind. I wondered how he was doing as the new Hell's Super, and if that role was a better or worse damnation for him. Flo popped into my head constantly, but I tried not to think about her. It simply hurt too much.

And of course I thought about Lilith. She may have been a succubus, but she was also my friend. Since a succubus was a demon, she was really one of the few people in Hell I could continue to have a relationship with.

A relationship. Yes, our friendship had become a little more intimate of late. As I thought about Lilith, my mind went back to my first night as a demon, before I'd checked into Beast Barracks.

Chapter 2

As the door to Lilith's two-story Colonial closed behind me, I had a feeling of dread, like I'd just received an audit notice from the IRS. If so, though, Lilith, in her sexy homemaker dress, three buttons open at the top, was the most appealing government worker I'd ever seen, so all in all, things could have been worse.

"Come over to the bar, darling," she said, escorting me gently but firmly by the elbow, as if I were a blind man in need of assistance. If I were a blind man, though, the smell of her pheromonal presence would have been plenty to keep me on course.

Lilith had a completely equipped wet bar in one corner of the living room. The bar was a pretty spiffy affair: a stainless-steel sink, a fridge for ice and beer, one of those fancy wine chiller boxes like what you'd see in a Hammacher Schlemmer catalog, cocktail glasses and an impressive array of bartending equipment, and a rack full of upside-down wine glasses. Not to mention limes, olives, other garnishes – and a whole lot of booze.

The sexy succubus – well almost by definition all succubi are sexy, I mean, who's ever heard of an unsexy one – was focused on a crystal pitcher full of cloudy liquid. She was stirring things up with a glass stick – there's probably a name for those things, but I've never learned what it is.

When the drink was a uniform pink, she sighed with pleasure. "Perfect!" she purred, filled a couple of collins glasses with ice and poured the contents of the pitcher into the glasses. I looked with suspicion at Lilith's favorite cocktail, the crackhead slammer, a combination of cinnamon schnapps, peppermint schnapps and Dr. Pepper. I'd never had one, and the combination of flavors promised to be nastiness incarnate.

Keeping a glass for herself, Lilith handed the other to me, then led me to the patio out back. She took a seat on the chaise lounge she'd reclined on earlier in the day, when I'd first discovered her home in the suburbs, and I resumed my previous post in the chair next to her.

So far I had said nothing. My emotions were a muddle of shock, despair, loss and anger, some of it directed at her, since she'd been a part of the con that had tricked me into becoming a demon. Lilith seemed to sense that I was troubled – shit, who wouldn't be troubled, if he'd just been tricked into being a demon? – so she said, gently, "Go ahead, Steve, out with it. But maybe, before you start, you'd like at least to take a sip of your slammer?"

It was a reasonable request, so I took a taste. It was hardly my beverage of choice – I'd always been a martini sort of guy – and the slammers cloying sweetness was a far cry from the dry edginess of gin. Still, the slammer was better than I expected. Besides, I'd just been tricked into becoming a demon, and I definitely needed a drink, so I slammed half of it back on my second sip.

I could feel the alcohol go to work on my nerves. My tension eased a bit, and I took another swallow. Then I sat still, staring into the drink like a fortuneteller examining tea leaves, trying to predict the future, which for me was pretty damn predictable. I was a demon, now, and I'd have to start doing demonic things. Such was my fate. "You know," I said at last, slowly, "I'm pretty mad at you right now."

Lilith sighed deeply. Her chest rose and fell with the breath, straining the fabric of her dress. Despite my anger, I was rapt in contemplation of her magnificent mammaries. "I know, Steve.

But what was I to do? Azazel appeared to me right after you left my house today and revealed himself as none other than my Lord Satan. He gave me an explicit order to help him, well, bamboozle you," she said, lowering her eyes, in shame, or perhaps just an excellent imitation of it. "What else was I to do?"

"You could have said no," I grumbled.

The succubus looked at me in surprise. "No I couldn't!"

"Oh, right, right," I said, then felt all the despair of my predicament fall upon me. "You're a demon, like me. You have no free will at all, do you?"

She held out her empty hands, which were as lovely and perfect as everything else about her. "No, not really. I mean, if I'm left to my own devices, I can make certain choices, like what dress to wear or whether to drive to work or take the bus. But for the important stuff, especially a moral decision, I have no say at all. I have to do what I'm told, or, in the absence of a direct order, follow my basic nature."

"Like I do now." I slammed back my crackhead slammer. I stared into my glass, seeing in its emptiness some metaphor for my predicament. "Hey, where can a guy get another drink around here?"

"Sit tight," she said, hopping off the chaise. "I'll get the pitcher."

While she was in the kitchen, I thought about what she said. Demons were like animals in a way. Like trained seals. Or dogs. Obedient. Eager to please their masters. *But who tells their masters what to do?* The answer was obvious. They followed their natures, just like Lilith did. In her case, that was toward lascivious activity. In Satan's case, in that of Asmodeus, Beelzebub and all the other devils in Hell, their tendency was toward evil. They were the bosses, so if they said "be evil," their underlings would oblige. Without hesitation.

But does that mean, then, that I'm evil because I have no choice but to channel the will of my masters? The thought was depressing.

At that moment, Lilith returned with the half-full pitcher, as well as a terrycloth robe thrown over her arm. She handed the latter to me. "I, I thought you might like to get out of your bunny costume."

"So you think it makes me look like a rabbit too?"

When I was ready to leave my apartment for the last time, before coming to see Lilith, as per orders, I found a red, plush body suit, with a fake pointy tail and a set of clip-on horns lying on my couch. The implication was obvious. I was to abandon my coveralls, just as I was relinquishing my old station as Hell's Superintendent of Plant Maintenance, and dress myself in what was obviously some sort of neophyte demon garb. I felt ridiculous doing it but figured I had no choice. "I don't know if I'm allowed to take it off," I said with more than a little resentment.

She smiled, a gentle smile that seemed at odds with a person having a demonic nature. "That's just Satan's little joke. All the new recruits get some hazing. Besides, you had to wear something. The HOOTI coveralls were no longer appropriate."

HOOTI: that's the acronym for Beezy's division in the Underworld: Hell's Office of The Interior. Plant Maintenance was a department in that operation.

"Once your horns and tail start to grow in, you'll be able to wear anything you want, except when you're at Beast Barracks, where they'll expect you to wear a uniform like the other recruits. Go ahead, put the robe on. You won't feel so ridiculous."

I pulled the horns from my forehead and tossed them on the bricks of the patio. "Uh, would you mind turning around while I change?"

Lilith's mouth turned up in a pert little smile. "I've seen it all before, you know. Well not yours, but a bunch like it."

I'm being prudish, especially in light of, well, never mind. "Still, would you, please? I'd appreciate it."

"Sure," she said and put her back to me.

With my own back to her, I unzipped the body suit and dropped it to the patio as well. The robe slipped over my shoulders easily, and I tied it at my waist, feeling much more comfortable. "Thanks, I ... "

Lilith was reading my orders, an intense look on her face. She looked up at me and flushed. "You, you dropped this," she said, handing it back to me.

Quickly, I grabbed the paper and put it in one of the pockets of my robe. "Then you know what I'm supposed to do, what we're supposed to do."

"Steve," she said breathlessly, closing the distance between us, "so what? It's what I've wanted to do since the first time I saw you in 'Flo Does The Super.'"

That was a porn film made on the sly by a couple of devils who had surreptitiously filmed the only time Florence and I had made love. It was still a sensation all over Hell, playing regularly in most of the theaters. I blushed.

"Oh, that's right," I said, putting my back to her again. "You're a succubus. It's what you do."

"Steve Minion!" she shouted. "You turn and face me, right this instant!"

I don't know if the hurt in her voice was what made me spin around so fast, or if her tone of command made me do it. After all, as a demon, she outranked me, and that sounded like a direct order. Whatever the reason, I obeyed without hesitation.

And saw that she was in tears. "Why, why are you crying?"

"Because I'm crazy about you, and you know it!" she said, wiping furiously at her eyes with a cocktail napkin.

"But you're a succubus. Why does one more man, more or less, make any difference to you?"

Lilith was biting down on the crook of her index finger, trying to will away the tears. "I don't know, but it does. I may be a succubus. I may have sex with a lot of men, but I don't have sex with every man I see – I wouldn't have time. Maybe I *don't* have free will, but I have some choice in my life, and I choose you. Damn it, I choose you!" She stamped her foot on the ground in frustration.

And my heart melted. Lilith had never been anything but unfailingly kind to me – well, that and unabashedly flirtatious – and even though she'd played a part in my becoming a demon, it was not by her choice. I knew she cared for me. What's more, I knew I cared for her back.

Funny. You always hear about the whore with a heart of gold. Lilith was a succubus who, at least as regards me, had a heart of, hell, I don't know what. Rubies? Platinum? Diamond? Emerald? Whatever, it was a whole lot more precious than gold.

Probably ruby. They were like cinnamon drops, which were her favorites.

I closed the gap between us and held her. She cried softly into my shoulder, and I stroked her hair, muttering nonsensical endearments, but mostly trying to communicate that it was okay, that I knew she'd had no choice in her involvement with me becoming a demon. "I know you care for me, Lilith," I said at last.

"You, you do?" she sniffed, holding me tighter.

"And I care for you too, very much." I kissed her forehead, between her horns, and held her more tightly to my chest.

Now, you have to understand that almost any succubus would take that as an invitation to, well, ingratiate herself, but Lilith just held on tight, giving my neck an occasional kiss, nothing more. "It's, it's been hard, Steve. I love you. I've never loved anyone before, except my parents and sisters. And it didn't feel like this."

She had told me before that she loved me, but I hadn't entirely believed her. I did now, though.

Gently I turned her face up toward mine. I kissed her eyes, her cheeks, and finally her lips. It was a very tender kiss, and she almost startled when I did it. I don't think she was used to tenderness. Passion, lust, yes, but not tenderness.

And then I sat down, with a plop on the end of the chaise lounge. "It's just that … "

"What?" she said, sitting down next to me. "It's Flo, isn't it?"

I sighed. "Yeah. I love her, you know."

The words seemed to hurt her, which I never wanted to do, but Lilith and I had always had an honest relationship – well, we did, if you discounted the "get me to agree to become a demon" ploy – and I didn't want to lie to her. She gave me a final hug then let go, just sitting beside me on the chaise.

"She's lost to you, you have to understand that."

"I do," I said with a sigh. "It doesn't change my feelings."

She swallowed hard then nodded. "Steve, why did you do it? Why did you agree to become a demon, knowing that by forfeiting your humanity, you would lose Flo?"

How to explain this? I thought for a moment, then said, "Lilith, I believe you when you say you love me, but you're new to this whole concept. Love is, well, love is putting someone before yourself. Love is taking the fall so that your loved one can be safe, stay protected, which is what I tried to do when I thought Flo was at risk. Love is … "

"Love is never having to say you're sorry."

"Oh, you saw that movie?"

"Yeah," she said, wiping her eyes again. "I didn't quite get it."

"That's because it was sappy and trite. True, loving relationships are full of heart-felt apologies. Humans and, I suppose, even demons, make lots of mistakes, though humans probably make more because they have free will, so can muck things up more than the rest of the creatures in the universe. Heart-felt apologies," I repeated. "Just like now, when I tell you I'm sorry to have doubted you." I kissed her on the cheek again.

We sat together for a long time, neither one talking. Then at last, Lilith ventured, "Steve?"

"Yeah?"

"You know we have to do it. Satan's orders. I don't know why he did it. Maybe to reward me for my cooperation, maybe to break you away from your human attachments."

Especially Flo. I shrugged. "Maybe both."

She nodded. "Maybe. Anyway, it's there in writing. You have to. Flo is beyond your reach, and you can never get her back. And here I am. I love you, you care for me, and I know you are attracted to me. So what are we waiting for?"

I smiled sadly. "Nothing, I suppose."

Lilith grabbed the pitcher, and I picked up the two glasses. We went over to the hot tub. Steam was rising from the water.

Lilith poured out the last two slammers. We toasted each other, emptied our glasses in a single, long draught, then set them on the side of the spa. The beautiful little redhead took off her shoes and unbuttoned her housedress. She was naked beneath it, and I marveled at the supernatural support her full bosom seemed to have. Lilith got into the water with a soft splash; her breasts floated on the water; they were like two full moons reflected in a pond. I untied my robe and let it fall to the ground by the spa then slipped in next to her.

Only later did it register to me that there was a starry sky above us, which was completely impossible, since there are no celestial objects in the skies of the Underworld. Yet Satan's attention to detail was not lost on me, and for once I didn't resent it. It was very romantic.

Awkwardly, I kissed the beautiful redhead, caressed her soft horns, her erect nipples. They felt much alike. Then I kissed her with more assurance, held her lush body against mine; the swelling between my legs grew to gargantuan proportions.

"Go ahead, Steve," she said breathlessly. "Put a flag over my head and do it for Old Glory."

I smiled fondly, and pressed my body more firmly against hers. "Now that," I said, "would be a sin."

Forgive me, Flo.

Chapter 3

I stayed up all night, thinking about my encounter with Lilith, my feelings for her, those for Flo, and the connection I still felt with my human friends in Hell. Satan's attempt to wean me from those other relationships had mostly failed, but not entirely. No, not entirely. I felt a bond now with Lilith that was more than the casual friendship and mutual attraction that had been there before.

And my time in the Corps was changing my attitudes about demons. Most of them were not bad sorts. True, there was an occasional demon who relished the idea of doing evil, of inflicting pain on others, but most of my colleagues had simply elected to get out of their eternal punishment and make the best of a bad situation. There was no denying that the lot of a demon was far better than that of the damned.

Unbelievably, I could see myself becoming friends with a few demons. Max, Gomer and even Sarge were alright guys.

When I thought of Sarge, I glanced at my wristwatch. Clocks in the Underworld were notoriously unreliable, but Mickey's little hand was almost pointing at four, and his big hand was lined up with eleven. If my watch was right this morning, I had five minutes to meet Sarge for my early morning fencing session. I grabbed my pitchfork and hurried to the practice grounds.

Sarge was already there, waiting for me. "Well, maggot. I thought you were going to be late."

I blushed. "Almost was. Spent the night thinking about things."

My drill sergeant eyed me appraisingly. "You know, Minion, you probably think too much."

"You're not the first person to tell me that."

He nodded. "Your life as a demon will probably go better for you if you operate more on instinct than you're used to. Just act and react. Like now!" He jabbed his pitchfork at me, and I just barely turned it to the side before he skewered me.

"Your speed saved you that time, not your skill. You rely too much on how fast you are, like a strong demon – well, you're that too – but like Digger relies too much on his strength. There are times for both, but it's best if you have skill as well as talent. Allow me to demonstrate."

I nodded, and saw the sky. A dull red glow was peeking over the eastern horizon. It looked like a sunrise, though of course we didn't have any of those. Still, the day was beginning in earnest. "Boy, that's pretty," I said.

"What?" Sarge said turning.

I used the opportunity to lunge at him, but he caught the tines of my pitchfork and casually redirected my speed and strength to a patch of earth about five feet away from him. I lost my balance and came up spitting sand.

"Devious, trying to distract me with the sky. Excellent! I didn't know if I could expect deviousness from you. That's highly valued in the Corps, you know. Shows you have some brains." He smirked. "I'm still waiting to see a little skill, though. Try again."

We circled each other, and I looked for a weakness in his defenses. There were none, though he found plenty in mine. He beat me time and again. "No, no, no maggot! Remember what I just said about you thinking too much? Well, in this case, forget all that. Fencing, whether with a pitchfork or an epée, requires strategy. Size up your opponent. Look for his strengths and, as importantly, his weaknesses. In your case, Max continues to beat you because you think you're so fast, he can't possibly keep up. If this were a race, that would be true. But all he has to do is watch you, look for your tells."

"My tells? Are we talking poker, now?"

He grinned. "Same concept. Most people communicate what they're about to do before they do it. For example, when you get nervous, you tend to get sarcastic."

"I do?"

"Oh, yeah. I'd have thought you'd have figured that out by now."

I rubbed my jaw. "Wish I had. That might have saved a few, ah, unfortunate encounters with Satan."

"You have a speed tell, as well. Whenever you're getting ready to move fast, your whole body tenses up, as if it's ready to explode into motion. But what if you could maintain a neutral pose, somehow make that speed a surprise that comes out of nowhere? No tell."

"I think I could do that." By way of demonstration, I shook my limbs loose and in a nanosecond snatched Sarge's pitchfork from his hand. First it was in his grasp. Then it was in mine. I doubt he even saw me move. "Like that?"

His jaw hung open. "Damn, you *are* fast! But yes, exactly like that. I didn't see it coming. If you were like that in a fencing match, no one could beat you. Not even Max."

I handed Sarge's pitchfork back to him. "That's good to know, but I'd also like a little skill with the pitchfork."

"Well, you have that already. You're one of the better fencers, actually."

"But not as good as Max."

Sarge shrugged. "Maximus has a few techniques that he's practiced over and over. You'd be amazed what a few good moves can do for your success rate. In his case, he has beaten you every time with the same maneuver."

"Don't I know it!" I said with a frown. "He's really good at twisting my pitchfork from my grasp."

"You can move fast. Can you see fast too?"

"Yeah, I think so."

"Prove it. Watch me. I'm going to blink very quickly. You tell me how many times, starting … now!"

I watched. Boy, he really *could* blink fast. It was like he had an eye condition or something.

"Stop!" he said a few seconds later.

"Seven hundred and thirteen," I said without hesitation.

"Excellent. So, start watching your opponents with the same eye you just used to count my blinks."

We practiced for another hour, and by the end of the time, I was able to avoid Max's signature disarmament move every time. I watched for Sarge's own tell, and just when I could sense that he was going to snag my pitchfork, I moved unexpectedly. I sped up; I slowed down. I moved my fork a little closer to his body; I reared back. There was no pattern. I was one with my pitchfork. I even managed to beat Sarge two out of three times. At the end of the session, Sarge threw his pitchfork into the sand and plopped down next to it. "That's it! Max will never be able to beat you again."

I grinned and sat down beside him.

"But I'd advise that you let him," he said, after a minute of silence between us.

"Huh? Why?"

"You're too good Minion. It's the only thing he or anyone else in camp has ever surpassed you in. Let him leave camp today thinking he's better at you at this one skill. For that matter, let the other cadets think the same thing."

I thought back to the "showoff" comment from yesterday and nodded. "Understood, sir. But thank you for the practice. If

I'm going to be a demon, I'd at least like to be a good one … at least I think I would."

Sarge used the butt of his pitchfork to scrape his personal sigil into the dirt. It looked like a demon tail, but it had three V's at the end instead of only one, like the sergeant chevrons on his sleeve. "Why do you say it that way?"

"Have you heard how I became a demon?"

My superior pursed his lips and nodded. "You were tricked into it."

"Yes. I'm probably a fool to say this out loud, and especially to you, Sarge, but, well, I'm still having some issues with the whole situation. Unlike the others here, I never really wanted to be a demon."

He nodded slowly. "I've been wondering when this would come up. Fortunately, it's time for the next phase of your training."

"There's another phase?"

"Yes," he said. "Up until now, we've focused on building up your natural attributes — strength, speed, coordination, handling a pitchfork. The next phase deals with demon decorum, or how to act like a demon. We start this afternoon, and in your case the timing is perfect. Physically, except for teleportation, which no one here can teach you, you're already better than any demon on Level Eight, and that includes me, as much as I hate to admit it. But you still need to learn about stealth. You need to learn demon attitude, demon dirty tricks."

Sarge frowned. "This whole teleportation thing: it's a new one for me. Many demons have experienced teleportation, but devils have provided the transportation. To do it under one's own power, though." He whistled. "Well, I was amazed to see it on the recruitment poster, and it wasn't there for very long." He looked at me critically. "In fact, I think it was there just for you, because the ability is almost unheard of among our kind, Other than Adramelech, I don't know of another demon who can do it. Not even very many devils are able to teleport, so we'll have to see who among the major devils could teach you. Perhaps TNK-el..."

"TNK-el! That duplicitous little shrimp? No way!!" TNK-el had been deeply involved in the elaborate plot to trick me into becoming a demon.

"Hey!" Sarge said, looking back and forth nervously, as if he expected TNK-el to appear at any moment. "He may be small, but he's one of the most powerful devils in Hell."

"You're kidding," I said, astonished. "I knew he was a friend of Satan's, but I didn't know he was anything special."

"Well he is, but your animosity toward him is noted. I'll find someone else. For now, though, you and most of your colleagues are about to begin your lessons in trickery, bad deed doing, that sort of thing. Maybe by the time you develop your skills in those areas, you'll feel more like becoming a demon was the right move for you."

"Do you, do you like being a demon, Sarge?"

"Oh, yeah!" he said, grinning. "The life is great. Much better than when I was one of the damned."

"I get that, of course, but don't you feel bad about torturing people? I mean, you were human yourself once."

He shrugged. "No, not really. Remember, these people are down here for a reason. They're *supposed* to be tormented. It's my job to torment them, and if I didn't do it, there are others who would do it anyway. Besides, once I chose to be a demon, I never really thought about it anymore."

"Well, I do."

"Hmm. Perhaps we ought to have you spend some time with the company shrink. Though it's rare, you're not the first demon to have difficulty settling into the role. But there's time for that later. Let's just get through the regular training and see how you feel at graduation."

"Okay." I looked over at the old demon. "You're awfully nice for a drill sergeant, you know."

"Well, don't say that in public!" He grinned again. "Seriously, all that yelling we do out on the field, well, it's mostly for show. I mean, we need to get you obeying orders without question or hesitation, but in the absence of free will, that's pretty easy anyway." He shook his head. "I think we've all just seen too many war movies. The 'bust your ass' drill sergeant is what everyone expects, isn't it?"

I thought back to John Wayne movies, to 'An Officer And A Gentleman,' in short, to just about any film that had a boot camp component. The sarges all acted pretty much the same. "Yeah."

"Well, don't worry. In public, I'll treat you like shit, just like the rest of the recruits. In private, though, I don't really see the point. My purpose is to turn you into the best demon you can be." He looked at me critically. "Besides, you don't strike me as the type who responds well to intimidation tactics."

I thought about the many times I'd stood my ground against Satan himself, and smiled wistfully. "No, not really."

"Didn't think so. In private, then, I'll try to help you through this transition as best I can." Sarge got to his feet and helped me up. "Don't worry, Minion. It will all work out."

I bit my lower lip. "Hope so," I mumbled.

After morning maneuvers, we had a fencing session. I made a point of losing to Maximus, though now that Sarge had opened my eyes, so to speak, I could see Max's technique as if it were an old movie running in slow motion. After laying me on

34

the ground, my demon friend grabbed my arm and popped me back on my feet, a big grin on his face.

"Bravo!" I said, applauding, and the rest of the cadets joined in. "I didn't even see it coming."

Well, lying at least is becoming easier. It's a start.

"Thanks. Now, I've gotta run. My discharge papers came in too. I have to boogie up to New Rome now."

"You'll be back for graduation though, won't you?" asked Gomer.

Max gave the little guy a squeeze around the shoulders. "Wouldn't miss it. I want to walk with my friends, like you and Mignon here."

"That's Minion."

"Really?" He grinned. "And with all of the cadets in our class. See you soon," he said, then headed to the bunkhouse to get his gear.

After lunch, the rest of us were gathered in the camp auditorium, a theatre-style facility with a sloping floor down to the lectern in front.

The camp commander, a dapper devil in khakis named Cringe, stepped to the podium. He was carrying a swagger stick, no doubt his pitchfork in a transformed state. "Good afternoon, recruits!"

"Good afternoon, SIR!" we all shouted in unison.

"Today we will be working on one of the most important skills you will need in the Corps: your laugh."

Our laugh? He's got to be kidding.

"We are very fortunate today to have a guest lecturer. This particular devil, in addition to being one of the princes of Hell, is known throughout the Underworld for having patented the famous devil laugh, which is the pattern for the demon laugh as well. Cadets, I give you Beelzebub the Great, Lord of the Flies!"

35

Beezy, all seven hundred non-corporeal pounds of him, waddled on stage to enthusiastic applause. I was clapping louder than anyone, which got me a few puzzled looks; not everyone in the Corps knew of my long-time association with Beelzebub. He had been my direct supervisor for sixty years and was about the only one of Hell's royalty who I really respect.

The old devil, who was dressed in his usual white suit and signature black fez, took his place behind the lectern. At over seven feet tall in his natural state, he towered over the furniture. Beelzebub wrapped his hands over the edges of the podium; his mitts looked like two ham hocks. "Thank you, Captain Crunch."

"That's Cringe, sir."

I snickered, and Beezy caught my eye. His face was impassive, except for a small twitch on the right side of his mouth. "Of course, Captain Cringe. My mistake."

He turned back to his audience. "A demon's laugh is like a calling card. All of you will soon be charged with tormenting the eternally damned. In this regard, you are stand-ins for devils and, ultimately, for Lord Satan Himself."

The cadets nodded. They seemed to understand that this was an important responsibility.

"The demon laugh is the exclamation point on the punishment. Do something evil. Make the laugh. Threaten someone. Make the laugh. We spent a great deal of time in R&D coming up with the perfect, creepy, hellacious laugh. You must all master it. Allow me to demonstrate. Ahem," he cleared his throat. "Bwahahahahahaha!"

The hackles on the nape of my neck rose. The sound of his laughter creeped me out. Yep, nobody could do it better than Beezy. Not even Satan.

"A Bwa followed by six ha's. Exactly six, no more, no less. Get it? Now let's have one of you try it." He pointed to someone in the audience. "Cadet, what's your name?"

A familiar demon stood up. "My name's Caleb, sir, but everyone here calls me Gomer."

"Gomer. Gee, I wonder who came up with that?" He shot me another quick look. I shrugged.

"Very well, Cadet Gomer. Do the laugh."

I saw Gomer's skinny chest expand to double it's size as he took a deep breath. "Hayuk. Hyuk Hyuk Hyuk Hyuk Hyuk Hyuk."

One of the ham hocks slammed down hard on the lectern. The eyes of everyone in the room opened wide, everyone's except mine. I was used to Beezy's temper. "Not Hayuk hyuk! Bwaha, etc. Now, try again."

A look of intense concentration came to Gomer's eyes. He may not have been the brightest or most talented of demons, but he always tried his best. "Bwak bwak bwak bwak bwak bwak bwak!"

Beezy closed his eyes, pinched the narrow ridge of his nose. "Not Bwak bwak. Bwa ha. Jeez, you sound like a chicken. I think you need to spend a few hours in the language lab, Cadet Gomer. Crunch!"

"Cringe, sir," the captain said with all the deference he could muster, which was considerable in my estimation, considering Beelzebub had just dissed him twice in front of the cadets.

"See to it."

"Yes sir."

"Who wants to try next?"

Since no one wanted to antagonize the Lord of the Flies, there was not an immediate volunteer. But group dynamics can be a funny thing. The pressure for someone to step forward can be overwhelming. Finally, one demon who seemed to have a death wish – or would have, if he wasn't already dead – stood up. Kurt, a young-looking fellow with dirty, blond hair and a stoned look around his eyes, stood. "I'll give it a shot, sir. bwahahahAHaHA!"

My old boss frowned. "You have the correct syllables, and the correct number of them, but you're crescendoing through the laugh. It should be exactly the reverse. You start with an explosion of air on the Bwa. It should be the loudest part of the laugh, then you should get softer, ending on a breathy 'ha.' Minion!" he shouted abruptly.

I jumped to my feet. "Yes, sir!"

"You, of all the demons in this room, should know how to do the laugh. You've certainly heard it often enough. Let's hear your version."

"Very well, sir." I cleared my throat. "Bwahahahahahaha."

He frowned. "Technically accurate, but it lacks heart. If this were the Olympics, you'd probably get a nine point five for skill and about a three for artistic merit. Here, I know." Beezy held up his right hand, and what looked like a severed head appeared in it. "Catch," he said, throwing the head to me.

I snagged the object. It was a ceramic piggy bank, complete with a slot on top. The bank was in the likeness of Thomas Alva Edison. I frowned. Edison was perhaps my least favorite human in all of Hell, and Beelzebub knew it.

"Now, Minion. Throw the thing as hard as you can to the floor and then do the laugh."

He didn't have to tell me twice. As I thought of how intensely I disliked Edison, my face twisted into something that must have been very ugly, at least based on some of the reactions of my colleagues in the room. With all my strength, I threw down the piggy bank, shattering it in a thousand pieces. "Bwahahahahahaha!"

Beezy held up two cards, each about ten inches square, and each with the number ten written on it. "Perfect on both scores. All you needed was the proper motivation."

My ex-boss turned to the cadets in the room. "Eventually the laugh will become second nature, but for now, visualize your least favorite person in the universe. It could be someone from your lifetime or your afterlife. Think of slapping them hard, or crushing their skull. Then laugh. Kurt! Again!"

The blonde demon thought for a second and then released a hearty "Bwahahahahahaha!"

"Excellent! You, and then you!"

One demon after the other gave up a pitch-perfect laugh.

"By Pluto, I think you've got it!" he said, with satisfaction.

"Thank you, Lord Beelzebub," Cringe chimed in. "I think I speak for all of us when I say how much we appreciate you taking time out of your busy sch … "

"Dismissed," Beezy barked.

Cringe looked like someone had squeezed the air from his lungs. His swagger stick morphed back into a rather limp looking pitchfork. "What, what he said."

As I stood to leave, I noticed Beelzebub walking in my direction. "I knew Edison would be good motivation for you."

"Yeah, well, I'm not proud of it, but I really don't like him very much, as you know."

"Not proud of it?" Beezy grabbed my elbow and led me to a corner of the room. "Come on, Steve. You're a demon now. Hating a human is perfectly appropriate and acceptable."

My old boss stared at me with his piercing eyes. He seemed to be showing far more concern for me as a demon than he ever did as a damned human, which was understandable, I guess.

"What's wrong? Sergeant Faust said you're showing incredible talent, maybe even arch demon level talent."

"Really?" That surprised me. In all of Hell, there were very few arch demons, and they were generally desk jockeys, managing other demons. There was one, though, who had the raw might truly deserving of the rank, and when humans and demons thought about arch demons, Adramelech, the King of Fire, was the one who immediately came to mind. He was immensely powerful; unfortunately, he was also dumb as a stump.

"Yes, and if that's so, you could become one of the most powerful creatures in Hell, stronger even than some devils."

"You mean I'd be an Adramelech, but with brains."

"Bwahahahahahaha! Good one. But precisely right. No wonder Satan was so interested in you. He must have sensed your potential."

I shrugged. "Maybe. I'm doing well enough with basic demonistic skills, I suppose, but despite what Sergeant Faust said … hey, wait a minute. Faust? I've always just called him Sarge, but do you really mean Faust, as in Goethe, Christopher Marlowe Faust?"

"Well, yeah, sort of. His real name is Simon Magus, but since he was one of the originals for the Faust legend, we've all taken to calling him that."

"Simon Magus … Boy that rings a bell."

"It should. He was a contemporary of Saint Peter, a magician who got too big for his britches. Pete took him down, big time, and after he died, he ended up down here. Faust is, as best I can remember, the first demon we ever created."

"But never mind about that. We're talking about you here. The sergeant says you're doing great!" Beelzebub tried to say this with enthusiasm, but the attitude didn't suit him. Still, I appreciated the effort.

"Beezy," I whispered, "my heart just isn't in this. I may have been tricked into willingly becoming a demon, but I never really wanted it."

"I knew this was a mistake," he whispered to himself, though with my demon ears, I could hear him clearly, "but he just wouldn't listen."

"It will probably work out," he said more loudly. "Go through the rest of your training, and you should be okay. Here, take this." Beezy held out a hand. There was an amulet in his grasp. I lifted it by the gold chain and saw an ivory cameo of Edison, set against an oval of onyx. Instinctively I snarled.

"That's the spirit!" Beezy said jovially. "Put that around your neck, and whenever you need the proper motivation, just touch or look at the amulet. Your dislike of Edison will see you through training. Eventually you should adjust."

"Well, I wish I were as confident as you. Still, thanks. I appreciate your concern," I said, slipping the amulet around my neck. My distaste for the Wizard of Menlo Park was so intense that the thing felt like it was burning my demon skin. I snarled again.

"Good one. Now laugh!"

"Bwahahahahahaha!" I ranted, wiping a bit of drool from the corner of my mouth.

"Excellent! Keep it up." He glanced up at the sky, seeing something I certainly couldn't. "Oh, look at the time! Gotta go." In a small explosion, enough to char my face slightly, Beelzebub went up in smoke. When the smoke cleared, he was gone.

Chapter 4

The next morning, after roll call, inspection and breakfast, Sarge gathered us together on the practice field.

"Up until now," Faust said, "we've worked on getting you physically fit for the demanding duties of a demon. And the laugh of course." There ensued a hearty round of "Bwahahahahahaha!"s from the guys. They'd all been practicing, in the shower, while on KP, guard duty, etc., and had the signature demon guffaw down pretty well.

"But being a demon isn't all about breaking rocks with your face, running faster than a Ferrari and laughing like a lunatic." Sarge sat down, cross-legged, on the grass. That there was healthy, green grass at all in Hell was a bit of a wonder, but then no human ever got to see the Beast Barracks encampment, so they'd never know. Fort Fury, as the place was called, was actually fairly pleasant, as far as Hell was concerned. I don't think I'd seen anything in the Underworld as nice as this except up on One, where the Virtuous Pagans and unbaptized babies hung out. Oh, and Amorous Acres, the suburb where Lilith had her house.

"First, let's talk about personal hygiene. It's important not to take baths. A smelly demon is an effective one. By definition, demons are disgusting, and it's important that your smell be as repulsive as possible."

I raised my hand. "Sir, my girlfriend is a succubus. Do I really have to smell like a latrine around her?"

He conceded the point. "That's a reasonable concern. I guess you don't have to stink, at least not all the time. Just make certain you foul yourself up as much as possible before you show up for work. Oh, and try not to floss."

Gomer's hand shot up this time. "But, Sarge, I don't want to lose my teeth."

"Oh, shit, guys," Sarge said, with uncharacteristic familiarity. "You're immortal. If you can exist forever, do you really think your teeth and fangs are going to drop out of your gums? And yes, Minion," he said, anticipating me, "you can floss before you suck face with your girlfriend."

"Good to know," I muttered. Lilith would be glad too, no doubt.

"Now, let's talk about the most important role of a demon. Who can tell me what that is?"

I winced. The answer was pretty obvious, but I kept my mouth shut, and left it up to my friend, Chuckles, to respond.

Chuckles, was a short, squat demon-in-training. That wasn't his real name, of course, but many of us got nicknames in camp, nicknames that stuck and eventually became a demon's new "nom de guerre." There were very few of our kind who went by the names they'd had in life. I realized, ruefully, that I'd probably still go by Minion, unless I managed someday to achieve some high rank in the demon chain-of-command. There aren't too many generals named Minion. For now, though, I was pretty sure I'd still be saddled with the name I'd been born with.

Anyway, Chuckles was called Chuckles because he had a broad, comical face that his horns did nothing to detract from, with blunt features that looked like they'd been drawn on. Since he looked like a clown, and since he had mastered the sinister demonic laugh far more quickly than most, we'd christened him Chuckles. Well, not really christened. That would get us in a boatload of trouble down here, but you know what I mean.

Chuckles said, "A demon's main job is to torment damned humans. Frequently, painfully."

Faust nodded. "Excellent, Chuckles, and exactly right. Now, tormenting them doesn't necessarily have to be physically painful. Adding psychological pain, by which I mainly mean fear, to the mix is even more exquisite ... harrumph!!" Faust was showing his smarts. It didn't pay for a sergeant to sound like an intellectual, though, so he took it down a notch. "I mean even more effective. Yes, the icing on the cake is when you can combine both."

"I would think," I said slowly, "that making them suffer without them knowing it would be the best."

"What do you mean?"

I mean I don't want to have to hurt people. "I mean that if someone is in great psychological pain and doesn't understand why they're so miserable, that would be more soul-wrenching than just sticking them with a pitchfork." Everybody looked at me uncomprehendingly, so I tried to explain. "It's like having major chronic depression. You feel terrible but see no reason for it. Then you feel even worse because you don't think you have the right to feel so bad. See? Now that's truly diabolical."

The other demons-in-training looked at me blankly.

"Maybe," said Sarge, rubbing his chin in thought, "but that kind of subtlety is the province of devils, not us demons. Stick to more obvious forms of torture, got it, Minion?"

I sighed. "Got it, Sarge."

"Good. Now, we have a bit of good fortune. Today happens to be 'Take Your Demon To Work Day.' All of you were influenced by one demon or another in your decision to enlist in the Corps. I can vouch for all of those demons. They know their stuff. They will be arriving in a few minutes. You will be shadowing them all day, watching some real pros ply their trade, so pay attention!"

At that moment, Hell's Elevator arrived with a ding, and twenty demons stepped onto the grass. I'd wondered who I'd be shadowing.

"Hey, Minion!" yelled a voice. Of course. It was Karnaj.

"Hi, Karnaj," I said, shaking his hand when we came over. "I guess we're headed for the mines?"

"You bet. Let's go."

The platoon and its complement of mentors crowded into the Elevator. Stops needed to be made on each level, including the bazaar on the Eighth Circle. The Elevator did a sideways jog and dropped off Sourpuss, a dour-faced member of my class, with a long hook nose. Apparently, he and his mentor were going to spend the day pestering the humans who worked in some of the shops.

I didn't catch where everyone else was going, but I did hear that Chuckles was going with his "dad for a day" to New Rome. Daddy in this case was named Bozogart. Like my colleague from Beast Barracks, Bozogart, who went variously by Bozo, Zogar, Zogart and even Bogart, had a clownish appearance. He was even tricked out in a clown outfit. They were going to be performing at the human version of the Palace, which is where devils and demons went to watch a show. The human analogue was called the Dungeon, and the acts there were intended to scare the crap out of the poor schmucks who were consigned there for Eternity. These unfortunates had the misfortune to be both avaricious and fraidy cats. Specifically, they had coulrophobia, an irrational fear of clowns.

It's actually a fairly common phobia. If it weren't, why would they have made all of those horror movies with clowns as the villains? Also, ever notice how many kids are actually frightened by those pasty-faced wisenheimers? It's not really a surprise, if you think about it. From a very young age, kids are subjected to huge creatures with white skin, gigantic red lips, noses the size of red golf balls, who are dressed in garish costumes and then proceed to torture defenseless balloons by contorting them into all those bizarre shapes. Sounds scary to me.

So that's where Chuckles was off to. Gomer and his mentor, Goober, were headed for the Fourth Level and the dirt farm where Nicky worked. I hoped that my two friends didn't run into each other. They wouldn't have known, of course, of me being a common acquaintance, but I didn't like the idea of one friend tormenting the other.

That's all I learned before the Elevator stopped at Level Six. Can't say I was thrilled to spend my day in the mine. After all, this was where Satan had tricked me into becoming a demon. But orders were orders, so I determined to make the best of things.

The mine was its usual bustle of activity. Damned souls were flowing into the mine like those African termites going into their giant mounds. Workers were pushing carts full of sulfur from the inside of the mine to an open train or a boat at the river dock, each waiting to receive Hell's most precious cargo. Demons not yet called in for the day's job of torturing their human charges were hanging around outside, smoking and drinking coffee.

Nabob, a friend of Karnaj's, was staffing the front desk, just outside of the mine. That was Karnaj's normal station, and it's where the time clock and time cards for the thousands of mine workers were kept. I'd met Nabob before. We'd had drinks at the Palace once. He, Karnaj and a few other demons had been trying to talk me into joining the Corps. They'd been unsuccessful, but I ended up joining anyway in the end, so they were pleased. "Hi, Bob," I said. Nabob always preferred to be called Bob. Can't say I blame him.

"Hey, Minion. Good to see you."

"Are we going to work the desk today?" I asked Karnaj.

"Nah. Bob's going to cover that. I mean, you can blow the break whistle if you want to and get on the PA system to yell some obscenities. That seems to bug the shit out of the mine workers. But we're going to wander through the mines and see some of the other ways you can torture people here."

Ah, swell," I said, trying not to roll my eyes.

"It *is* about break time," Bob said, meaningfully.

"Well, we should take advantage of it then." Karnaj turned to me. "Want to give it a go?"

"Why not?" This kind of torment I thought I could handle.

"Need any pointers?" my mentor asked me.

"Don't believe so. I've watched you do this before. Let me think." Remembering some of the things I'd seen Karnaj do, I pulled the break whistle, cleared my throat and shouted into the microphone of the PA system. "Break time! Ah, smoke 'em if you got 'em. Oh," I added, a new item that would personally piss me off. "We're out of coffee, so don't even try to make it to the break room!"

I waited about ten seconds, just long enough for someone to pull out a pack of cigarettes, retrieve a cancer stick, strike a match but not get the thing lit. Then I pulled on the break whistle again and yelled into the mike. "Break's over, you lollygagging motherfuckers!"

I looked to Karnaj and Bob. "How'd I do?"

Karnaj stroked his beard and nodded. "Pretty good. I mean, I recognized many of my own lines, and imitation is the sincerest form of flattery, so I liked that. That coffee bit, though:

47

that was original. I liked it. Might even try that one myself sometime."

"Well, back when I was a human, if you'd made me go without coffee, it would be torture. I'd get a headache … "

"You should probably sound whinier though," Bob suggested, while Karnaj nodded in agreement. "The whine seems to really irritate them."

"Still, a very good start. Nice job," Karnaj said.

At that moment, a worker came up to the time clock and punched in. "Let me see your timecard," I growled.

"Okay," said the woman, a damned soul who appeared to be in her fifties. Probably died of cancer or something. I did my best to frown as I examined the card. "You're late," I growled again.

"Actually," she said, "I'm early."

"Are you doubting the word of a demon?" Bob snarled.

"No. No sir," she said meekly.

"Besides," I said, showing her the card, on which the time clock had, as I'd expected, stamped the incorrect time, marking her fifteen minutes late, "your card says otherwise."

"You know what we do to late employees, don't you?" Karnaj pulled out his pitchfork which morphed rapidly into a cat-o-nine-tails. He whipped her bloody.

My gorge rose, and I turned away quickly. I hadn't expected further repercussions for her tardiness, though it was predictable, I suppose.

"Now get in there and try to make up for lost time," Karnaj said.

"Yes sir," she groaned and dragged herself inside.

My stomach settled down – out of sight, out of mind – and I turned to the other two. Fortunately, they had not noticed my nausea.

If the day was intended to introduce me to some subtle approaches to tormenting the damned, it was a bit of a failure. From my perspective, demons weren't particularly creative in how they hurt humans. A whipping here, a poking there, a little Hellfire, a pie in the face if some human's comment merited it. All really painful and/or humiliating, I could speak from personal experience, but not exactly exquisite torture. Hell, I thought some of the stunts I'd pulled on Thomas Edison or Henry Ford over the years were much more inventive.

Ironically, thinking about those stunts made me feel guilty now, when as a demon I should have been proud.

We were near the end of our day traveling through the mines, when we came on a large work crew. It was being led by Digger and included my old "pal," Ford. Seeing the monstrous demon, my face flushed.

"What's wrong, Minion?" Karnaj said.

"Oh, nothing," I said and tried to think of a good excuse. "Ford is not one of my favorite humans."

"Then go ahead and pitchfork him or something."

"Well, I … "

At that moment, one of the massive wooden braces that supported the ceiling cracked and started to collapse downward. By reflex, I rushed beneath it, flexed a little and held it up. I didn't even break a sweat.

"Let it go," Karnaj hissed behind me.

"But if I let go, the ceiling will collapse on all of the workers!"

"You dummy, it's *supposed* to collapse on them! We have a cave-in every day. Look at Digger!"

I glanced over at the head of Hell's sulfur mine. He looked puzzled then, seeing I was supporting the roof, frowned.

Karnaj gave me a quick spin, knocking me off balance, and I lost my grip on the beam. It and the ceiling collapsed, burying half the work crew. Digger, satisfied, nodded, and went back to work.

The moans behind me almost made me retch, but Karnaj's voice kept my attention away from the suffering.

"That was a close one. Honestly, Minion, I would have thought you would have expected a cave-in."

"Sorry," I said. "It was just reflex."

"You *are* strong though. Jeez Louise!" he said, admiringly. "You held up the entire ceiling by yourself. Digger is the only other demon here who could have done that."

At the end of the day, Karnaj randomly picked someone from a work crew and began to stick the poor soul repeatedly with his pitchfork. "You should skewer at least one human a day," he said, breathing heavily as he jabbed. "It's good exercise, not to mention pretty much *de rigueur* activity for a demon. Care to join in?"

"Uh, sorry, I can't," I said, trying to hide my revulsion.

Huh?" He stabbed the butt of his victim about ten more times. "Why not?"

"I haven't been certified yet. It's, it's a new regulation," I lied.

"Oh, well, let me just finish up then." He drove his pitchfork deep into the poor schmuck's ass, then twisted, mutilating the gluteus maximus. "There, that should do."

"Moan." Using his elbows, the bleeding human dragged himself to a corner of the chamber in which he'd been working. Like a dying animal, he wanted to be alone in his misery. Unlike a dying animal, he'd be back at work the next day, ready for more fun. Tonight, though, after his body had healed, he'd be washing out his white coveralls, trying to get both his own blood and the yellow dirt of the mines out of the fabric.

"Come on," my mentor said, turning away from his victim, "let's get a beer in the break room. I want to introduce you to the rest of the team."

My little feat of strength did not go unnoticed by the other demons. After I got a cold one, a nice craft beer called Devil's Backbone that was made especially for the demons, the mine's supervisors all wanted to try to arm wrestle me. Apparently, this was a standard form of entertainment, and I felt obliged to participate.

We went to the center of the break room, where a large flat stone served as the gaming surface. Two smaller stones were put opposite each other to serve as seats for the contestants.

There wasn't much competition. I easily beat all of them. In fact, I could have probably taken two at a time and still won.

"ME TRY NOW!" said a deep voice from the entrance. It was Digger.

"Now we'll see something!" said Bob. "No one has ever beaten Digger."

I was intrigued. There also wasn't much choice in the matter, so up went my arm, and down came Digger's. It had to come down, since the mine's overseer was so fucking huge. Just grabbing his hand was a challenge.

Physically, Digger had the advantage in weight and leverage, but from the moment Karnaj yelled "Go!" I could tell that I was the stronger. Digger strained against me, but I hardly felt his effort. I could slam his arm to the stone any time I wanted.

The urge to beat him was strong, since I was still peeved with him for his role in making me a demon, but then I looked at his face. Digger was turning red with effort. The poor, dumb brute didn't understand. He had never lost before, yet he knew he was about to.

Unbidden, Faust's advice came back to me. I needed to let other demons beat me occasionally, or they'd feel resentment. Besides, I felt sorry for Digger. He was a mental midget, and if he wasn't the strongest, what was he? Nothing, really. Slowly, so as not to make it look like I was throwing the contest, I let Digger push back my arm, until my hand was an inch above the table. I was still holding him, and if I wanted, I could have reversed our positions in a moment. Instead, I gave a groan and allowed Digger to shove my fingers into the stone. My hand made a four inch depression in the rock.

The applause was thunderous. The demons came up and patted Digger on the back. Some of the demons started yelling, "Still number one! Still number one!"

Digger looked at me. "Minion very strong. Strongest demon I ever wrestled. BUT DIGGER STRONGER!" he yelled gleefully.

"Well," said Karnaj, as we finished our beers. "That's about it for today. Let me walk you to the Elevator." I shook hands with the other demons and we headed out.

"You know, Minion," Karnaj said casually, as we walked to the lift. "The others may not have spotted it, but I did. You threw that contest with Digger."

"Don't know what you're talking about," I mumbled.

"It was well-done, though. The other guys: they look up to Digger because he's so strong. I, well, I just like him. He's a simple soul, really. He tries hard, and he does a good job as head of the mines. And he's really proud of his strength."

"That's good to hear," I said, when the Elevator landed on Six. "See you."

As the door closed behind me, I heard Karnaj whistle. "I never thought I'd see a demon stronger than Digger. Shit! That was really something."

Chapter 5

The weeks passed, or at least they felt like weeks. We continued to train our bodies. I got even faster and could now blast across the desert at the speed of a Japanese bullet train, creating a showering wake of sand behind me. My strength grew impressively; I could bench press two dragons in the gym. Running the pole between the two, and finding a bench high enough and sturdy enough to bear up under fifty thousand pounds – not to mention a really stout pole – was a trick, but the Corps' personal trainers managed it. My abilities were still overshadowing those of my colleagues, most of whom had hit their upper limits, while my talents were still growing. I remembered the advice of Sarge, though, and made it a point to lose an occasional fencing bout with my pitchfork.

I still had not managed much control over my teleportation powers. At least once a day I'd accidentally trigger the ability, and I was usually left sprawled over a jeep, smooshed inside a sewer pipe or something else equally inconvenient. The worst was one time when I sneezed and found myself in the middle of a sand dune. Boy, digging my way out was no fun at all. It was dark in there, too. Faust said he was continuing to look for a devil who had time to train me; meanwhile I just hoped my unmanageable new ability wouldn't get me in any trouble.

One morning, after breakfast, we were gathered in the main auditorium of the academy. Captain Cringe again introduced our morning speaker.

"Today, you begin your study in stealth and guile, and for your introduction to the topics we have brought in a guest speaker."

"Who is he?" shouted a demon from the back row named Harlan. Harlan was a bit of a smart ass, but since I like snarky people, he and I got along pretty well. "Is he a lawyer?" The rest of the demons in the room gave an appreciative snicker.

"Close," Cringe said, trying to suppress the smirk on his face. "Of course, he's a demon now, but in life, he was the son of a lawyer and helped run the government for a while in Florence."

"Oh," Harlan continued. "Even worse. A politician." The snickers grew more enthusiastic.

"And who better to teach stealth and guile? Our speaker this morning literally wrote the book on strong-arm tactics used to maintain order. In fact his very name has come to be associated with, and I quote from *Wikipedia* here, 'deceit, deviousness, ambition and brutality.' Please give a warm welcome to Niccolò Machiavelli!"

A tall, thin demon stepped out from behind a curtain and took the captain's place at the lectern. His face was long and narrow; his hair was cut short, making his demon horns show prominently on his strong brow. When the applause quieted, he began to speak. "Thank you, thank you very much. Before we get started, I wanted to announce that after the lecture, I'll be signing copies of my book, *The Prince*, in the lobby. You should all buy a copy, especially since it is required reading here at the Academy."

From the side, the captain nodded. "All proceeds for today's sales will go toward the renovation of the mess hall, which I'm sure you agree is a good cause." There were many hoots from the audience.

Machiavelli nodded. "Over the years, my name has been transformed into an adjective. The term 'Machiavellian' has come to be a stand-in for a kind of ruthlessness and, as your commanding officer said, deviousness that is necessary to effectively rule others."

The demon pulled out his pitchfork and transformed it into a pointer. "There are a number of lessons to be learned from my book. True, it was written as a treatise on the nature of power, how to get it and how to keep it, but there is much in *The Prince* that can apply to being a good demon. You know, I based much of it on my experiences with Cesare Borgia. Many of the Borgias are in Hell, including Cesare and his dad, Roderick, aka Pope Alexander VI. So is the pope's daughter, Lucrezia, famous for her poisons as well as for being a major babe. If you want to fact check anything in my book, or get further details, I refer you to them."

"Today, though, I'm not going to provide a synopsis of *The Prince*. I hate lecturers who just repeat something I can read on my own, don't you?" There was some grumbling in the audience. Not all the demons present were scholars like Machiavelli. "I want to focus on a few concepts and a couple of key words today, and give you some examples of how to practice the principles behind each."

"Let's start for a moment with the nature of damnation. As we all know, Hell provides a personal form of torment for each of its inmates. Yet there is a common thread that runs through all human experience down here. Can anyone tell me what it is?"

I watched Machiavelli's performance with approval. As a former academic, I had spent many hours behind a podium, lecturing to a group of students with disparate levels of understanding and insight. The group of beginner demons in the room was not unlike a class of freshmen taking Economics 101. There were razor-sharp intellects in here and also people, like Gomer, who probably should have been taking welding classes in a community college. Yet it was the instructor's task to teach them all. This resulted in a sort of dumbing down of most concepts. It wasn't until you got to upper division courses that you could count on students that, if not uniformly bright, had enough aptitude for a topic that you could speak with confidence that they'd "get it."

I had a pretty good idea what our speaker this morning was driving at with his question, what answer he was seeking, but I kept my mouth shut – unusual for me, I know, but there's a first for everything – to see how the others in the room might respond.

When no one in the auditorium responded immediately, he tried again. "Let me ask this in another way. When you were damned humans, why did you feel tortured?"

Asking it that way got immediate responses. "The pain?"

"The misery?"

"The smell?" Gomer offered.

Machiavelli nodded. "All good answers, but not what I was going for. Anyone else want to offer a response?"

Chuckles, who was sitting in the middle of the auditorium, raised his hand.

"Yes, you in the fifth row?"

My friend cleared his throat. "Loss of control."

Bingo. He may look like a clown, but Chuckles is one smart cookie.

Apparently, Machiavelli agreed. "Excellent, Demon … ?"

Chuckles coughed in embarrassment. "Er, Chuckles, sir."

"Demon Chuckles. And don't be embarrassed by your new name. I'm sure most of your future charges will find it ironic." Chuckles's large lips parted into a rather gruesome smile that made me shudder involuntarily.

Machiavelli faced the audience. "Chuckles is correct. Think about all the tortures down here. Remember your own personal damnation before electing to join the Demon Corps. Being cooked in a vat of boiling oil, spitted and turned over a fire, spending eternity talking to your in-laws, driving a cab blind, having sex with someone you find repulsive. Things are either done to the damned, or the damned do them to themselves, and pay attention to the way I say this, *against their will*. They are powerless to avoid their torment. They have lost control."

"You lose control when people or circumstances take it away from you. You lose the ability to choose an alternative."

I frowned. This line of reasoning was striking a little too close to home.

Losing control: like when I chose to become a demon and forfeited my free will. By that definition, I'm still in Hell. Well, of course I'm still in Hell, but in some ways, as a demon I don't have any more control than I did as one of the damned.

Coffee's better though.

"That's part of the demon's job," Machiavelli continued. "To take power from the damned, take away their control. And how do we do that?"

"Stick 'em with our pitchforks!"

"Hurt them!"

"Scare them!"

I felt vaguely ill.

"Yes, yes, of course. All of that. But how? Oh never mind." Our lecturer was losing patience, which was never a major virtue for any demon. "I'll tell you. You keep them off balance, make them insecure, surprise them."

"There are a number of tools you already know about that you've been practicing. Your strength and speed, for example, are, to the damned, supernatural. Humans find your powers

58

scary, and that makes *you* scary. Then there's your pitchfork." He grinned maliciously as he brandished the pointer, which morphed back to its original three-tined state. He swung it briskly through the air. "The pitchfork is an icon for evil. Hurts like Hell, too, when properly applied to the epidermis of the damned, by which I mean poking the shit out of them."

"But there are other tools available to you, skills you have that you must continue to hone. The first is 'stealth.' Now, who in the audience wants to give me a definition? Come on now, not all at once," he said with a sardonic grin, when no one came forward.

At last Gomer spoke up. "It's being a good sneak. You sneak up on a person without them hearing or seeing you."

Machiavelli nodded. "Not a bad definition. And how does one do that?" Various answers were offered, including wearing dark clothing, taking advantage of low-light conditions – Gomer offered up the importance of not wearing squeaky shoes – and so forth. "Let's look at a few good examples of stealth. Ironically, the best ones I know of how to be sneaky can be found in slasher movies of the late Twentieth Century. I have a video here ... "

Lazy. He's going to make us watch a movie.

His choice of video was excellent, though. He grabbed all the best sneaky scenes from the 'Halloween' movies. Boy, that Michael Myers character, creeping up on victim after victim, scared the crap out of more than one demon in the room. Machiavelli burned up at least thirty minutes of his time with the clips, along with the discussion he led afterward.

"The second tool you have is guile. Trickery is a great way to keep your human charges off-balance. Allow me to demonstrate." Machiavelli brought out three walnut shells, half shells actually, and a pea. These he placed on the flat surface at the front of the lectern. His visual aid would have been hard for a human in one of the back rows to see, but since we all had demon eyes, we had no difficulty.

"The shell game is the classic, simple con. Note, I put the pea under this shell. Now I shuffle the three around a little." His hands moved rapidly. "Where is the pea?"

Oh brother. "Nowhere," I said. "You've palmed it."

"Have I?" Machiavelli said innocently. He lifted up the middle shell, and the pea was under it.

Of course, since I was faster than all the other demons in the room, including Machiavelli himself I was pretty sure, I'd seen him take the palmed pea and deftly slide it back under a shell. My colleagues couldn't follow the speed of his movements, though, so deciding it was not to my advantage to show off again, I oohed and ah'd with the rest of them.

Machiavelli covered the pea again and reshuffled the shells. He moved with blinding speed, but I was still able to track his motions. He had again palmed it. "Now where is the pea?" he asked me.

I shrugged.

He flipped each shell over in sequence. They were all empty. "By the way, you were correct the first time when you said I'd palmed the pea. I slipped it back under too fast for you to see."

Says you.

"And I've done the same thing again," he said, holding the elusive pea between his right thumb and forefinger for all to see.

The applause was enthusiastic, and I tried to suppress my smile. These recruits had to have seen devils perform all sorts of magic in their time, yet here they were being impressed by a simple sleight of hand.

Machiavelli had shell game sets for each of the recruits, and he had one of the teaching assistants distribute them to the audience. Shouts of pleasure, like those of children opening their presents at Christmas, echoed around the room. I merely rolled my eyes and pocketed my own set.

"As you know, unlike devils, demons don't have a great deal of magic at our disposal. We're strong and we're fast. We can blast a little Hellfire, conjure up a pie when needed. And we're mean. Not to mention evil. But since we don't have much magic, we have to trick people sometimes. Guile, guile, my young colleagues, will stand you in good stead. So practice hard with your shell game. It's good exercise in trickery. Then look for other ways you can fool people."

"In conclusion, let me just offer the following advice: don't let humans know you're coming and cheat them at every opportunity. These skills will serve you well to keep your charges off-balance, frightened, and generally miserable. And after all, that's the whole point, isn't it?"

After the applause died down, he added, "Don't forget to pick up your signed copy of *The Prince* in the lobby. Thank you." He bowed deeply and left the lectern.

Chapter 6

For weeks, the shell game was all the rage in camp. My fellow demons played with their new toys obsessively, trying to elicit an ooh or an ah from a demon who had the exact same trick in his possession. The whole exercise was completely moronic, in my opinion. As for me, my shell game remained unopened, still shrink-wrapped and in a pocket of my trousers.

One day, Faust stopped me in the hall. "I've noticed," he said with mild annoyance, "that you haven't spent much time practicing the shell game."

"Sarge," I said, trying to keep any hint of disdain from my voice, "I grew up in New York. I learned how to play that game before I turned ten." And watched it performed on the sidewalks of Manhattan or in the middle of Central Park by hucksters who made their living that way.

"Then indulge me. Try to fool me."

"Sarge ... "

"Do it."

With a sigh, I took the game from my pocket and broke it out of its plastic. I used the top of a trash can as a flat surface, placed the pea in the center, covered it with a shell and put down the other two shells on either side. "Shuffle, shuffle, razzle, dazzle. Abracadabra, SHAZAM and Presto!"

"You don't need to be so sarcastic."

"Sorry. It's kind of my signature style. Anyway, where is the pea?"

"Your right palm," he said confidently.

"Is it?" I said opening my empty right hand then did the same with my left.

Faust scratched his head. "I could have sworn you palmed it." With a claw, he flipped over the three shells. They were empty too.

"Give up?"

"Yes. Where is it?"

"Check your right coat pocket."

With a frown, Faust dug in his pocket. He looked startled when he touched the pea. "All right. I guess you don't need much practice with the shell game." He tossed me the pea and I snagged it with my left hand. "I'm going to have to find something a little more challenging than that." He thought for a moment, then an evil expression came to his face. "You're too fast for any demon I know. Think you're fast enough to put one over on a devil?"

I got very still. This could get me in trouble, and Sarge knew it. Still, I was curious. "Who?"

"How about TNK-el?"

I thought about that little creep, about how he'd played me for a sucker, about how he'd contributed to my current situation, and my blood boiled. I didn't know if I was fast enough to pull a fast one on him, but I was itching to try. *But what?* I thought about it for a few moments, and it came to me. "Bwahahahahahaha!"

"Very good!" Faust said. "At least you've been practicing your laugh."

"What? No, that was completely natural and unforced." Which gave me a mildly uncomfortable sensation. Maybe I was getting into the demon mentality a little too enthusiastically. Still, I was thinking about sticking it to a devil I had a grudge with, so I didn't feel as bad about it as I might if I'd planned on doing something to someone else. "If you can arrange for the two of us to leave camp for an hour or so, I think I might be able to pull it off. And if I can't manage it, I'll take the wrath of Shrimp Imp."

"I can do that. Just don't call him 'Shrimp Imp' to his face. TNK-el has a terrible temper, and plenty of firepower to back it up."

The camp had its own elevator button not far from the mess hall. The lift didn't usually stop here but hung around Beezy's office, but since Hell's Elevator could move horizontally as well as vertically, it would, as needed, divert from its normal route. Less than a minute after we pressed the button, the Elevator appeared.

"Hey Sarge. Hey Steve," said the demon who possessed the Elevator. "Where to?"

"Five," I said, "if you would, and as close to the hospital as you can get us."

"No problem."

"Thanks. Say, what's your name, anyway?"

"Otis."

Makes sense. "Thanks, Otis."

The demon Elevator let us off right on the edge of the large plaza before Hell's Hospital. As I stepped onto the concrete, a wave of trepidation swept over me. This was the first time I'd been anywhere near the hospital since the day I agreed to become a demon. Somewhere inside the tall twin metal towers of the building was Flo, the love of my afterlife. Flo, the best person on either side of the mortal divide. Once, we had been quite the item, but that was all past. We had not seen each other since having coffee the morning before my transformation, and I was sure she would find me repellent now. Out of shame, I stuffed my tail into my trousers, pulled my cadet cap forward in a futile attempt to hide my horns.

"Are you all right, Cadet Minon?" Faust asked with concern. "Demons don't usually sweat."

I mopped my brow with my sleeve. It came back sopping. "Just a bit nervous."

Sarge thought for a second. "Oh, yes, Florence Nightingale works in the hospital, doesn't she?"

"Yes. Unfortunately, TNK-el is a bit besotted by her, but that means he spends a lot of his time here. If I'm going to trick him, I have to find him first. He's likely to be inside somewhere."

"Are you sure?"

I thought about the devious little creep. TNK-el had helped Satan play me for a sucker, but his attraction to Flo seemed genuine. "Not sure, no, but it's likely. Listen, Sarge, I, I'd rather not run into Flo, so I'm going to slip in and out as quickly and quietly as I can. Let me reconnoiter the waiting room. I'll be right back, okay?"

"Sure. I'll just take a look at this lovely statue." Faust was referring to a giant figure of Satan, holding a caduceus in the air. The sculpture was the centerpiece of a large fountain. The source of the sulfur-tinted water, or what I could only hope was water, was the Devil's pecker.

It's not as strange as it sounds. There are fountains all over Earth, from Rome to Cincinnati, with little cherub-like figures providing the water through their pee-pees. Anyway, Faust thought the statue was quite attractive. Being a sergeant in a perpetual boot camp, I guess he didn't get out very often.

While he was admiring the view, I did a few leg stretches then bolted for the entrance to the hospital. I was running as fast as I could without actually plowing into anyone. In three seconds I dashed into, around and then out of the waiting room, rejoining my NCO (non-commissioned officer for those who don't spend time around military types or do crossword puzzles). "It's okay. Coast's clear." He nodded, and we stepped inside.

The waiting room was less busy than usual. The few people in there were filling out admission and insurance paperwork. Flo was nowhere to be seen; I'd made certain of that. Neither was TNK-el. Sometimes he'd wander the floor of the waiting room, tripping patients, then sticking them in the butt with his pitchfork, but there just weren't enough victims in the lobby today to make it worth his while.

"Well, well. Steve Minion," said a familiar voice behind me. It was Uphir, demon physician and chief administrator of the hospital. Uphir, a little puce-colored demon who regularly tortured Flo with his antics and, in the past, occasionally me, seemed to have an unerring sense when it came to me. I could almost never appear in the hospital without him knowing about it. Since it was his domain, of sorts, though, his prescience in this area made a certain sense to me.

For once I was glad to see him. "Hello, Uphir."

Astonishingly, Uphir held out his hand. I'd always found him a bit on the belligerent side, not to mention filthy and generally repulsive, and I looked at his hand as if it was a live crawfish. He wanted to shake, though, so I obliged him. "Welcome to the Demon Corps, Steve."

"Er, thanks, Uphir."

"And is that Sergeant Faust behind you? Faust, you old dog," Uphir said, shaking Sarge's hand too, "I haven't seen you since Beast Barracks, what was it, oh, eight hundred years ago?"

Sarge smiled. It was a slightly sick smile, which gave me some comfort. There are demons and then there are demons, I suppose, and some are more repulsive than others, Uphir being in the ninety-fifth percentile on the yucko scale. Still, we were part of the same team now, so I mentally shoved down my revulsion and tried to make nice. "Say, Flo isn't anywhere nearby, is she?"

He looked at me with a mixture of pity and amusement. "No, she's up on the sixth floor, arguing with a proctologist."

I sighed with relief. "Do you have any idea where TNK-el is?"

"Yes, of course. I know where everyone is within my hospital. Amazingly, he's not sniffing around Flo's skirts." He grinned. "I hope that gives you some comfort."

"A little. Where is he?"

"Well, he's not in the waiting room, torturing people here, and he's not with Nightingale. The only logical other place you'd find him is ... "

"The cafeteria, getting a ... "

Uphir finished my sentence for me. "Slurpee. Say, Simon, how's Minion here doing in Beast Barracks?"

Sarge examined his claw, and nodded in satisfaction. "I probably shouldn't say this in front of the maggot, but he's the best."

"The best what?" Uphir said, hanging in anticipation on Sarge's assessment.

"The best. Period. The most powerful demon in all of Hell. More powerful than Adramelech, even."

I gasped.

"Y ... you're kidding, right?" Uphir asked, swallowing hard.

In all my interactions with the demon physician of the Underworld, he knew he'd held the upper hand. He was a demon, a highly placed and very powerful one. I was one of the damned. He used his superior status in Hell's hierarchy to occasionally treat me like shit. I imagine that learning I was more powerful than he was not the high point of his day.

"Oh. Well. Good, good for you Minion. Steve-o. I mean Steve." He smiled pathetically at me. "If there's anything I can ever do for you, just let me know. Now, if you'll excuse me, I'm going to do a back transplant."

"A back transplant?" I said, puzzled. "What's that?"

"Oh, I have a former NBA player with some bad lumbar sections. I'm going to implant a spine from a giraffe. They're almost the same size, so it should work out okay."

"Best of luck with that." I grinned at him in a way that I hoped looked malicious, though in fact the description of the surgery nauseated me. Still, demons were supposed to revel in thoughts of such creative torturing of the damned, so I tried to look enthusiastic.

He smiled again, a sickly smile, since he was probably uncertain about the nature of our future relationship, and quickly left the waiting area.

"Did you really mean what you told Uphir, I mean, about me?"

Faust started laughing. "Maybe, maybe not. I really don't know. You're powerful, but more so than Adramelech?" He shrugged.

"Then why did you say it?'

"I read your dossier and know you and Uphir have some history. I've always hated that little creep, and he's risen far too high for his talents to merit. It was worth a million watching him squirm like that, don't you think?"

I grinned. "You betcha." I was liking Sarge better all the time.

"So what's the plan?" he said as we headed toward the staff cafeteria.

"You go on ahead of me – the cafeteria is behind that door on the far right of the hallway – order some coffee, and just watch. I'm going to piss the great TNK-el off and then slip away without him ever knowing who's responsible."

Faust looked skeptical. "If you don't get creamed by him first."

"Yes," I agreed. "If I don't get creamed by him."

"Man, you must have a death wish."

"Irrelevant at this point in my personal evolution," I said, looking up innocently.

"Point taken." He headed down the hallway and soon disappeared through the cafeteria door. Taking a deep breath, I followed.

Step one: stealth. The cafeteria door was of the type that swung back and forth, in and out, so people could come and go with their hands full, particularly handy on the going out part if you'd picked up a coffee, sandwich and Twinkie to eat on the job. In the door's center was a large circular window. I stood to one side of the glass and peered into the room, but couldn't see anything but a large set of scrubs. The door flew open and flattened me against the wall.

"Ooh … "

"Get out of the way, bub," said a demon RN, his hands full with a quartet of Venti coffees. I assumed he was a registered nurse, because the hospital didn't employ any demon nurses who had less than their BS, that's Bachelor's of Satanism. An LPN, that's Licensed Perfidious Nurse, could do most jobs in the hospital just fine – after all, they weren't trying to cure cancer here but inflict it along with an assortment of other maladies – but that only required an AA, Associates of Antagonism degree. Unfortunately, credential inflation is not confined to Earth but is a universal phenomenon. LPN's could dispense minor pain, like jock itch or bloody noses, but you had to be an RN if you wanted to inflict serious torture as a nurse in Hell's Hospital. That's just the way it was.

The RN, a hulking bruiser of a demon, looked at me and rolled his eyes. "Stupid place to stand, anyway," he said, and left.

After peeling my ectoplasm, along with a little paint, from the wall, I tried again to look furtively through one side of the glass. Sarge had already grabbed a coffee from the urn in the corner and was sitting at a table with a good view of the cafeteria line, a long affair of glass and chrome not much different from what you'd see in a middle school back on Earth. A demon was scooting one of those plastic trays along the chrome runners. The tray was laden with a burger and fries. He dispensed his own drink, a Diet Coke I noted, though why anyone would worry about his weight down here seemed kind of stupid. Still, some people develop a taste for artificial sweeteners and actually prefer the diet variety to the original. Go figure. He reached the register at the end of the line, where a demon who could have been Cookie's twin rung him up.

I couldn't see TNK-el anywhere, but he was so fucking short that he might have been below my line of sight. I stood on my tiptoes and tried to gain higher ground. The glass turned blue again, and once more I was peeling myself off the wall. A little woozy from my second squeeze play in under a minute, I glanced in again.

"Clang!" A diminutive creature had jumped from the floor and was walking along the rails of the cafeteria line. It was TNK-el. He walked past the salad bar, the vats of baked beans, the entrees, even the desserts which included, I noted with distaste, large slices of coconut cream pie, and headed straight for the cashier.

"A grape Slurpee," he said brusquely. "And put it on my account."

"At once, my lord Tinkle," said the Cookie clone.

"That's TNK-el!" the devil yelled, brandishing his pitchfork. "Accent on the second syllable. And there's no "I" in TNK, so don't pronounce it."

"Yes, Lord TNK-el!" The cashier looked nervous, as if he'd had an unpleasant encounter with the irascible devil before. He went to the Slurpee machine and grabbed a plastic cup.

"Not the small, you idiot! I want the super size."

"As you wish, sir."

TNK-el hopped off the runner and stood before the cashier station, tapping his foot impatiently. I guess that's why he got back on the floor. If he'd tried that tapping thing up on the railing, he'd probably have fallen through.

The cashier topped off the Slurpee, snapped on a plastic lid and stuffed a straw in it, then placed the concoction on a tray which he placed on the chrome rail with such care that the drink seemed more an offering to the gods than a frozen concoction of sugar and artificial grape flavoring. TNK-el was still focused on his foot taping routine. "Your Slur ... "

Step two: a little guile and a whole lot of speed.

This was my chance. *Steady boy.* I took a breath, slipped through the door and took off running at my top speed.

A wind seemed to pick up in the room. Demon fur fluttered in the air, not mine, which was plastered to my hypersonic body, but that of the customers in the room. A stack of napkins blew off a table and fell to the floor. I was going about a thousand miles an hour, I figured, no mean trick in the small confines of the room. With a hop, skip and a jump, I grabbed the Slurpee and vaulted over TNK-el then hightailed it to a hiding place I'd spotted behind a vending machine in the far corner of the room.

" ... pee, huh?" The cashier was staring at an empty tray.

That's when TNK-el looked up. "So? Where is it?"

The cashier looked around wildly. "I put it right here. It just, it just disappeared."

The shrimp imp's eyes narrowed, and he lifted his pitchfork. "Slurpees don't just disappear. Are you trying to pull a fast one on me?"

"Never, my lord. Never. Here, I'll draw you another one right now." The demon rushed back to the Slurpee machine and filled up another super sizer.

This time, TNK-el did not take his eyes off the demon. The devil saw his Slurpee flow into the cup, witnessed the addition of both plastic cap and straw, and saw the cashier place the drink on the tray.

TNK-el never took his eyes off his Slurpee. He was reaching up for it with both hands when the drink seemed to vanish.

Now I was crouched behind the vending machine, two Slurpees in the crook of my right arm.

"Hell and damnation!" screamed the little devil. "What the fuck is going on?" He scanned the room with all the maniacal paranoia of Captain Queeg in the 'Caine Mutiny.' Everything seemed normal. It wasn't, because from his vantage point, he couldn't see the nervous but exhilarated young demon cowering behind the vending machine. I reached behind me and snagged a salt shaker from a nearby table with my left hand. With a deft motion, I tossed it to the far side of the room. It clanked against one of the metal legs of a chair, and TNK-el spun on his heels toward the noise.

Step three: misdirection.

I was already in motion again, this time running up the wall and across the ceiling. When I was immediately above the little devil, I released the two Slurpees and gave out a loud whistle.

By the time TNK-el looked up, I was already out the cafeteria door. I peeked back through the glass in time to see gravity drop the two purple drinks right in his face.

The ensuing obscenities were most gratifying. TNK-el was blinded by the purple concoction, but that didn't stop him from sending a blast of Hellfire at the ceiling that put a ten foot hole in the asbestos tiles. Then, still wiping Slurpee from his face, the little creep destroyed the railing on the cafeteria line with a swipe of his pitchfork. He continued to shoot Hellfire indiscriminately in all directions, which cleared out the room pretty quickly. I got out of the way of the door just as it flew open. Devils and demons, all except TNK-el, who was still standing in the center of the cafeteria in a destructive rage, bolted from the room.

Sarge was one of the first out, and I trotted up beside him, matching his pace as we hurried for the hospital exit. "How'd I do?"

Faust's teeth were gritted, and he was actually sweating a little. "Not a word until we get back to camp."

We hurried to the Elevator. Otis wasted no time picking us up, and in a minute we were back at Beast Barracks.

"That," Sarge said, panting slightly as we headed toward our own cafeteria, "was one of the most reckless, dangerous stunts I've ever seen."

"And?"

Faust couldn't help himself. He started laughing, tears coming from his eyes. He had to lean against a wall to keep from falling over. "And one of the funniest things I've ever seen! How did you do it?"

I took a penknife from my pocket and began to sharpen a nail that had gotten chipped one of the two times I'd been thrown against the wall outside the cafeteria. "Oh, stealth, guile, some simple misdirection and a whole lot of speed."

"Well, I couldn't see a damn thing. Slurpees disappeared and reappeared, and you were nowhere in sight."

I explained exactly how I pulled it off.

Sarge nodded. "I give you an A for sneakiness, an A for guile, and an A plus for speed. I've never seen anyone else move so fast they were invisible, except maybe Beelzebub when he's swatting a fly."

"Thank you," I said with pleasure. "Beezy's my mentor, you know."

"I know."

"Learned everything from him."

"Don't know about that. Beezy usually doesn't mess around with stealth and guile. He doesn't need to."

I nodded. "Good point. Satan loves them both, though, and I've spent more than my share of time with the Earl of Hell. Guess I've picked up a thing or two from him as well. So I get three A's. Cool."

Sarge was still snickering. "Yes, oh and some extra credit for having nuts as big as cannonballs."

"So what's next?" I asked, rubbing my palms together in anticipation. I was really pumped from getting some minor revenge on a major devil.

"Teleportation. And I have just the instructor for you."

Chapter 7

The next morning, after roll call and breakfast, Sergeant Faust escorted me to a desolate patch of Level Eight.

In the interest of full disclosure, all patches of Level Eight are pretty damn desolate. Some, however, are more interesting than others. This was not one of them. For as far as the eye could see there was, well, nothing. The landscape was unusually flat. Sand was everywhere in evidence, but other than that, there wasn't a cactus, a hill or anything in sight. "Is it my imagination, or is this the most boring stretch of landscape ever conceived?"

"That's intentional," Faust said. "There's nothing here for you to run into, except the ground itself."

"Oh."

"If you'll, ah, excuse me, I think I'll make a hasty retreat before your instructor shows up." Sarge took off like he was dodging rocks that an exceptionally accurate pitcher was throwing.

"How will I recognize him?" I yelled.

Sarge had traveled so far, so quickly, that I could barely hear his response. "Won't be a problem ... "

"Hello, Minion!"

I spun on my heels. "You!"

"Yes, me," said the Lord of Hell, doing his signature eyebrow arch. He was dressed in a warmup suit, a ball cap with the word "COACH" stitched across the front and his usual sunglasses. Around his neck was a whistle and in one hand, a clipboard.

I was nonplussed. Of all demons, only Adramelech could teleport, and he was as stupid as an S is curvy, so I pretty much expected a devil to be my instructor. But for Satan himself to teach me. Why was that?

"Because," the Devil said, "I wanted to. Beezy could have done it, or one of the other princes of Hell, but really, there weren't many other options. Very few in Hell can teleport. TNK-el *was* an option," he said, raising one eyebrow, "but … "

He left the conjunction suspended in midair, and like anyone who feels the need for resolution, I completed the sentence, "but if he knew what I'd just done, he would have spent his time shake-and-baking me instead."

Satan grinned. "Precisely. By the way, that was a completely outrageous stunt you pulled yesterday."

I shrugged.

"If TNK-el knew you were the one who humiliated him, he'd dismantle you."

"Ah … does he know? For that matter, how do you?"

"I know, foolish young demon, because I'm Satan." The Earl of Hell gave me a withering glance. "You should understand by now that, if I'm of a mind, I see almost everything that goes on down here."

"But TNK-el doesn't?" I asked hopefully.

Satan grinned. "No. Tink is very powerful, one of the most powerful devils in Hell, despite his small stature, but he isn't omniscient."

"And … and you won't tell him?"

"My badness, why would I want to do that?" Satan asked, all smiles. "Admittedly, he's sort of a friend of mine, but he's more like a frat brother. We share some things in common, like both being former cherubim and one-time roommates, but we're not really friends. I have no friends, as I've told you before, not even Beelzebub, who *would* be my best friend … provided I had any friends at all. Which I don't."

That was a pretty convoluted statement, but I understood exactly what he was saying.

"By the way, the trick you played on Tink was absolutely spectacular!" Satan burst out with the patented "Bwahahahahahaha!" laugh. "If he had been able to spot you, I would have given your spleen to him. But, damn, you completely fooled one of Hell's great devils!"

"You saw that?"

"Of course, Minion," Satan said. "Aren't you listening? I'm nearly omniscient down here. TNK-el, however, as powerful as he is, isn't. He has no idea who played that trick on him. He actually suspects me, which I suppose is the highest compliment you could possibly receive for your hijinks."

"Speed, strength, skill with a pitchfork. Stealth. Guile. I was right!" Satan trumpeted with satisfaction. "You have the stuff of demon greatness about you."

"Even more than Adramelech?"

Satan's mouth puckered up, like he'd just sucked on a lemon, when I mentioned Adramelech's name. "What an asshole," he murmured. "One of my biggest mistakes was making him the greatest of all arch demons. Sure, he's the most powerful demon out there, or he has been, until recently," he said, eyeing me meaningfully, "but he has power without intellect. He's … "

"An idiot," I said.

"Bwahahahahahahaha! Exactly so, youngster. You, however. Well, you have his potential in terms of strength and demonic talent, but you're … "

"Not an idiot, " I said, completing his sentence again. "I don't know if I'm as strong as the top Arch Demon of Hades, but I *do* know that I'm smarter than he is. You don't need to tell me."

"Precisely, Minion! I have known for a long time that you could be a prince among demon-kind." Satan sat down on the sand. Suddenly he had grown pensive. "All of the devils in Hades were former angels, as you know. The demons, though, the demons were my chance at creating my own mini-me's. In Adramelech, I found a human with enormous physical potential, but not the caliber of mind I wanted. Adramelech mirrors, on a smaller scale, my own strength, but he has the intellect of a mollusk."

I nodded, finally understanding. "But you saw something in me."

"Yes," he said, eyeing me expectantly.

I sat on the sand, scraping random sigils in it. "I don't know if I have or will ever have the strength of Adramelech, but I have been surprised by my speed and strength."

"Yes, young one." I felt like I was talking to a particularly reprehensible Obi-Wan Kenobi. "And I've even given you the gift of teleportation. I know you are faster, and you may very well be as strong as Adramelech is right now, and you are certainly smarter. You will be my greatest creation! Bwahahahahahahaha!"

"Do you," I said slowly, "do you think you could stop laughing like that? You're creeping me out."

"I am? Good," he said, satisfaction in his voice. "What's the point of being the Prince of Darkness if you don't scare people?"

"Well, that's true," I said, considering.

"But enough of these pleasantries. I'm here to teach you to teleport. Tell me what your experiences have been thus far."

I frowned. "Not very good, I'm afraid. I haven't figured out how to trigger a teleportation. The only times I've done it have been accidental, and I've usually done something like sneeze or cough or hiccup. Something stupid like that."

"That makes sense. It's all in the sphincter, Minion."

"What? You're kidding."

He shook his head. "Nope. Have you ever been in the middle of a pee, and for some reason or other you have to stop before you're done?"

"Well not recently, but sure."

Satan conjured up a life-sized drawing of a body. It looked much like something you might find in *Gray's Anatomy*. The book, not the TV show. There were some differences, like the horns and tail and a few internal organs that seemed shifted, but otherwise demon anatomy looked much like the human variety. "The sphincter is the organ for teleportation. All you have to do is concentrate on where you want to go, pinch down on the old sphincter, and voila! You will just have teleported."

A lightbulb went on in my head. "Oh, so that's why a sneeze or cough or hiccup would trigger an accidental trip."

"Yes. Everyone reflexively tightens the sphincter in those situations. You might want to minimize them, if you can, or at least strengthen your sphincter and your control of it."

"Don't know if I can always stop a sneeze. How would I strengthen my sphincter?"

"I advise Kegel exercises at least twice a day." A prescription pad materialized in Satan's hand. He scribbled out something, tore off the top sheet and handed it to me. The rest of the pad disappeared.

"What does this say?" I asked, trying to puzzle out his execrable handwriting. Satan had many writing styles, but this time he chose the one that looked most like an MD's.

"Just some instructions on proper form for doing Kegels."

"Ah, gee, thanks." I stuffed the note in my pocket. There would be time to decipher what it said later.

"So let's have some practice, shall we?" Satan said, rubbing his hands together. "Your teleportation range will be limited, because you have such a small sphincter. I, on the other hand, have the largest sphincter in the Netherworld, just like I have the largest di … "

"Got it," I said, hastily.

"Why, half my body must be sphincter," he said with obvious pride, "which is why I can teleport anywhere in Hell or Earth in an instant. Why I can even teleport to Diyu!"

Diyu is the Chinese version of Hell.

"Neat." I hoped I didn't sound sarcastic. I wasn't meaning to, but Satan was currently engaged in his signature Sin, the Sin of Pride, and paid me no mind.

"So my teleportation power is almost unlimited, and it's all because … "

"You have a large sphincter."

"Just so." He examined me critically. In fact, it felt like he was staring right through me, like he had X-ray vision or something. "You actually have a larger than normal sphincter for either a demon or a human, though your penis is nothing to write home about."

"Hey!"

"The Kegels will strengthen your sphincter, not only giving you more control over your power, but increasing your range. I doubt, though, that you'll ever manage more than a mile or so."

"That sounds pretty good though, I mean, I suppose I could do a bunch of rapid mile teleportations and get somewhere pretty quickly."

"That's the spirit! Now that you understand the basics, you're ready for a test flight. Put your pitchfork down in the sand. We'll practice teleporting with objects later, but first the basics." I jabbed the tines of my pitchfork into the ground, where it vibrated for a moment before settling down.

"Teleportation is a lot like golf. It's a target game, so you want to rematerialize with some precision. Wait here." Satan disappeared and reappeared a couple of hundred yards away. He pointed at the ground next to him, and a large black X appeared.

Aim for that, Satan's voice said in my brain. I guess he didn't see the point of yelling.

I stared at the X with all the concentration I could muster then tightened my sphincter and ...

Landed right on top of the Lord of Hell.

"Get off me, Minion."

"Yes sir. Sorry sir."

"Humph," he grumbled, getting to his feet. "It's been a long time since I taught this to anyone. I should have seen that coming. But!" he said, brightening, "That was a pretty good first attempt. You got the distance exactly right, and you were only off the mark by about a yard. Let's try again."

He teleported back to our original spot, made another large X in the sand, then stepped back about ten feet.

Now.

I landed right on top of the X. Admittedly, I landed with my chest, knocking the wind out of me, but, I was dead-on perfect.

"Excellent. Now teleport back to the original X, but this time try to keep your feet under you."

"Yes sir."

I hopped back and forth between the two X's about a dozen times, slowly improving my landings, until I could consistently hit the spot on two feet. "Good job, Minion," Satan said. "Now let's check your range." The Devil pointed. "Aim for the horizon, and try to reach it."

I pawed at the sand with my feet, like I was an athlete preparing to do the standing broad jump, or a thoroughbred at the gate waiting for a race to start. I stared at the horizon, which looked impossibly far, but I concentrated, pinched my sphincter and teleported.

Seconds after I landed, Satan popped up beside me. He made a note on his clipboard. "Almost two miles! I'll be damned. Well, I already am damned, but still. That was great Minion! I don't think Adramelech can do that, even now after a millennium of practice. Now teleport back to your starting point."

I made the same distance, but I was fifty feet to the right of my pitchfork. "It's hard teleporting to an exact spot when you have no reference points," Satan said, as we walked back to where we'd begun our lesson. "If you'd thought to concentrate on your pitchfork, though, you'd have been right on top of it."

"Is it possible to get back to a place you've teleported to before, even if it's as unmemorable as this?"

"Yes, you'll be able to do it in time. Now, pick up your pitchfork and practice teleporting with an object in your hand."

That was pretty easy. "Can I teleport someone with me?"

"Sure, but it might cut down on your range. Now," he said leering evilly. "how about teleporting to a moving target?"

"Is this anything like shooting skeets?" I asked, thinking to stick my pitchfork in my secret place rather than just tossing it to the ground. Satan nodded approvingly.

"The skeets analogy isn't bad. You have to compensate for the speed of the traveling object. Like Wayne Gretzky famously said, you have to skate to where the puck is *going* to be."

"And what's my puck?"

In answer, Satan whistled, and BOOH swooped down from the sky. BOOH, the storied Bat out of Hell, and one of my closest friends, was the size of a small airplane. His landing kicked up a bunch of sand, and I almost sneezed, but caught myself before teleporting across the desert.

"BOOHsie," Satan crooned. BOOH was the Devil's courier, pet and dearest companion. "BOOH, head out about five hundred yards, then take off and fly an arc over that stretch of sand, okay, sweetie?"

It was all I could do not to roll my eyes.

"Minion here is going to try to teleport onto your back. For now, keep the speed down to, oh three or four hundred miles per hour, okay?"

"Urm." That was BOOH's gentle way of saying yes, and a few other things. Usually when he vocalized, BOOH made a loud "Skree!" Over time, I'd learned his nuanced way of talking. His body language helped too.

BOOH took off, shooting straight into the distance then, hanging a sharp left, he began flying the arc.

"Okay, Minion. Concentrate."

This was a bit unnerving. I have a slight fear of heights, and even though I'd gotten over the worst of it by flying many times on BOOH's shoulders, or gripped in his claws, this looked a little dicey to me.

"Now Minion."

I swallowed hard, closed my eyes, and concentrated on the task.

I wasn't even close.

"I know you have a little acrophobia," Satan said, as I got off the ground, spitting sand, "but if you're going to hit a moving target, you really need to keep your eyes open."

"Right, right. I knew that."

"AGAIN BOOH!" The giant bat repeated the maneuver but in reverse. I did slightly better this time, and I watched BOOH's butt, a mere ten yards ahead of me, as I plummeted to the desert floor.

"Close, but no cigar. Both of you, AGAIN!"

It took me about twenty times before I could consistently land on BOOH's back, but I got it, and I could still manage, even after Satan had BOOH double his speed. On the last run, BOOH flew me down to Satan. When we landed, I gave BOOH a high five.

"Well done, both of you. Here," Satan said, handing me a piece of paper.

It was some form of certificate, with an embossed seal at the bottom. My name was on the top, and Satan's signature was at the bottom, on a line that said "Flight Instructor."

"VFR? What's that?" I asked.

"Visual Flight Rules. It means you're certified to teleport to anywhere you can see."

"What about places I can't see?" I was wondering if it were possible to hop between Circles of Hell.

"That's IFR, Intuitive Flight Rules. You're not certified for that yet, but it's not hard, as long as you've been there before and can conjure up a good picture in your mind of the place. But that's something you can practice on your own." Satan was looking bored. It was tough having a ruler of all Hell with ADD, but what are you going to do? "I'll keep an eye on your progress, and when you have it down, I'll send you your IFR certification. Now it's *my* turn to fly." With that, Satan disappeared.

"How you been, BOOH?" I asked my friend, as we sat down on the ground.

"Urm. Skree." He pointed at his back and I nodded.

BOOH often got an itch in the most inconvenient spot, right between his shoulder blades. I think it was a little bit of mange, or maybe it was just seborrhea. I just hoped it wasn't the heartbreak of psoriasis. Anyway, I took out my pitchfork and turned it into a back scratcher then climbed on my friend's back and started scratching away. "Ooo ... " he said contentedly. That was a new sound, but there was no doubt about what it meant.

"Skree?"

"I'm okay, I guess," I said, continuing my ministrations. "Everyone tells me I have great potential, but the real test will be when I have to start torturing people. I think, BOOH," I said softly, "that's going to be a problem for me."

"Urm."

"You're right, of course. We'll just have to see. There!" I said, after having thoroughly scratched his back for about five minutes. "Better?"

BOOH nodded.

"Well, I guess I'd better get back to the base. Great to see you. When this Beast Barracks stuff is over, perhaps we can get together for a longer visit."

The giant bat stood and shook out his wings. Then with a final nod of his head, he took to the skies. I watched until he disappeared from view, which took all of a couple of seconds. BOOH maybe couldn't teleport, but he flew like a bat out of Hell.

I guess that's self-evident.

The rest of the afternoon, I practiced teleporting to places I couldn't see. The camp was less than two miles away, well within my range, so I visualized the front gates and tightened my sphincter. That worked pretty well, though I scared the crap out of the two cadets standing guard.

Teleporting by memory actually seemed to work better when I closed my eyes. There were fewer distractions that way. I hopped all over the compound. That most powerful of physical laws in Hell, by which I mean Murphy's Law, that is, if something can go wrong, it will, did not seem to apply to demons. For example, there were a couple of times when the place I visualized happened to have a very solid occupant, a demon, a jeep, a recently-placed dumpster, consuming the space. I did not materialize inside any of those things. I suppose if I'd sneezed or something, I might have. After all, that happened before I'd learned how to properly teleport. Or maybe, with a little experience, a teleporter can make a last minute adjustment and avoid a calamity like that.

The whole intuitive approach to teleportation, in many ways, was easier than teleporting to a place I could see. As a final test, I decided to try moving between levels of Hell. The different circles were about a mile apart, easily within my range, as long as I only hopped one level at a time. I closed my eyes and visualized Glasgow by the Kraken on Level Seven, dockside, near the Throat of Hell on that Level. "Beam me up, Scottie," I said under my breath.

With a pop, I found myself on the pier. One leg was wet; I was standing in a half-full bucket. Yet I'd done it, and I did a little triumphant fist pump. Next I visualized the sulfur mining camp on Six. I found that the more detail I could summon up about my destination, the more precise I was in the teleport. I hopped up a couple of more levels. Then as a final test, I attempted to speed teleport, doing a series of jumps and covering four levels of Hell in four seconds.

Shit. It was really cool.

By the end of the day, my sphincter was a little sore, but I wore a great big smile on my face. I'd done it, mastered what had seemed to me unmasterable. I also gave the Devil his due. He was a hell of a teacher; because of my time in academe, I knew good teaching when I saw it.

Around dinner time, I made a brief stop at the mess hall to make myself a sandwich. I saw Sarge and gave him a smile and a big thumbs up, but I wanted to be alone that evening so took my dinner back to my bunk.

Lying on my pillow was a sheet of paper. It was my IFR ranking, and like the VFR one, it was signed by Satan himself.

Chapter 8

We were only a few weeks from receiving our commissions as demons-in-full, provided none of us washed out. I gathered this wasn't a very common occurrence. Little surprise there. Supposedly, becoming a demon was an irreversible process, so a failed one could not return to the ranks of the damned. Perhaps there was a pit somewhere in an out-of-the-way place where a handful of defective demons spent Eternity, but if so, no one knew where it was.

One afternoon, Sarge released us early, with instructions to take the time to send out graduation invitations to all of our friends. "You can invite no more than six guests. That's all the tickets each of you gets. Any more and the bandstand couldn't handle them all."

Inviting guests to our commissioning: this struck me as bizarre. After all, we were from the ranks of the damned, and it was unlikely that a human friend would or even could turn up to cheer the success of a graduating demon who might very well be torturing the crap out of said friend the next day.

Even so, there were some people I wanted to invite. None of them were humans, of course, but having traveled extensively across (and through) the nine Circles of Hell, there were a few non-humans I was friends with. There was Lilith, of course. And graduation just wouldn't be a celebration for me if BOOH couldn't come. I would of course invite Charon, along with his big brother Mortimer, aka, Death. I wasn't really all that close to Morty, but Ronnie wouldn't come on his own. He was a bit of an introvert, not to mention a workaholic, not nearly as gregarious as his older sibling. Getting Charon away from the River Styx was nearly impossible, and as good a friend as he was, he was likely to decline, which meant his brother would decline too. I shrugged. This whole invitation stuff was complicated. Good thing this wasn't a wedding or a baby shower. You have to invite lots more people, and somebody's feelings always get hurt.

After those four, I racked my brains for who else to invite. I decided on Bik, the young fire giant who ran Hell's boiler room down on Nine, Prometheus and Sisyphus. That meant I was overbooking by one, but if the airlines could do it and have things work out, I figured I could too. Besides, Prometheus and Sisyphus were as much workaholics as Ronnie. I'd be lucky to have three guests, though BOOH, who I was pretty sure would make it, was so ginormous, he'd take enough space in the bleachers for a good dozen.

I doubted anyone would have the guts to turn away BOOH, though.

Filling out the invitations took no time at all, especially with my super speed, though I noticed that a consequence of my revved-up reflexes was a regrettable deterioration in penmanship. The addresses were legible, but just barely. With a shrug, I dropped them in the mail box.

I looked at the base clock tower. There were still hours before mess, so I had some time to kill. Practicing teleportation seemed a good idea, not to mention loads of fun, so after getting permission from Sarge, I winked out of camp.

First I hopped around Level Eight, popping up first at the bazaar. The demons and humans crowding the market were surprised when out of nowhere a demon jostled them. "Sorry, sorry," I said, then popped away to a quiet spot near Beezy's office.

"Having fun, Minion?" Beelzebub rumbled through his screen wall. He was sitting at his desk, his readers balanced on his nose while he processed some paperwork.

"Yeah!" I said with enthusiasm. He shot me a look. "I mean, yes sir."

Beezy flattened some flies on his desk with his flyswatter. "Looks like you have it down pretty well. How far is it you can teleport, now? Satan told me, but I forgot."

"Around two miles. Satan says I might eventually be able to do a bit more."

Beezy nodded. "That's pretty good. Only the princes of Hell can do more than that."

"It's pretty keen!"

The Lord of the Flies took off his readers and laid them on his desk. He sighed. "Minion, demons don't say 'keen.' That makes you sound like the Beaver."

"Oh," I said, vaguely disappointed. "How about gnarly?"

He considered. "Better, but now you sound like a hippie."

"Okay," I said, getting peeved. "Funner than Hell. Does that work for you?"

"Don't be impudent," he said, but without much irritation. "But yes, that will do. Now, if you'll excuse me, I'm examining the specs on a new fire pit."

"Later, sir," I said.

He waved vaguely at me and went back to his work. I teleported to Seven, then quickly to Six, by the time clock near the center of Slothtown. The clock hands moved about twice as quickly there as elsewhere in Hell – when they operated at all, time and clockworks both being a bit FUBARed in Hell. The slothful, who were damned to an afterlife of hyperactivity, glanced constantly at the clock, looking nervous. So much to do, so little time in which to do it. Tsk, tsk.

Up and down and sideways I went, but as I traveled, I thought about all of the people I *couldn't* invite to graduation, former friends like Allan Pinkerton, Nicola Tesla, Louis Braille, Orson Wilde, Samuel Finley Breese Morse, Dora from Parts. Of course I thought with heartache about Flo. And Orson.

I had vowed to stay away from Florence, never wanting her to see me in demon form, though the desire to catch a glimpse of her, if only for an instant, was almost overwhelming. But almost as strong was my desire to see Orson. On a whim, I decided to spy on him. And that would be sneaky, which seemed like a good demon skill to practice.

I appeared in the abandoned steel mill six blocks down the street from my old office trailer. Not sure if they were inside or not, I decided to teleport to a familiar but hidden place inside. There was a crawl space above the sagging acoustical panel drop ceiling. As a human, I'd spent some time up there, trying to fix a leak in a pipe. I'd never been successful, but the experience gave me a clear memory of the space. Closing my eyes, I envisioned the crawl space, pinched the old sphincter and teleported.

"Oof," I exhaled softly. During Beast Barracks, I'd put on some weight – a couple of hundred pounds of demon muscle, not as bulky as the human variety, but still making me larger than I used to be. That made the fit within the crawl space a bit tighter than when I'd been human. I heard the ceiling supports groan under my weight, but they held.

Using a claw, I made a peephole in one of the tiles, and stared down into the office. Edison was carrying a pile of work orders over to a pile in the corner. And there was good old Orson, sitting at what used to be my desk, his now, examining some paperwork in his hand. The sight of my dear friend almost made me weep.

"I *hate* doing jobs for Sekhmet," he grumbled, slapping his hand at the work order.

"Why's that?" said Edison, coming back from the stack of ignored work orders.

"She-devils are the worst, much more demanding than their male counterparts when it comes to home improvement projects. It's like, 'Move the couch here.' So you move the couch here, and she'll say, 'That's not quite right. Try it over there. Oh, and while you're at it, put a hundred pounds of rocks on the sofa to make it extra heavy.' Then she'll make you do it again. Or you'll paint a whole room in Navajo White, but the color isn't quite right, so she'll make you do it over in Light Beige. I mean, jeez, how can she tell the difference? Off-white is off-white."

As I've said before, devils and demons are neither male nor female, but a little of both. However, they generally gravitate in outward appearance toward one or the other gender. Sekhmet looks like a woman … mostly.

"You're exaggerating, I'm sure," said Edison.

Orson shook his head. "No I'm not, Tommy."

Tommy? When did Orson stop calling him Big Prick and switch to a first name basis? I was vaguely jealous of their new-found familiarity, though at the same time recognizing that it's hard to work with someone on an eternal basis and not eventually call him by his first name.

Speaking of names, though: "I wish you wouldn't call me Tommy," Edison groused. "It's undignified."

Orson pursed his lips. "Well, I suppose I could go back to calling you Big Prick, but what would you prefer?"

"How about Mr. Edison?"

"No way. You work for *me*, remember?"

"You never let me forget it, so of course I remember."

"Tell you what," Orson said. "Since we're going to whitewash Sekhmet's fence, why don't I call you Tom?"

"Only if I can call you Huck."

The two laughed, and I was again stung by jealously.

Edison went to the supply closet and pulled out a roller. "No," Orson said. "We can't use that."

"Why not?"

"Makes the job too easy, so it's not allowed. Grab a couple of four inch brushes. That's the best we can do."

Edison shrugged, retrieved the brushes and a drop cloth. Orson went to a stack of newspapers in the corner. I think they were the *Underworld Gazette*, but I couldn't be sure. "We'll want some of these too."

"How are we going to carry everything? We'll have the ladder and, what do you think, three gallons of whitewash?"

My fat friend nodded. He rolled up the newspapers and stuffed them in the front of his coveralls. He looked now to be at the very least a D cup.

Edison, who in life frequently wore a bowler, slipped one on now. "What's that for?" Orson asked.

"I don't want to get paint in my hair."

"Good point," Orson said, pulling open a drawer. "Ordinarily, I'd wear a gimme cap, but since we're a team..." Hell's new Handyman-in-Chief pulled out a bowler of his own and placed it on his head. This made me smile. The two of them looked quaint, old timey.

Orson slipped his hammer out of its loop in his tool belt and replaced it with the paintbrush. Edison followed his lead. He draped the drop cloth over one shoulder. "I can handle the ladder and one gallon of paint. Can you handle the other two gallons?"

Hell's Super frowned, but nodded. "Let's go get the stuff from Dora."

The two headed out the front door. They'd make one stop

at the shed in back to get the painter's ladder then head over to the Parts building. I teleported to their next destination. Even from my vantage point behind the building, I could see the plume of Dora's cigarette, the smoke rising in the air until it blended with the rest of Hell's noxious atmosphere.

They didn't spend much time with Dora. I heard a little arguing. Dora hated giving anybody anything, even though it was her job, but then that's a hoarder for you. Eventually, though, she relented and gave them what they needed. Off the two went to the curb, where they tried to hail a cab. As usual, they were ignored. Hell's cabbies were not intentionally cruel, but being blind, they couldn't always see a fare. Also, the demon dispatcher often gave explicit orders not to pick up people.

For ten minutes, cab after cab passed them by. It was too far to walk to Sekhmet's estate, not with all the crap they were carrying, so if one of the taxis didn't pick them up soon, they'd be forced to ride a bus. Getting across town on a demon-driven bus could take all day.

I decided to cut them a break. As another one of the cabs prepared to ignore them, I quickly ran to the rear bumper and gave a quick yank, pulling the car to a stop, then ran back before I was seen.

The cab driver appeared startled, but when Edison opened the back passenger door and threw in the ladder, he knew he was caught. The two men piled in, Orson gave the address and they were off. I trotted along behind them, keeping just out of sight.

"Who built this thing?" Edison grumbled, as he stared at the privacy fence around Sekhmet's back yard.

"Steve and I did, a few months before, well, before I took over."

"This is the shoddiest excuse for a fence I've ever seen in my life."

I was sitting in a nearby tree. Staring at our handiwork, I confessed to myself he was right. Oh, the thing was solid enough, though Orson and I had had a devil of a time digging the post holes – hard to do when you're only allowed to use ice cream scoops – but the planks were all cattywampus, as if the builders had astigmatisms. We didn't. We just sucked as carpenters.

"Hey, lay off!" Orson snapped. "Steve and I may not have been good with a hammer and a nail ... "

"No shit."

" ... but we made a great team."

"Oh, you're not going to start that again, are you?" Edison whined. "Steve this, and Steve that. He was so wonderful to work with, much nicer than you. Blah, blah, blah."

Well. It was nice to know Orson missed me. I certainly missed him.

"Get over yourself, and get to work."

Edison was staring up at the fence. "Why is it nine feet tall?"

"Sekhmet likes her privacy. Mainly, though, I think it was to force us to bring the ladder. I can't paint the top, even on my tippy toes, and I'm taller than you."

"Whatever," Edison said, spreading the drop cloth. He fought with the ladder for a few minutes, poking himself in the eye at least once, before Orson took pity on him and came to help. Between the two, they wrestled the contraption open. The paint cans fought them as well, but the guys finally got the lids off, stirred up the chalky white concoction, and started to paint.

"You paint the high parts, using the ladder, and I'll work down here."

"Why can't you use the ladder? I don't like heights."

"Two reasons. I weigh almost four hundred pounds. The ladder and I don't get along for that reason alone."

Edison stared distrustfully at the ladder. He must have had some prior experience with the beast. "And the other reason?"

"Because I said so," Orson replied, sounding like a dad ordering around an unruly child. "I'm your boss, remember?"

Tommy frowned, his mouth forming a narrow line across his face, as he pinched his lips between his teeth. "Fine." He grabbed his bucket and paint brush and moved carefully up the ladder, stopping on the last legal step, about four feet in the air. From there, he could just see over the top of the fence. "Holy crap!" he gasped, and almost fell off the ladder.

I saw what had caught his attention. Lying beside the pool was a major babe. Sekhmet had the body of a Vegas showgirl, and she frequently dressed like one, except when she was home, where she preferred to spend her time lounging by her pool in a string bikini. That's what she was doing now, a straw hat covering her face to keep out the light.

The sin that had sent Edison to Hell had been Pride, but I saw a fair amount of the old Lust in his eyes as he ogled the she-devil. Yep, Sekhmet was quite an eyeful, except for the fact that…

Edison's "Holy crap," must have caught her attention. "Holy," is not on the list of words forbidden for use down here, especially when it's used in reference to fecal matter, but it is uncommon, and generally gets a devil's attention. Sekhmet raised up on her elbows, lifting up her hat to see who'd made the noise, giving Edison a full-on view of her delectable bosom … and her lion's head.

"Aaghh!" This time Edison *did* fall off the ladder, his bowler landing on the grass and rolling along its rim until it came to a stop at the base of the tree I was sitting in. As he slipped, the Wizard of Menlo Park's fingers got caught in an over-large gap between two boards, and there he hung, his body slapping against the fence, two feet off the ground.

Orson was a little preoccupied. He'd been working beneath Edison, and when Tom fell, he knocked over the ladder, along with his can of paint. Predictably, the can landed upside down on Orson's head. Drenched in whitewash, my friend began to curse a blue streak.

"Edison, you idiot!" he shouted, as he threw the can – and the soaked bowler – off his head and reached for a cloth to wipe away the paint.

"Help me, Orson!" Tom's fingers were turning purple.

Still muttering some pretty foul language, Orson crawled beneath Edison's splayed legs then stood up, taking the weight of the suspended man on his shoulders, and giving his assistant time to extricate his fingers from the two slats of wood. "Okay," Edison gasped. "I'm free."

"Good. Now get the Hell off my shoulders!" Orson leaned forward and dumped Edison on the grass, then both of them sat for a few minutes panting from their exertions.

"You realize, of course," Orson said at last, "that now we don't have enough paint to finish the job."

Edison hung his head in shame. "Yeah, I know. I'm sorry."

I had an almost uncontrollable urge to blast him with Hellfire and throw a pie at him, but someone beat me to it. (Good thing, since we hadn't studied pies in Beast Barracks yet.) While Orson wiped away the worst of the paint on his head, Edison started cleaning the pie off his own face.

Watching Orson and Edison work together had been a trip down memory lane. My old life had been a series of mishaps not unlike the one I'd just witnessed. To many, it might not have seemed very hellacious, but a damnation of being Hell's handyman was pretty horrible in my estimation. In a way, though, I missed it, especially the easy camaraderie Orson and I had shared.

Finally Orson stood. "Go retrieve your hat and head back to Dora's. Get two more cans in case something else happens. Meanwhile I'll keep working."

"Yes sir," Edison said contritely.

As he picked up his hat, Edison saw me high in the tree. "Hey, what … "

I teleported.

Chapter 9

There were still a few more weapons in the demon arsenal that I needed to master, as did the rest of the members in my platoon.

We started with conjuring and casting Hellfire. I don't know why Satan settled on fire as the way to punish the damned. I mean sure, it hurts, but he could have opted for bone-chilling cold, or pressure-related pain, like dropping sledge hammers on people's feet, or something smell-related, like emitting intense body odor at will. But while all of those were used in Hell, at least to some degree, fire-related torment was a required element in eternal damnation. So, while demons I suppose could get some continuing education credits by taking correspondence courses in other forms of torture, we all had to learn how to conjure and cast Hellfire before graduating from Beast Barracks.

Oh, I should tell you that Hellfire is a little different from the regular variety. First, it's a bunch hotter than that toasty campfire you roasted marshmallows over as a Scout. Second, there's the smell. Hellfire is permeated with the scent of sulfur. All demons can produce and direct Hellfire; it just requires a little practice to control it.

We started with blasting it from our pitchforks. That was pretty easy. Like a wizard uses his staff to focus and direct his magic (no, there are no wizards, Virginia, but we've all read *Lord of the Rings* or seen the movies, so I'm sure you get what I'm talking about), a demon can employ his pitchfork to dispense Hellfire with precision. The fire itself, though, comes from within.

After the gang had spent a morning of target practice,

shooting flames hundreds of feet with our pitchforks, we were instructed by the drill sergeants to put our weapons away and try to do it *au naturel* or I suppose, to be precise, unaided by any tool. My first efforts, in fact, all of our first efforts, were pretty ugly. I sent a huge ball of fire into the sky. No structure, no sense of direction to the blast. Pretty embarrassing, really. The worst of it was I scorched my nails, and I'd just had them done the previous day by the camp manicurist. Getting the charred outer surface of my nails removed, and resharpening them to resemble the claws of devils, not to mention obtaining that claw-like gleam from what was essentially human keratin, would require another hour in the chair, and the whole time I'd have to listen to Madge, my manicurist, jabber on about her problems, while she soaked my nails in Palmolive.

It took me about three hours to master the unaided creation and direction of Hellfire toward a target. In this one area, I found I wasn't particularly special. Many of the other recruits could make Hellfire as well as or better than I.

Next came cream pie throwing, or pieing as it's also known. I know it's stupid, but Satan has decreed for almost one hundred and fifty years that under certain circumstances, particularly when one human genuinely thanks or shows affection for another, the former – and sometimes the latter – must be smacked in the puss with a cream pie. It's a well-known fact down here that the Devil has a very low-brow sense of humor. Also, like me, the Lord of Hell is a film buff, and, at least according to urban legend, he got the idea about the pie throwing from seeing Fatty Arbuckle do it in a 1913 film called "A Noise from the Deep." I really don't know if this is the case or not, but pieing is now as ubiquitous in Hell as Hellfire itself. In my time as a damned human, I'd had many a pie hit me in the puss. In my case, the pie in question was always coconut cream, because I'm allergic to coconut. My former assistant, Orson Welles, got lemon cream, because he despises lemon. Others of my friends got flavors that in one way or another were equally noxious to them, like Dora getting grasshopper pie (she hates mint), Shemp Howard getting butterscotch, and so forth.

Throwing a pie is easy, but conjuring one up from thin air, not so much. For some reason, Satan insists that they actually be good pies, like what you'd get from your favorite pie shop back on Earth. I'm not really sure why he gives a fuck, but whatever else he may be, the Lord of Hell is a stickler for detail, so we had to be able to conjure a delicious pie at a moment's notice.

Pie conjuring, in fact, took us weeks to learn. First we started with the crust. Anyone who is a baker can tell you that making a good crust from scratch is difficult. I crapped up more than one batch. I'd hoped to be able to cheat by using a frozen pie crust shell, but Sarge caught me immediately. I got ten demerits for that. Realizing that he wasn't going to allow me to cut corners, I grabbed a copy of *The Complete Pie Cookbook* and learned how to make crust. Then I had to learn the recipes for the dozens of possible pies that might be especially odious to particular individuals.

Once I got pie conjuring down, though, the rest was easy. I now had the satisfaction of knowing I could make a really good pie and throw one with unerring accuracy. Learning to precisely throw pies was absurdly easy in comparison with learning to teleport myself onto the back of BOOH. The whole squad spent a morning creaming each other with pies. Fortunately, none of us was hit with pies we hated. Not a single coconut cream pie grazed my face, though I got my share of butterscotch. Don't know why Shemp doesn't like butterscotch. It tastes pretty good to me.

Anyway, this particular exercise was a blast. We were conjuring and hurling pies at each other for hours, laughing like lunatics, until the sergeants pronounced that we'd all passed pieing and called a halt to the festivities. Too bad. I could have tossed pies at the gang all day.

The next session was a necessary prequel to what I'd been dreading ever since I started in the Demon Corps. It was time to put all of our training to practical use. After all, the purpose of being a demon was singular: demons were made to torture the eternally damned.

"Frankly," Captain Cringe said to us during our last days at Beast Barracks, "I wouldn't give a crap if you practiced on real humans from the get-go, but Satan believes you should never touch a damned soul unless you are competent at torturing it. So … " he ended limply, as the manikins were brought out from a back room and placed on the long, narrow tables that filled the classroom.

I looked at the models and almost laughed. They looked like more elaborate versions of Resusci Annie, the dummies used back on Earth to train people in CPR. These, however, had more than a head, neck and torso. The manikins had arms and legs and hands and feet too. Calling them Annies wasn't quite accurate. They were female on one side, with breasts and other gal parts, and male on the other, masculine junk included. That way we could practice torturing both sexes, I supposed, without having to have two separate manikins. I mentally named my model Torture-ee Anne and Andy.

On the nose of each manikin was an analog dial. "What's this?" Chuckles asked.

"That's the Excruciometer," Cringe explained. "It will show you how much pain you are inflicting." Cringe nodded to the two sergeants standing patiently at the back of the room. They distributed clipboards to each of us. On each of the clipboards was a single sheet of paper. "Here is a list of torture techniques you are to practice. We've gone over these in class before, so if you've done your homework, you'll know the acceptable ranges for each maneuver. After each one, record the score from the Excruciometer in the provided box. Oh, and make sure you use a number two pencil. We're grading these with a Scantron machine."

"Mainly because it's too much trouble to grade by hand," Sergeant Faust said, handing me my clipboard.

"Precisely so, Sergeant." Cringe said. "You'll get your scores tomorrow and be able to see where you nailed it, so to speak, where you went overboard, and where you held back too much. All right? Good. Cadets, present pitchforks."

As one we all drew our pitchforks from our belts.

"Some of your torture will require use of your pitchfork, and some will require your hands."

"Do you mean we actually have to touch it?" Gomer said with mild revulsion.

"Don't be so squeamish!" said the other sergeant, a lupine sort of demon named Garrou. "This is a plastic manikin. If you can't stand touching something so obviously fake, how are you going to torture a real human? Now demon up, cadet!" he finished sternly.

Cringe nodded in approval. "You may begin now. You have the entire class period to complete the exercise. Any questions, ask the sergeants. I'll be having tea and scones in my quarters." With that he left.

And then we had at it.

Anne/dy was a bizarre, hermaphroditic simulacrum – cool word "simulacrum," and I wanted to see if I could work it into a sentence – but as I read down the list of torture techniques, I realized s/he was the perfect model for the job. There was the nipple tweak, painful for both sexes, but especially so for the female side of Anne/dy where there was more nipple to tweak. There was the nut jab as well as the nut vise, the latter requiring the cadet to transform his pitchfork into an actual vise. Then there was the pelvic exam for the Annie side, the prostate exam for Andy. Of course, there were many forms of torture that could be applied to either half of the manikin, like the butt stab, the foot puncture, the eye gouge. In those instances, it was dealer's choice.

I began my work with as close to a clinical detachment as I could. After all, like Garrou said, these were fakes, no real harm was happening to anyone. I rapidly worked through the worksheet. From my homework, I remembered the pain tolerances for each torture. It was important to be able to accurately gauge exactly how much pain could be endured. After all, you didn't want your subject to faint on you. There was a definite finesse involved in all this torture stuff. Funny that I'd never noticed it before, and it gave me new respect for demons like Uphir, who was a master at this, and even Gaap, the demon bus driver who reveled in slapping me over the face with a whip or sticking me with a cattle prod.

Yet as I got close to the end of my assignment, gouging the manikin and then recording the results from the Excruciometer onto my worksheet, I started to feel a bit ill. Perhaps I had too good an imagination, but I started thinking that Anne/dy could actually feel all the hurt I was inflicting.

And even if s/he can't, the time will come soon enough when I'll be doing these maneuvers on the real thing. I shuddered at the thought.

As I neared the last few procedures on my worksheet, I realized I was no longer applying sufficient pressure to Anne/dy.

We were working on the honor system, which seemed a bit odd to me since we were all unscrupulous demons, but I dutifully recorded my readings, even though I knew I'd be graded down on them. I'd pass the assignment, but I'd be lucky to get a low B or maybe a high C, and that was only because of grade inflation.

The buzzer rang, and I handed in my clipboard. Sergeant Faust looked keenly at me; he must have noted the slightly ill expression painted on my features. "Are you okay, Minion?"

"Not really," I said, gulping. "But I'll have to be. No free will, right?"

He nodded slowly but looked troubled.

That afternoon I teleported all over Hell. I tried to stay incognito, but I watched carefully as more experienced members of my new profession applied all the forms of torture I'd practiced on Anne/dy. All the demons, every one, seemed to take great pleasure in their work. I wondered if I would ever be able to. More, I worried that I *would* someday enjoy hurting my charges.

I returned to Level Eight a little before the dinner bell. I needed to burn off some energy, so I took a quick run – only a couple of hundred miles. At one point, I found myself in a desert portion of Eight that resembled not the Sahara but the Chihuahuan in the United States. It was a very arid landscape but lacked all that sand. There were, however, large boulders scattered on the ground. In my mind, I could picture Beezy doing this, tossing the large rocks idly as he contemplated some aspect of Hell or Eternity. Beelzebub was a restless and thoughtful devil. He spent a great deal of time alone out here, and these boulders were arrayed in a far from random fashion.

I looked for the biggest rock around; the one I settled on was twenty feet high, wide and deep. Who knew how many thousands of tons it represented, but I lifted it with ease, throwing it a hundred yards. Then I blasted it with Hellfire, first from my pitchfork, as if I were wielding an acetylene torch, then from my fingertips. I might have been wrong about my talent for slinging fire. Maybe it was because I was upset, but my flames burned white hot as they torched the rock, hotter than any the other cadets had managed during any of our practice sessions.

For good measure, I even threw a pie at the boulder. My choice was coconut cream, for even though I personally couldn't stand that particular dessert, I had to be able to conjure one up and throw it when needed.

I sat down on the ground with a thump. I could do it all, and then some. Every skill a demon or even an arch demon needed was within my possession. But what I'd feared from the beginning of Beast Barracks was being confirmed. My heart just wasn't in this.

My internal clock told me that it was dinner time, and even though I'd lost my appetite, I needed to get back to camp or get in trouble. Rather than running back, I did a series of rapid teleports, reaching the gates in seconds, just as the mess hall bell began to ring.

I picked at my food, then went to bed early. I lay awake all night, staring at the canvas that formed the roof of our bunkhouse, I remembered my nights as a damned human, tossing and turning in insomniac torture. Even though I knew, as a demon, I would rise the next day physically fit and ready for whatever task was required of me, I feared there would be a weariness to my soul that I would not be able to shake off.

At least there would be, if I still had a soul. I was no longer sure if, in forfeiting my free will, I had not also forfeited that ineffable essence that was the true me.

The end of Beast Barracks training was a nightmare for me.

As I'd suspected, I'd passed the test with Anne/dy, though my marks were lower than Sarge would have wished.

"What's going on, Minion?" he asked, as I filed into the torture classroom after breakfast. "You completely blew your last three procedures."

"Hand cramp," I stammered, shrugging.

"Yeah, right. Pull yourself together," he hissed in my ear. "It's for real now. Get it right, or there'll be Hell to pay."

"Har, har, sir."

"You know what I mean."

I sighed. "Yeah, I do."

The final two days were live-action repeats of the tests we'd performed on the manikins. I suppose I should have been grateful for the way the examination period was structured. On that first day, all of the real-human test subjects were volunteers. In life, they'd been masochists and enjoyed any pain we inflicted. Yet their hysterical laughter and anxious grins did nothing to assuage my misery. Whether crunching a guy's nuts in a vise or dilating a vagina to gargantuan proportions, my own stomach cramped in sympathetic misery. Many times I sought to ease up on the amount of pain I inflicted, but Sergeant Faust was onto me, and he made certain I did my job.

"Do it right, or I'll make you do it again until you hit spec," he said grimly.

Sweat pouring from my brow, I nodded. The subjects screamed in pain, and he was satisfied.

On the final day of our examinations, the masochists were swapped out for unwilling humans. They begged for release; they begged for relief. I noted with dismay that my colleagues, having gotten inured to the torture process by starting with manikins and then progressing to willing subjects, had an easy time putting it to these poor damned souls.

I was not so lucky. Under the watchful eye of Faust, I performed each method of torment competently if not enthusiastically. This time the screams were screams for mercy, for release from agony, but between the strict oversight of my superiors and the awful compulsion that came from a creature lacking free will who must above all things obey direct orders, I did my duty.

But there were tears in my eyes, and my soul screamed each time theirs did. At the end of the day, after performing my last act of torture, I raced from the classroom and retched violently on the sand outside.

Curiously, none of my colleagues, not even soft-hearted Gomer, followed my lead. In fact, they looked at me as if I were a freak or, worse, a traitor of sorts.

And yet, as pathetic as my performance in the torture chamber was, I somehow passed. All that remained was graduation, and I would be a demon in full.

Chapter 10

The sky was a vibrant blue on graduation day, which was pretty unusual, since the air tended toward a sickly yellow in Hell. But Management must have pulled out the stops to make this a festive occasion.

Bleachers had been erected along the side of the field where we practiced some of our military maneuvers; brightly colored banners attached to the railings of the seating billowed in the hot breeze. The emerald green parade field was precisely mowed.

All the soon-to-be graduates were in their quarters, ironing slacks and shirts, blackening boots, buffing demon horns. For the occasion, Madge had come to our barracks, sharpened everyone's claws and then polished them to a fine luster.

We even got out the silver polish to use on our belt buckles, making the camp motto, "daemonium in cogitatione semper," gleam brightly. For those of you who don't speak Latin, that roughly translates to "always think like a demon." This being too long to put on a belt buckle, it was of course shortened to its acronym: DICS. This made a sort of sense to me, since most people in Hell called demons a bunch of dicks, at least behind their backs. Sometimes the damned called them dickheads.

Yes, this was going to be a day of high pageantry, and everyone was really putting on the dog. We wanted to be the sharpest looking graduating class the camp had ever seen, which explained all of our spit and polish. Especially the spit, which we used to sleek up our tails and hair.

There's something special about demon spit. It's like a gel, thick and a little mucousy, and it does a wonderful job moussing up the old mane or smoothing out a rough spot in one's tail fur.

We had all stripped the sheets and pillows from our cots, tossing them in a large dumpster outside the bunkhouse. They were due to be burned. The next platoon of cadets would get fresh bedding, I supposed because no one, even a new recruit, wanted to sleep on sheets that had been previously used by a demon. Can't say I blame them. Most demons smell to high heaven – though I personally was trying very hard not to succumb to that odoriferous state – and a recruit would not yet have developed a graduate's tolerance for rankness.

I stared out the window of the bunkhouse, watched the bleachers begin to fill. Most of the attendees were demons themselves; there was always considerable pride when a new crop of graduates crossed the threshold into demonhood. There was of course no family gathering in numbers to witness the proud day; with few exceptions, becoming a demon was not viewed by many relatives as a point of pride. There were few friends in the audience, either. Damned humans weren't allowed to attend graduation exercises, and unless a family member or friend had become a demon prior to you, they wouldn't even know to attend, even if they'd been allowed and wanted to, which was unlikely.

I, however, had at least one demon friend who I thought might attend, and I scanned the bleachers with my demon sight, looking for her. She wasn't hard to spot. Lilith was seated on the front row. She wore a splendid green sundress, low-cut of course, with a ribbed bodice that clung tightly to her tremendous ta tas. The skirt was pleated and flared at the bottom; the wind lifted it occasionally, showing a generous amount of her shapely calves.

Lilith was very fair, like most redheads, even demonic ones, and while she was as heat-tolerant as any of her kind, she wore a broad-brimmed straw sunhat to protect her lovely and delicate features. Or maybe it was just for style, since there is no sun in Hell to protect against. In any event, she looked quite fetching. She also looked very excited. Her bright blue eyes were wide open, and she was scanning the camp eagerly; I hoped it was me she was looking for.

Since I had forfeited almost everyone else in my afterlife by becoming a demon – Flo, Orson, Allan, Nicky, Louis, all of them – I was grateful to have at least one friend who would be at my graduation. *Well, a bit more than a friend.* The thought made me blush.

Make that two. In the sky an enormous creature was flying in lazy, ever lower loops. It was BOOH, of course. I smiled, realizing he too had come to see me graduate. BOOH settled down on the top ledge of the bleachers, dead center. He would have overbalanced them, throwing the rest of the audience over his shoulders, like so many grains of salt, if he had not thought to spread his wings and use his power of flight to take some weight off the seating. He looked magnificent that way, like a grisly version of the great eagle on the back of a dollar bill, almost a part of the day's decorations.

And here's three. A flaming meteor dropped from the sky and landed next to my batty friend. Bik had managed to get away from the boiler room to attend.

In the center of the bleachers was a VIP box, which was currently empty. I assumed some major devils, as well as high-ranking demons, would fill it at the last minute.

"Hey, you knuckle-headed SOB's, are you ready for this?"

I turned to see Maximus enter the bunkhouse, dressed in Roman warrior garb, complete with goofy hat that looked like a red Mohawk growing from a helmet, body armor, sandals and a red cloak. In his hand was a sword, no doubt his transformed pitchfork. As I suspected, Max had already been made a

111

centurion. He'd go far in the Demon Corps.

"Max!" I yelled, delighted, and rushed over to shake his hand. The other demons joined me, pounding Maximus on the back, shaking his hand or giving him a guy hug (across the shoulders with one arm, from the side, no privates touching), demonstrating a camaraderie which a few months ago I would have thought demons incapable of.

"Minion, Gomer, Chuckles," he said, a broad smile on his face as he looked at all his colleagues in the room. "Great to see everyone!"

"We're so glad you came," Gomer said.

Max grabbed Gomer in a brotherly neck lock. "I promised, didn't I?"

"Yes, you did," I said, "but you'd better get changed. Inspection is in ten minutes."

"Okay," he said, taking off his helmet. "Where's my cadet uniform?"

"In your locker," Chuckles said. "All pressed and ready for you. Gomer even polished your boots."

"Thanks, guys." Max quickly swapped out his clothing and stored the centurion uniform in his locker.

And none too soon. A bugle sounded, and Sergeant Faust yelled at us from the door. "Assemble outside for inspection!"

Sarge walked up and down the double line of cadets, adjusting a cap here, an epaulet there, looking for his reflection in the spit-polished boots. At last he seemed satisfied. "At ease."

We stood at ease for about fifteen minutes. In the air, I heard the band play the familiar strains of "Hell to the Chief." Satan must have just arrived. Then a bugle sounded "Assembly." Sarge cocked his ear and, nodding, turned to us.

"You've done well in your training, maggots. You will all

make fine demons, I'm sure. All that remains now is the conferring of your commissions, which will be done by Lord Satan himself. Attention!"

We snapped back to our formal posture.

"Left face! Forward march!" In two rows, we marched to the parade grounds.

We stepped on field to the sounds of the camp's marching demon kazoo band. These were some serious kazoo players. Just tremendous. I didn't know kazoos could play so well in tune, though of course it was hard to tell the actual pitches, since kazoos mostly buzz, like bees swarming or people blowing through combs wrapped in waxed paper.

My favorite instruments were the six silver-plated kazoosaphones that wrapped like great serpents around the demon musicians playing them. The kazoosaphones laid down a magnificent oompah of tonic and dominant raspberries, while the soprano, tenor and baritone kazoos garnished the noisy fruit with melody, a complex countermelody and some impressive upbeats. The tempo was vigorously percussed by three bongos, a conga drum, a toy tambourine, the cymbals (as opposed to the symbols), and of course a glockenspiel. The drum major marched before the band, throwing his gargantuan pitchfork into the air; each of his elaborate tosses sent the fork spinning multiple times before it came back to his hand. He only missed once, though unfortunately that miss staked him to the ground. Still, the band didn't miss a beat. Unfazed, it formed two columns and flowed around him. Right after the kazoosaphones, bringing up the rear of the band, cleared his prone body, he managed to pull the tines from his flesh and gamely, if limply, followed in the wake of the band.

We marched past the bleachers. I could have done without the goose stepping. It seemed a little Hitleresque to me, but this style of march had the advantage of keeping our heavy boots away from our tails. Nobody wanted to step on a fellow demon's tail or to have his own so degraded. As we pulled even with the VIP box, Sarge yelled out the command to halt.

"Cadets!" he shouted. "Right face!"

We pivoted sharply, facing the bleachers.

"Hut! Present arms!"

We presented arms. This was as painful as it sounds and was accomplished by grabbing left forearm with right hand and right forearm with left hand then pulling … very hard. The arms popped out of their sockets with a sickening slurp. Quite painful, but it was one of the required maneuvers, we'd practiced it many times, so we were prepared for it. We waved our arms at the audience like a platoon of maniacs before popping our free-floating limbs back in the sockets at our shoulders. After collectively suppressing our shudders of pain – it was considered bad form to moan when presenting arms – we saluted those in the stands with our pitchforks.

The crowd went wild.

I was more than a little impressed by the VIPs in the box. Cringe, as camp commandant was there, of course, but he was little more than a figurehead, and he stood off to one side. Adramelech, the highest ranking demon in Hell, stood on the opposite side of the box. The King of Fire was powerfully-built, with a barrel chest. Said chest was covered with medals, including copper, silver, gold, and even lead and iron. The arch demon was in full military regalia, which would have made him look quite impressive if not for the dazed and crazed expression in his eyes, and the slight bit of drool that had gathered on his chin. I couldn't tell if he was demented or just stupid. Both probably.

But those figures standing in the middle of the platform

were who really caught my eye. In the center was Satan, Earl of Hell, resplendent in a red suit. He had his horns and tail on display, and a magnificent golden pitchfork in his hand. Such attire was unusual for him, since he usually thought pdd's (public displays of devilry) were gauche. To his right was Beelzebub, his white suit freshly pressed, his black fez held under his left arm as if it were a military hat. His omnipresent flies seemed aware of the formality of the occasion; they flew on either side of his head in perfect columns. To the left of Satan stood Asmodeus, Lord of Lust, in a black suit with red sash. Gone was his normal cockiness. He obviously took the day's ceremony seriously.

And then there were two ovals of light, one a bright gold, the other a sickly yellow-green. I could see figures inside. Within the disc of gold was Mammon, devil prince in charge of Greed; within the other was Belphegor, the purveyor of Sloth in Hell. Those two never left their realms, but were attending the ceremony in spirit if not body. Along with Beezy (Gluttony) and Satan (Pride and Wrath – he got a twofer – Pride for his Lucifer aspect and Wrath for his Satan one), the five devils represented six of the seven Deadly Sins.

Conspicuously absent was Leviathan, prince of Envy. Like Mammon and Belphegor, he tended to stay in his own back yard. I was surprised though that, with the other princes of Hell present in one form or another, he was allowed an excused absence. Judging from the irritated expression on Satan's face, Leviathan's non-attendance was a breach of etiquette.

The Earl of Hell cleared his throat. When he spoke, sans microphone, his voice rumbled across the field. "Cadets, today marks a milestone for you. You are about to join the Demon Corps, an elite order with a proud tradition. You are no longer human, but something new, something special, and you now join the ranks of Hell's hierarchy of power."

Swell. I felt a little ill.

Beezy, standing at rigid attention beside his boss, looked bored as hell. Lilith, though, was beaming at me, a look of possessive pride on her face. I held my face impassive, though the temptation to grin back at her was almost more than I could resist.

"As I speak to you now, your orders are materializing in the inside pocket of your jackets." I felt a tingle near where my heart used to be. "There is a grand party planned in your honor at the Palace in New Rome. Hell's Escalator is being set in reverse for the next two hours in your honor so you may easily reach it or any other level of Hell. But tonight is yours. Celebrate where and as you will and on the morrow, open your orders and report to your new assignments."

"And now, by the power invested in me by, well, me, I now pronounce you demons, with all the rights and privileges hereunto pertaining. Daemonium in cogitatione semper!"

"Daemonium in cogitatione semper!" the newly-made demons shouted with one voice. A little lump of pride formed inside me, until, that is, I said to myself, "Always think like a demon? Why the fuck should that make me feel so proud?" Still the mood was infectious. It was hard not to be pumped.

"DICs, DICs, DICs, DICs!" chanted the crowd.

As if he'd almost forgotten an important duty, Captain Crunch stepped forward hurriedly. "Demons rule!" he shouted.

"Humans drool!" we yelled in return, finishing the time-honored phrase.

"You are now demons, my children," Satan said with obvious pride. "My will be done … So there!"

Sarge gave a subtle hand gesture, and we all whipped our caps from our foreheads, tossing the hats high into the air. We grabbed our pitchforks and together sent forth a massive blast of Hellfire. The caps were incinerated. Satan waved his hand to one side, as if brushing away a fly, and a gust of wind caught the ashes, blowing them from the field.

"Dismissed!" Satan commanded, then he just disappeared, while the entire sky momentarily went black. Asmodeus was next. Assuming the form of a lightning bolt, he zipped into the sky. The two orbs of Mammon and Belphegor glowed with power, flashed in cadence – bing bong – and were gone. Adramelech, not having the brains to come up with a flashy exit, just teleported away. Cringe walked awkwardly off the dais.

As the stands emptied, BOOH and Bik launched into the sky. They flew above me in a tight circular formation. They must have been planning to do this all along. Then, like the Thunderbirds or the Blue Angels, they broke formation and flew off rapidly in opposite directions. Very classy. Thinking the maneuver was a salute to all of the graduates, my colleagues on the ground applauded. That was fine by me.

I looked back to the stands. Only Beelzebub remained. He stepped to the front of the VIP box, gripped the railing with his large hands. He sought me out in the crowd then locked eyes with me.

What now little demon? Can you adapt, or will this destroy you?

I gulped. This was the first time Beezy had unambiguously demonstrated he was telepathic.

And his question was right on target. I'd been wondering the same thing since being tricked into enlisting. He didn't need to search my mind; my mournful look must have been a clear enough answer. Beezy just shook his head.

I shrugged. *Damned if I do; damned if I don't.* With that thought, I gave the only devil I'd ever respected a brisk salute.

He returned it, then smiled, a little sadly, I thought, before leaving in signature style by means of a thermonuclear explosion. The large mushroom cloud that marked his departure reached to the underbelly of the next level of Hell.

"All right, DICheads," Faust said to us, a broad smile on his face. "Get out there and raise some Hell."

Chapter 11

I had not taken three steps from formation when Lilith was in my arms, embracing me. "Oh, Steve," she whispered in my ear. "I'm *so* proud of you." Then she gave me a kiss that took my breath away.

"Wow!" said Gomer.

"Who's the babe?" asked Chuckles.

"Guys," I said to my comrades, "this is Lilith, my, my girlfriend. I told you about her, remember?"

"Holy shit!" Max said. My centurion friend had left camp for New Rome weeks before I'd told my colleagues that I had a girlfriend. "A succubus! A genuine, glorious succubus! Minion, you old bastard, you've been holding out on me! Don't you think you should introduce us?"

I made a round of introductions, while Lilith practically preened under the admiring gazes of so many handsome young demons. Yet I was touched that all the while, rather than flirting with them, she nestled into me, kissing my cheek, nibbling on my ear.

"Girlfriend indeed!" Max said. "I see there's not much hope of separating you two."

"Not a chance," Lilith said with an impish grin. "However, I wanted to invite all of you to a small party I'm throwing up on Two. I promise a good time will be had by all."

A large portion of the platoon had already decided on going to the Palace for the gala celebration. They expressed their regrets then headed to the bunkhouse to pick up a few things prior to heading for the Escalator. Max, Gomer, Chuckles and a few others accepted Lilith's invitation, though. She gave them her address, and they promised to be there in an hour. Then they headed off to get their gear.

Lilith kissed me again, then whispered in my ear, "Oh, I forgot to tell them some of my sisters were going to be there."

I grinned broadly. "I think that will be a pleasant surprise."

She frowned. "You stay away from them, though. You're mine."

"Whatever you say, dear."

"Don't you need to get your stuff from the bunkhouse?"

I shrugged. "I don't really have any stuff. Not anymore." Well, there was the pea game, but I felt that I could somehow do without it. Not having any possessions I valued, like my old tool belt or putty knife or rolls of duct tape, saddened me, but I tried not to show it to Lilith. This was a day of celebration, and I was determined to stay as upbeat as possible.

Besides, I do have this really keen pitchfork now.

Lilith stared with dismay at the crowds building before the Escalator. "We should head for the Escalator now. The Elevator is likely even more jammed."

I looked at my freshly buffed claws. "Oh, I don't think that will be necessary."

"What do you mean?"

"Do you trust me?"

She looked startled. "Of course I do, but why?"

"This," I said, wrapping my arms tightly around her. Then I closed my eyes, visualized the docks on Level Seven and teleported us there.

"Oh, Steve," Lilith said. It was now her turn to nearly swoon. "That was *so* hot! You really *can* teleport. I mean, I know it was part of your signing bonus, but I can hardly believe it! Not even many devils can teleport!"

"Yeah," I said, trying to sound modest, but secretly bursting with pride. "I can't travel as far in a single hop, but Satan says I can already teleport farther than Adramelech. I can do two miles, and my range is still growing."

"Hmm." She nestled against me. "How long would it take you to teleport us to my place?"

"That's five more hops. About ten seconds, I guess."

"That would give us an hour to, you know ... "

I got us there in five.

After we finished with our urgent errand, we showered together, lathering each other up. Amazing how long it took me to get her breasts clean, not that they were particularly dirty, maybe a little sweaty, but then there was also a lot of surface area to cover, and I wanted to take my time and do an especially good job. You understand.

Then we dressed for the party. She had a tuxedo waiting for me in the closet – she had always liked me in a tuxedo. I needed a little help sticking my tail through the small hole in the trousers tailored to accept my pointy appendage. Lilith had selected a hot red cocktail dress that showed off her assets, and all of her numerous other things, to great advantage. She was just slipping her second shoe onto her dainty foot when the doorbell rang. The first of our guests had arrived.

All of my new demon friends had spent the hour rummaging up something appropriate to wear. Some of the outfits were a little odd. Max was back in his centurion outfit which, I had to admit, suited him well. Chuckles actually wore a clown outfit, but it was tailored very tastefully. I thought he looked great. Even Gomer managed to look dapper in a white suit that reminded me of the one Atticus Finch – or Gregory Peck, take your choice – wore in 'To Kill A Mockingbird.' There were other demons with them. Kat, who in life had been a woman, wore a glam off-the-shoulder evening dress. There were a few other formerly-female demons who attended. They all looked just fine.

Then some of Lilith's sisters showed, much to the delight of my demon friends. They had brought a few incubi with them, so there was a nice mix of personalities and sexual proclivities in the house. It wasn't long before everyone was paired up. Some succubi were with "male" demons, some incubi with "female" demons, some succubi with "female" demons, some incubi with "male" demons, succubi with succubi, incubi with incubi. You get the idea. There was someone for everyone.

Soon Lilith's living room was full to bursting, so she opened the back French doors. While I'd been at Beast Barracks, she'd had a pool installed. Many of the gang yelled in glee. It wasn't often that you had an opportunity to immerse yourself in water in Hell, at least it wasn't for this crowd, since none of them were recruited from Level Seven, where drowning in the ocean was a common occurrence. Lilith had tents erected on the lawn near the pool and told everyone there were swimsuits for everyone inside.

Lilith had had the party catered, and demons in white shirts and black ties, pants too, weaved through the throng of party-goers, distributing champagne, beer, wine, cocktails, you name it. There were also canapés, including those little egg rolls and meatballs, which Lilith knew were my favorites.

It would have been nice if some of my human friends could have attended, but I knew that was impossible. Still, when there was a knock on the door, Lilith, who had been handling the hosting duties up until then, sent me to the door. I opened it, and Charon was there. I was so happy to see him, I hugged him.

Good to see you too, he clacked out in Morse code. Lacking a tongue, Charon couldn't speak, but I'd always been able to understand him. Funny thing, though, other demons in the room could too. I guess it was a power of demonhood, the ability to understand everyone in Hell. Behind him was Sisyphus, the ancient Greek king who was the symbol for eternal punishment. These were the two hardest working guys in the underworld, and I knew Lilith had pulled some serious strings to get them the night off. I shook hands with Sisyphus and asked what he wanted to drink.

"Mead, I think."

"Lilith do we have any mead?"

She gave a little moue. "Fresh out. Sorry."

"That's okay," said the gregarious Greek. "How about a rum and coke?"

"Coming right up. And a white wine for you, right Ronnie?"

Indeed. Ronnie always drank white wine. Since anything he swallowed inevitably fell through his bones and went on the floor, he never imbibed anything that might stain a carpet. He was thoughtful like that.

"Thanks, hon," I said, kissing her cheek, after getting them set up with their drinks.

She dimpled prettily. "I thought you should have some old friends as well as new ones here tonight."

At that moment, there was a loud thump in the back yard. I looked out and saw a furry monster drinking out of the pool. The sight made me smile broadly.

"You didn't think I'd forget BOOH, did you?" Lilith said, giving my arm a squeeze. "Oh, Bik sends his regrets. He is in the middle of rebuilding some Venturi tubes down in the boiler room."

"That's okay," I said. "I was just glad he was able to make the graduation."

The party went on until the wee hours of the morning. I must have drunk a quart of martinis – not really sure, since things were a blur there for a while, until I sobered up. I do remember that at one point in the evening, we all put on swim suits and played volley ball in the swimming pool. Even Charon joined in. He was on our team and turned out to be one hell of a server, owing, I think, to the fact that he was hitting the ball with the hard bones of his right hand, without any flesh to absorb some of the impact.

BOOH, being a little large to join us, draped a wing across the width of the pool, forming a net. He was also the official scorekeeper and rules enforcer. You really didn't want to get caught by BOOH in an infraction, because he'd grab you with his claws and toss you into the hot tub, where you had to sit for ten minutes in a time-out before you could rejoin the game.

Lilith and all her sisters wore bikinis, but, and maybe it was just me being prejudiced, I thought none of the other succubi could hold a candle to my red-headed lover. Her black bikini stayed on by magic. Certainly the spaghetti straps alone couldn't have kept that skimpy top up. And the thong, well, come on, a thong bottom is hardly a bottom at all. I think our side scored more than one point because the demons on the opposing side were paralyzed by the sight of all her scrumptiousness, just like the boys in Dogpatch were by Stupefyin' Jones.

After the game, we all got out, and dried off. Some of the attendees left at that point. Charon and Sisyphus wanted to get back to work, so we said our goodnights. Some of the new graduates who had paired off with Lilith's sisters and cousins or their incubi friends, left arm in arm, heading for private spots were they could be connubial. Those of us who remained, me and Lilith, BOOH, Max, Gomer and Chuckles played some strip poker. Three of Lilith's sisters, Liliths Two, Three and Four I mentally called them, since all succubi are named Lilith, watched from the side, bringing the guys drinks and generally cheering everyone on, or kibitzing when someone blew a hand. Because BOOH was too big to fit in the house, we played outside by the pool.

Interestingly, the night's big winners were Lilith and BOOH. Neither one had to take off a stitch of clothing, which my friends thought was a real shame in Lilith's case. She just laughed and said we should see her play bridge – that was her game – and her sisters agreed, saying no one could turn a trick like she could. BOOH was always a winner too. I tried to figure out how they could both win, never losing a hand, but my besotted brain never could figure it out. Just as well, though. No one really wanted BOOH to take anything off, not that he had anything to take off anyway.

After the game, BOOH gave me a big hug and then took off. Liliths Two through Four linked arms with my friends and led them out the front door. I was pretty sure that for Gomer, Max and Chuckles the evening was far from over. Gomer particularly looked excited. His eyes were as bit as saucers.

And that left only me and Lilith. The caterers had departed hours earlier but had done an excellent job cleaning up. We only had a few glasses to put in the dishwasher.

After the pool shenanigans, we had put back on our party duds. My tie had been hanging loose around my neck for hours, though, since we'd begun the poker game. Lilith, however, had stayed perfect in her ensemble. Now, though, she popped off her four inch spikes. We sat on the couch together, me rubbing her feet while we stared at a fire in her hearth. A fire was pretty gratuitous. Hell was way too hot to require one, and we'd spent half the party in the pool, so it would probably have seemed to some a stupid thing to have going. The fire, though, burning in the hearth, was a gentle thing, and we snuggled up together, staring into its flickering heart.

"Thanks, Lilith," I said, nuzzling her neck, and taking great delight in almost getting her to purr. "It was a great party."

She smiled affectionately at me. "It was my pleasure, Steve. I really wanted to do something special for your special day. I …" she hesitated, "I know this hasn't all been easy for you."

I leaned over and kissed her lips softly. "No, it hasn't, but hush. Tonight has been magical. To be with friends, to be with people who care for me … " I thought of Flo, Orson and my other friends, but shook my head. They were lost to me. But BOOH, Charon and even my new demon chums, well, it was nice to know I had friends. And then there was Lilith.

Our gentle kisses turned a bit more passionate, and it wasn't long before our hands were exploring each other's mystery lands. I took her there on the couch. Then she, flushed from our activity, took me by the hand and led me to the bedroom.

We had sex for hours, and it was wonderful.

Demons don't have to sleep, but Lilith, after what I guess was our twelfth time copulating in the wee hours of the morning, decided to lie in a languorous half-doze. She looked beautiful lying beside me; her skin gleamed a post-coital pink. I looked at her with affection. She was a wonderful lover, and I really cared for her, but …

… I could not put Flo from my mind. She was lost to me forever, this I knew, yet I loved her anyway. The first and only time we were intimate, we had made love, and as much as I cared for the darling she-demon drowsing next to me, I could not bring myself to call our sexual acts lovemaking. Perhaps I was just splitting hairs, but …

If you're not with the one you love, love the one you're with.

That was an anthem of sorts for my generation back on Earth. I reached my majority during the sexual revolution, the era of free love some called it, after the Pill but before the calamity of AIDS descended upon the world like the Angel of Death among Ramses' Egyptians. AIDS took all the spontaneous joy out of the sexual act, but for the first decade of my adulthood, I lived and loved without fear.

If you're not with the one you love, love the one you're with.

If I could not be with Flo, Lilith was an awfully fine substitute.

With a fond if rueful smile, I kissed the nape of her neck, then spooned her and dozed for the few hours left before reporting for duty.

Chapter 12

"Oh crap!"

"What?"

Lilith and I were dressing, she for work as the personal assistant to Asmodeus, Lord of Lust, me to report for my first assignment since graduating from Beast Barracks. As ordered, I had spent the previous evening forgetting about future responsibilities then this morning opened the envelope in my cadet coat pocket to see where I was to go. "Satan wants me to report to him personally."

Lilith walked over and read the orders over my shoulder. "Really? He must have something very special in mind for my sweetums." She kissed me on the ear.

I'd thought about the many times I'd done jobs for Satan directly. They were never pleasant experiences. Satan, the ultimate imperious, impatient boss, was terrible to work with. "It gets better. I have to be there in five minutes."

"You can make it. You're already dressed, and you can teleport. So, since we have a little time, how about a quickie?"

"Goodness, I mean, badness, you just can't get enough, can you?"

She smiled at me mischievously. "Well, I *am* a succubus."

"Listen, I'd *love* to, but I don't dare risk being late. Satan has no tolerance for tardiness."

"Okay," she said, a trifle disappointed. "We'll do it when you get home from work."

"Whenever that is. I really have no idea what I'll be doing or the conditions of my deployment." I picked up my pitchfork, preparing to go.

"Don't worry. Satan likes to keep his workforce happy.

You'll either be able to come home at night or at least with some frequency."

Home. I looked around the bedroom. It was a very domestic scene, but it didn't feel quite right. "Well, I guess I'll find out soon enough."

"Before you go," she said, turning her back to me, "could you hook my bra strap?"

Despite my nerves, I smiled. "Surely you can do that on your own."

"In my sleep, but I like it when you do it."

"Unhooking it is more fun. But okay." Leaning my pitchfork against the bed, I hooked the clasps for her. The back seemed okay – the fabric wasn't twisted or anything – but I wanted to do a good job for her, so being the responsible type, I decided to make certain the front was okay as well. The cloth felt properly in place, even though it seemed to be straining a bit. Then my hands, of their own volition, began to explore. Lilith purred with delight, then continued her cat impression by rubbing herself against me. I was going into mindless rut mode, when she suddenly gasped, "I thought you said we didn't have time for this!"

"What?" I said, coming to my senses. I shook my head to clear it, grabbed my pitchfork and kissed her on the cheek. "Right. Wish me luck."

"Luck, darling."

And then I teleported. Three, Four, Five, Six, Seven, Eight and down onto the white shag carpet of Level Nine – BING! – right before Bruce's desk. "Demon Minion reporting for duty."

"Well, well." Bruce the Bedeviled, Satan's personal assistant, stood. He was called "the Bedeviled" because Bruce was in love with Satan, especially in his Lucifer aspect, but Satan wouldn't give him the time of day. Like me, Bruce had recently become a demon. "Here you are, Steve Minion, demon deluxe. And on time too, for a change."

"Well, being able to teleport helps a lot with that," I said with some pride.

That didn't sit well with Bruce. He frowned. "Yes, I heard you'd been granted that power. You would have thought I, as Satan's personal secretary, would have been given it too."

"Why Bruce," I said, looking at him in mock amazement, "are you questioning our lord and master?"

Satan's assistant turned pale. "N … no. I'd never … "

"Besides, you're his secretary … "

"Assistant."

"Whatever. Anyway, you never leave your desk, so what do you need teleportation powers for?"

"Exactly so," said a deep voice. Satan had stepped out of his office. He was in his typical office attire, black suit, black shirt, black tie, dark sunglasses. I popped to attention, saluting him. "Very nice, Minion, but skip it for now and come in." I followed him through the double doors. They closed behind me.

Satan's office looked pretty much like it always did, a broad, black indeterminate expanse with a large rosewood desk some thirty feet from the entrance, a spotlight from an unknown source shining down upon it. The Earl of Hell's favorite red La-Z-Boy recliner was behind it and a cushioned office chair in front. Just as I was heading for the chair, though, Satan snapped, "Attention!"

I assumed the position – attention, that is. Satan walked around me, examining me from all sides. He looked at my freshly manicured nails, sharpened to where they were indistinguishable from the real thing, that is, from devil claws. He examined my horns, tested their pointiness with a finger, went behind me and jerked on my tail briskly. I almost yelped but held my tongue. Then, as if he were buying a horse or something, he pulled back my lips and examined my slightly sharper-than-human teeth, including my elongated canines. He nodded once then walked around his desk. Without warning, he yelled, "Think fast!"

An anvil was flying at my head at high speed. I grabbed it easily with one hand.

"Take the anvil, place it on Bruce's desk and come back in here, and do it all just as fast as you can."

He didn't have to tell me twice. In a nanosecond, I was out the door. I accomplished my task and was back in front of Satan's desk in the blink of an eye.

He rubbed his chin. "Very strong and very fast, not too fast for me to follow your motions, but certainly far beyond Bruce's ability to see you. To him, the anvil must have seemed to magically appear on his desk. Now, blast me with Hellfire."

"Uh, beg pardon?" I scratched my head.

"I said blast me with Hellfire, nitwit! And not with your pitchfork. That focuses your fire. I want to feel your raw power. Give it to me straight from your fingers. Show me what you've got."

I shrugged. "If you say so, sir." Summoning up all my will and all my demonic strength, I sent the hottest blast I could manage, straight at his face. He was unfazed, of course, but still he smiled.

"Quite hot, for a demon. Hotter than most devils are capable of. You seem to have turned into a fine specimen, as I suspected you would. And your teleportation abilities make you virtually unique. Well, all that plus the fact that you have a brain bigger than a slug's."

A clear slam at Adramelech.

He looked at me, his eyes glowing with enthusiasm. "I was

right about you. You will be my greatest creation ever! Bwahahahahahaha!" When he laughed, he sounded more like a mad scientist than a devil.

"But, sir? How did you know I was going to be so fast, so strong? So, well, so good at being a demon?"

The Lord of Hell scratched his chin, looked up thoughtfully into the darkness above before answering me. "As a human, you demonstrated many character traits that almost always make for a powerful demon. You were very strong-willed, very independent. Not to mention being smart and having more than your share of guts and raw determination. A human with those traits who agrees to be a demon, surrendering that very strong free will you had, is almost always a special catch."

I looked at him in surprise. "That's it? That's all there is to it?"

The Devil shrugged. "Well, no. Identifying a special demon isn't exactly a science. If it were, I wouldn't be saddled with Adramelech." He thought for a second, trying to put it into words. "Look, it's kind of like art. I can't tell you what makes for good art, but I usually know it when I see it."

"The same for demons?"

"Yes. I saw the makings for a great demon inside of you."

Satan sat down and motioned for me to do the same. The chair was unusually comfortable, by far the most comfortable I'd ever been granted during an audience in his office. It sure as hell beat the "chair of tacks" I sat in one time.

The Earl of Hell picked up some paperwork from his desk. "There is this one issue, though … "

"What?" I said leaning over the desk and trying to see what was in his hand. He glanced at me sharply. "I mean, what, my lord?"

Satan slapped at the paper with one hand. "Your final exam

in torturing. It was less than stellar."

I gulped. "Well, you see, I ... "

"No excuses!" he said, sharply, taking off his sunglasses and eyeing me closely. His eyes, sometimes black and sometimes red, depending on his mood, were an impenetrable jet today. "A demon with your power and your potential — I'm not sure there's a demon in the entire Underworld who could challenge you, even now, and you're just a newbie — should have aced that exam." He paused. "Okay, okay, I said no excuses, but why did you do so poorly?"

The Lord of Hell could have plucked the answer from my brain, but he granted me the privilege of answering myself. I tried to be as honest as possible, which is always the best thing to do with Satan, since you can't hide your thoughts from him anyway.

"Well, I'm still having a bit of trouble with the whole torturing damned humans thing. I mean, I know that's my job and all. It just makes me uncomfortable."

"Uncomfortable enough to barf all over Beast Barracks?" he asked, one eyebrow arched impossibly high. "Explain."

Even the memory of the incident made my mouth taste of bile. I swallowed, trying to keep down the nausea. "Torturing people, it's, well it's a bit repulsive to me. Like eating sushi."

"What?? You don't like sushi?"

"Not really, no."

"Man, you really are a wuss."

"Hey! I mean, hey, sir! I DID pass."

He looked at me with derision. "A Gentleman's C from the star recruit at Beast Barracks is practically a failure."

I looked down at my pitchfork, feeling ashamed and unashamed at the same time. I was a jumble of emotions about this whole torture topic. "I think it has something to do with being tricked into becoming a demon. My heart isn't in it."

"Why you ungrateful little putz! I've made you the most powerful demon in existence, and you tell me 'my heart isn't in it?'" He threw a boulder at me in disgust, which I knocked to the side.

I looked around the room desperately, hoping to find someone to take my side. There was no one, and at that moment I wished Beezy were there. "Sir, I'm trying. I really am. I'll do my best to improve."

"The only way to improve is with practice, which I promise you, my young demon, you will get in plenty."

"Swell, my lord." I could already feel my stomach knotting up. "Meanwhile, perhaps there are other ways I could be of service?"

Satan frowned and slipped back on his sunglasses. "Perhaps you can. In fact, I already have an assignment for you."

The Devil rose from his La-Z-Boy, by which I mean he levitated, floated to a spot a few feet behind his desk and dropped his feet to the floor. I'd seen St. Peter perform a similar move once before. It was really cool. Satan began to pace back and forth. "Did you notice a conspicuous absence at yesterday's graduation ceremony?"

"Yes, sir. Leviathan wasn't there."

"That's *Lord* Leviathan to you. Protocol, you know."

"Yes, sir."

"Anyway, all Princes of Hell are expected to attend the ceremony. Expected by *Me* to be there. Leviathan, Mammon and Belphegor I allow to attend virtually, since they prefer not to leave their realms. Even in that I am being generous, don't you think?"

"Yes, sir, though I imagine you'd rather not have Belphegor, I mean, Lord Belphegor personally attend, in any event."

"You got that right. Repulsive, isn't he?"

Belphegor, as the Lord of Sloth, would have a very difficult time motivating himself to travel all the way from Six, where Slothville is, to Eight. He was also a repulsive, smelly, slug-like demon who would not have made the best impression on anyone at the ceremony.

"But the main reason I don't force those three to come is that they do good jobs overseeing the punishment of humans who were damned for Greed, Sloth and Envy, as well as managing their respective circles in Hell. As reward, I indulge them in certain ways. Besides, it's pretty impressive to see those glowing orbs on stage. In some ways it's way cooler than having those princes show in person, don't you think?"

"Yes, my lord. I thought the orbs were very impressive."

"You know, Minion? One thing has certainly improved since you've become a demon."

"What's that, my lord?"

"Your manners."

"Thanks." I cringed at the slip. "I mean, thank you, my lord."

"Anyway," he continued. "This is the first time Leviathan has failed to appear for a graduation. I want to put him on notice that there will not be a second time."

"Are you going to see him, my lord?"

"Good grief, no! Me going to *him*? Ridiculous. Undignified. Besides, I don't like water."

"You mean like Dracula doesn't like water?"

"No, you idiot. Not like Dracula. I could appear there. I could even keep myself dry. But I don't like his waterlogged domain."

"So, you're going to order him to come to you?"

"In a way, but doing it directly would look like I'm coming groveling to him. You *do* realize what this is all about don't you?"

"No, sir, I guess I don't."

"Hmm. More polite, not as smart." Satan made a note to himself on a pad at his desk. "Leviathan is the Lord of Envy, right?"

"Yes sir, and … oh!" I said, a lightbulb going off in my head.

"Correct, young demon. Leviathan envies my power as Lord of Hell. He doesn't like taking orders from me."

"But, but you're his boss!" I was, for some reason, mildly outraged. "Besides, he doesn't have free will, any more than I do now. It should be impossible for him to disobey a direct order."

Satan smiled. "Now you're getting it."

"How did he do it?"

Satan blasted me with flame. It tingled, but didn't really hurt. He nodded, satisfied. Apparently, he was going to test me periodically. I didn't take it personally, though. That probably had something to do with my absence of free will too.

"I didn't give him a direct order. It's always been, well, just understood. Usually when I leave things ambiguous, devils and demons fall all over themselves trying to figure out what I want them to do anyway. However, such an approach does provide a loophole, a loophole that in Leviathan's case I intend to close."

In Satan's hand, a rolled parchment materialized. "I want you to take this to him. Don't worry, it's waterproof."

"What's it say, my lord?"

"That's not really any of your business, now is it?"

"No sir, sorry."

"Still, curiosity is a sign of intelligence, and since your IQ seems to have dropped a few points recently, I'm glad to see a little curiosity, so I'll tell you. This is a direct order that he must in future attend all graduation ceremonies. Since, as you say, he has no free will, he will have no choice but to comply. It also says a few other things," Satan cursed, and I got a pretty good idea of what the other things were. The Lord of Hell handed me the scroll. "Young demon, your first assignment is to find Leviathan in his underwater kingdom and deliver this to him."

"Could you just magically transport it into his hands?"

Satan zapped my head with a bolt of lightning.

"That tickles," I said.

"Good. It would have split a human's skull. But back to the scroll. You still don't seem to get it. If I send a lackey, excuse me, I meant a minion, Minion, with the message, I maintain my dignity. If I teleport it to him, well, it's complicated. Devil pecking order stuff that you probably wouldn't understand."

"No doubt, my lord. But sir, the ocean on Seven is pretty big. Any suggestions on how I might find him?"

He stared at me keenly for a second. "I do, but I think it would be good for you to figure this out for yourself. Work the old brain cells, if you know what I mean."

Great. "Yes sir. I'll figure it out." *Somehow.* "Do you want me to wait for a reply?"

Satan laughed. "Why the Hell not? Get his reaction and then return here for your next assignment."

"Er, my lord?"

"What?" Satan was growing irritable, his famous impatience to the fore.

"After this assignment, will I continue to report to you directly?"

"Yes. You see, I've always had big plans for you. After your probationary period, during which we'll work out the obvious kinks in your demonic personality, you are going to become my factotum."

"I thought that was Bruce's responsibility."

The Lord of Hell shook his head. "Bruce does a good enough

job maintaining my calendar and greeting guests, but he couldn't handle what I have in mind for you. You're going to be my troubleshooter."

"Oh, kind of a demonic version of Hell's Super."

"In a way. Now, take that message to Leviathan. No! Stop!"

I had just closed my eyes and was preparing to shift to Level Eight. I opened them again.

"Don't ever teleport in my office! Only I get to do that, understand?"

"Oh, sorry. I didn't know."

He humphed. "Well now you do. Take it out into the lobby. Dismissed!"

Chapter 13

With a barely audible pop, I appeared at my usual landing spot on Level Seven, a rarely-used stretch of dock along the waterfront. By habit, I raised my right leg, making me look a little like a flamingo, I suppose, except for the horns and tail. It had taken three changes of socks to teach me the habit of keeping my foot nearly even with my left kneecap. Fool me once, shame on you. Fool me twice, shame on me. Fool me a third time, well, I was just being a doofus, especially when it came to wet socks, which served as a very persuasive object lesson, as most anyone would agree.

So I'd learned to materialize while slightly off-balance, kind of like an Olympic gymnast might nail a landing, even if the dismount was a little on the wobbly side. I was mildly pleased with this modest new skill, but I didn't need it this time. Someone had moved the bucket, so I stood on one foot looking stupid. Fortunately, as I said, not many people came to this section of the pier.

I looked around the harbor. About a half mile away, and maybe two hundred feet above water level, hung a lone outcropping. That looked just perfect for the beginning of my modest scheme for finding the Leviathan. Eyes open, I concentrated on the bit of rock and …

Landed with a skid that almost sent me tumbling into the drink. There was bird or some other kind of shit on the stone, making things a bit slippery. Cursing, I scraped the crap off my dress boots, noting idly that I still wore the dress uniform of a cadet. Perhaps, if I asked nicely, Satan would let me wear something that didn't scream demon newbie. I also realized that my clothing was not the best choice for my current assignment.

"Screech!" Flapping above me was a harpy. Apparently, this was her preferred perch, and I was poaching.

"Oh, get lost," I said in irritation. Harpies had always been one of my least favorite creatures in the Underworld. They had the worst personal hygiene of anyone, making BOOH smell like a daffodil by comparison. They also cursed like sailors, and had terrible tempers. In the past, there had been little choice but for me to put up with their shenanigans, but my recent change of status had altered the equation in my favor.

The harpy dove at me, her sharp talons poised to rip some ectoflesh off my body. These winged creatures, in addition to being foul and belligerent, were a little short on brain cells. They attacked anything that moved, even if that thing that moved was higher on the Infernal food chain. I torched her with a blast of Hellfire, turning her feathers to a fine powder that blew away in a gust of wind, revealing a pink and scrawny body not dissimilar to that of a plucked chicken. She swore at me the whole time she fell, and she was only silenced when her body disappeared below the water. Judging from the bubbles rising from her point of impact, she was still cursing me out underwater.

I guess I really *didn't* know my own strength. My intention had been to discourage her from hassling me, not to render her flightless. Still, harpies are a tough breed. In a few moments, she scrambled onto the shore beneath the outcropping.

With my demon sight, I saw her flip me the bird, a particularly apt obscenity, considering harpies have always reminded me more of vultures than women. They're really a mixture of both, like a chimera is a combination of lion, goat and serpent or a griffin is a mix of eagle and lion or an accountigrat is a blend of tiger, rat and tax accountant.

But I digress. The noxious creature would grow her feathers back quickly. When harpies molted, which was infrequent but regular, usually happening at the most inconvenient times for whatever damned human they happened to be harassing – the creatures re-grew their plumage in less than a day, so this particular specimen would be back up on her rock in no time. I shut her from my mind and turned to the task at hand.

My assignment: deliver Satan's written orders to Leviathan. Before teleporting from Satan's anteroom, I'd stuck the scroll and my pitchfork in my secret spot. That would keep both hands free, something I felt would be important. Funny how, as much as I liked my fork, it was a tad inconvenient to carry around. Even putting it in my belt was not a perfect solution. Sometimes I'd trip over it or get my tail wrapped around it. Stuff like that.

Sarge had been right. Most of the senior demons I'd encountered only had their pitchforks in evidence for formal occasions; it seemed only relatively junior members of the Corps regularly carried their weapons openly. Following the leads of Uphir, Whizzer, Karnaj and other experienced demons I knew, I usually stored the pitchfork in my pocket universe. For reasons of protocol, I planned on pulling out my pitchfork when it came time to present myself to Leviathan. For now, though, it and the scroll would stay safely tucked away in my hidey-hole.

Job one was to find the Lord of Envy. Satan was right. Figuring that out was simple, once I'd given the problem a moment's thought.

Fact one: Leviathan spent all his time in the ocean, either as Moby Dick or, more commonly, the Kraken, a giant squid-like creature.

Fact two: The Prince of Envy liked nothing more than attacking the poor schmucks who populated the port city of New Glasgow, the docks of which were my landing zone on

Level Seven.

Fact three: All I had to do was sit back and wait. Sooner or later, Leviathan would breach, destroy some ships or the docks themselves, drowning a few hundred damned souls in the process.

I used Hellfire to scour the harpy shit from the rock. Then I made myself comfortable.

Less than an hour elapsed before the sky darkened. A storm was coming in from the sea. High waves beat against the weathered dock of the bay; cold rain pelted the people of the town, who went scurrying for cover. They knew what was coming.

A mile off shore, a tsunami was rushing toward land. When it hit, the dock shattered, and the bodies of longshoremen scattered like billiard balls hit hard by a cue ball. Then the tentacles of the Kraken shot out of the water.

That didn't take long.

I slipped off my uniform, until all I had on were my boxer shorts. Then like Johnny Weissmuller leaping off the Brooklyn Bridge in one of those Tarzan movies from the Thirties, I did a swan dive off the rock.

As I've told you before, I have a slight fear of heights, but it had mostly been drummed out of me by repeatedly leaping or being pushed through the Throat of Hell. Hell, compared to falling all the way from Gates Level to Level Nine, this was like hopping into the kiddie pool at a neighborhood park. Or at least it was until I crashed into the water and went below its surface.

I didn't know what to expect. Even damned humans can't be killed by submerging them in water. They can only drown, that is, their lungs can fill up with liquid, their bodies can writhe in desperation for a gulp of air that will not come. But, well, and not to be harsh or anything, they're already dead, and drowning is just one of many forms of torture, like being parboiled in molten lava or sitting through a sales presentation for a timeshare. They'll be around to drown another day. And another. And another.

Being a demon, there was unlikely to be any actual drowning in my future, but I had no idea how unpleasant being underwater might be. Turns out it was like having a cold, stuffy nose, congestion, a little post nasal drip. Pretty minor fare.

I pulled out of my dive just yards from the ocean floor, which so close to shore was no more than a few hundred feet. With my demon eyes, I could see pretty well down there, well enough to spot the huge, bulbous form of the Kraken. Leviathan was busy destroying the harbor and paid no attention to a simple demon taking a swim. The devil prince made short work of the pier. Planks of wood floated everywhere, along with a fair number of longshoremen and sailors, all bug-eyed, mouths open, hands clawing at their throats. Leviathan had a few of them in his tentacles, and he squeezed them to jelly before discarding them and grabbing some more. His actions were distasteful to me, and I felt the bile rise in my mouth, making my cold feel more like I had a stomach virus instead.

Fortunately, Leviathan was getting bored. After he'd juiced about fifty of the damned, he turned away from New Glasgow and headed back out to sea. I started swimming, trying to keep up with him.

On land, I was pretty damn fast. Underwater things were slower, but I acquitted myself okay, I guess. Maybe not Aquaman fast. Perhaps Aqualad fast. Fortunately for me, Leviathan was in no hurry. He seemed to be meandering along the ocean floor. Occasionally he'd pick up the husk of a sunken ship. He'd shake it like a child shaking a snow globe at Christmas. A time or two a shiny bauble fell out, catching his attention, but he never spent more than a moment with it. No doubt, the Kraken had seen it all before.

I followed him about five miles, until we came to an underwater city. Atlantis it wasn't. There were some structures, but they were constructed of rusted oil tankers, pipelines, sea derricks, a few large clam shells, in short, whatever Leviathan could scrounge from the ocean depths or pluck from the shores of New Glasgow.

Still, I suppose it was home to him. In the center of his small domain was a throne he'd cobbled together from a couple of container ships. Next to it was a giant motion picture screen. I noted that he was showing 'The Little Mermaid.'

At least he has good taste. That's one of my favorite Disney movies.

The throne was designed to hold a large creature at least somewhat humanoid in appearance. As soon as I made that assessment, Leviathan transformed into a being that could sit on that throne … sort of. Like the harpy I'd just pulverized, the new Leviathan looked like a composite. He had the head of a bearded king, complete with crown, a long white body with finned tail and blowhole on his back, and eight tentacles instead of two arms and two legs. He was part Triton from the Disney movie, part Moby Dick, part Kraken. TriDicken, not to be confused with turducken, which is equally bizarre, though no doubt tastier.

I reflected that this could just be a phase for him. He might assume all sorts of shapes for his personal amusement. Certainly there was no one else around to amuse him, not even a demon jester. Leviathan was the most solitary of all the princes of Hell. He kept no devils or demons in his personal entourage, though I knew he had an army of them in New Glasgow and in Covetown, the latter city being where most of

144

the damned envious were spending their eternity.

Covetown was a strange place. It too was a port city, appropriately located on a small cove about a hundred miles from New Glasgow. It wasn't named for the cove, though, but for the synonym for Envy.

I'll give you a second to grab your Roget's to check that out.

Because the cove was small, and because the torments of the covetous (oops, I let it slip out anyway, sorry about that) were subtle, the demons there really had little to do. Two damned humans might be sentenced to an eternity of dinner together in a tony restaurant. No matter what they ordered, they each wanted the other's entrée. So they'd switch, and then immediately want their original order back again. Change partners and dance. Didn't seem much like torture to me, but then Envy had never been one of my moral failings.

That's just one example. Other people would not get a promotion and stew for decades over it. Or a person would get a new car, then feel like shit when a neighbor would get a nicer one. So neighbor one would trade in his or her new purchase on a Mercedes instead of the perfectly nice new Lexus. Neighbor two would get a Bentley. Neighbor one would counter with a Rolls. You get the idea.

So the humans in Covetown pretty much took care of their own eternal damnation, though the devils and demons overseeing them would periodically have to step in and destroy everything, forcing the competition to start over. There wasn't much for Leviathan to do in Covetown, and truth be told, he probably would have been bored. Also, the cove of Covetown was pretty small for him to fit into.

New Glasgow, or Glasgow by the Kraken, as it was also known, was a different matter. It should be remembered that while the princes of Hell had purview over specific deadly sins,

Envy in Leviathan's case, they also had oversight over the entire circle in which they had established residence. New Glasgow had its share of the envious, but it was more heterogeneous than Covetown. All seven of the Deadly Sins were represented.

The big city was also a better target for Leviathan's ministrations. This particular devil prince seemed to prefer the bold, the audacious, and New Glasgow allowed that more than did the smaller town, so he let his underlings handle things in Covetown, while he concentrated on the main port city.

Leviathan settled down into his throne and started watching the movie, his tentacles tapping idly on the arms of his chair. A great white shark swam by, and he snatched it, stuffing the fish in his mouth as if it were nothing more than a sardine. He picked up a cup made from a diving bell and began to drink.

Okay, so now I'd found the Eighth Circle's devil prince, but how to approach him? Sneaking up on Leviathan seemed unlikely, and probably dangerous, so I decided on the direct approach. I knocked a couple of clamshells together, just to get his attention, then I swam up to him and bowed deeply. "My Lord, Leviathan."

Despite my best efforts, I still surprised him, and he reflexively threw the diving bell at me. As all devil princes, he was lightning fast, much faster than even me, but the water slowed the speed of the projectile and I was able to dodge it. "My Lord, Leviathan!" I said again, a little desperation creeping into my voice. "I come in peace." That sounded stupid, but it's the first thing that popped out of my mouth.

Leviathan eyed me up and down. "What in Hell is a butt naked demon doing in my domain? And why is your schlong so dinky?"

Whoops! I looked down and realized that I must have lost my boxer shorts when I dove into the ocean. I turned several shades of scarlet. "The water's cold down here," I said by way of explanation.

"Well, cover than up. I don't want to see your privates."

There wasn't anything I'd brought with me, except the scroll and pitchfork in my pocket universe. There was also a sandwich left over from last night's party, but I didn't think that would cover my nakedness. On a nearby rock, a small octopus was exploring. I grabbed the creature and placed him like a fig leaf in front of my manhood. The creature found the dangly thing modestly interesting, so he wrapped his tentacles around it and settled down for a nap. *As long as he didn't – ouch – squeeze.* "Better, my lord?" I gasped.

The devil rolled his eyes. "Marginally. At least it's in keeping with my underwater theme. Now, what do you want?"

The octopus was squeezing so hard that my balls had turned purple. It liked that so, being an octopus and capable of changing color, it matched the shade. Despite my discomfort, I had to admire its eye for color.

"I *said,* what do you want?"

"Sorry, my lord." I opened my secret place pulled out my pitchfork, which I put to my forehead in a gesture of obeisance. I zipped up the space quickly, so my sandwich wouldn't get waterlogged. "I come bearing a message for you."

"Yes? From whom."

"From Lord Satan, Earl of Hell, my Lord Leviathan." *And, incidentally, your boss, though you seem to have forgotten that.*

Leviathan roared and shot a blast of air from his blowhole. "That meddling tyrant! Why doesn't he leave me alone?"

I shrugged. "Hey, don't shoot the messenger ... my lord."

He went all squinty eyed on me. He was both pissed off and suspicious. "So, where is this message?"

Quickly opening my hidey-hole, I stuck my pitchfork back in

and pulled out the scroll, then again closed the space. "Here, my lord. Lord Satan put it on waterproof paper so the ink wouldn't run." I handed him the parchment, which he took in one of his tentacles.

Now, in his present form, Leviathan was about the size of a blue whale, that is, around a hundred feet tall, or a little less, since he was sitting down. The rolled-up scroll looked like a matchstick in his grasp. "I can't read this minuscule thing without changing form." Well, he probably could, if he really wanted to, which he didn't. He tossed it back to me. "Read it to me, demon!"

"Yes, my lord," I said, snagging the scroll.

"Call me sire. I *am* the king of the seas, you know," he said with pride.

"Yes, my lord, I know that. But I don't think Satan would like it if I called you that. He's really both of our sires, sir. You know... " I ended lamely.

Leviathan roared again, shooting a pillar of hard water at me. Despite my speed, I was unable to completely avoid it, getting the wind knocked out of me.

"Satan! Hell, I am so tired of hearing his name, of his insufferable pride. What makes him think he's so great? I'm as powerful as he is," the great devil grumbled, looking more than a little dissatisfied. "By rights, I should be the ruler of Hell."

Right. This is where the envy thing comes in. Out loud I said, "My Lord Leviathan, I am but a humble servant. Allow me to read the message, and I will leave you in peace." *Before you leave me in pieces.*

"Very well. Proceed. I want to get back to my movie, so be quick about it."

"Yes, my lord." I cleared my throat and began to read. "MEMORANDUM. To: Leviathan, Prince of Hell, Patron Devil of

Envy. From: Satan, Earl of Hell, The Antagonist Supreme, Ruler of the Nine Circles. Date: Whenever. Re: Obedience."

"New paragraph."

"Listen, Fish Face, where the Hell do you get off skipping Demon cadet graduation?"

"Fish Face!" Leviathan screamed. "How dare you!" He stretched out a tentacle to grab me, and I quickly scuttled back about twenty feet.

"Not me, sir." I responded hurriedly. "Just reading here."

Leviathan spat black ink from his mouth into a spittoon he'd fashioned from an old oil drum. "Just get on with it."

"Yes sir." Looking down the page, I winced. "Just remember, uh, that I didn't write any of this."

"READ!"

"Ahem … I don't require much of you devil princes, in your case just to ensure the proper punishment of the Covetous, as well as other sinners on Seven, and to attend an occasional official function. In fact, of all the princes, you generally get left the most alone. I know you like that, and I don't particularly want to see your ugly puss anyway."

"You, Mammon and Belphegor have been allowed to attend ceremonies virtually. I thought I was being more than generous in permitting that, even though Beelzebub and Asmodeus faithfully show up in person for every graduating class."

"Well, no more Mister Nice Guy. Up until now, I have made my desires implicit, figuring you were smart enough to figure things out. Apparently, you're even stupider than you look."

Ouch. I looked up at Leviathan. He was turning purple with rage – even more purple than my dick in the grasp of my eight-limbed fig leaf – but he was somehow restraining himself, which was impressive, since devils are not particularly well-known for their restraint.

I read the remainder of the missive in a rush. "Since you can't seem to take a hint, I'll be more explicit. I order you, from now on, to attend all graduation ceremonies *in person*. You may NOT just watch it on TV. You'll have to get off your butt and hie on down to Eight. Oh, and come in a proper size, no taller than ten feet. And put on some clothes, man! I don't want a fish tail on my platform, and I don't want you to scatter a bunch of scales up there, where someone might trip on them."

"This is a direct order, and seeing as how you have no free will, you have no choice but to obey me, your superior. See to it, minion!" I was shocked. Calling a devil, especially one of the princes, a minion was just about the biggest insult there was. Shaken, I finished lamely, "That's all it says sir, though Lord Satan's sigil and seal are at the bottom."

I looked up to see how Leviathan was taking this. That was right when one of his tentacles grabbed me. The Lord of Envy was furious, and he tightened down on me like one of the poor sailors I'd recently seen him squeeze to a pulp. Being a demon, I was made of sterner stuff, but the pressure he was exerting was enormous, and soon my face was as purple as my privates.

I released the scroll, sending it floating in the water toward him. I glanced up. There must have been a mile of water above me. Concentrating, I contracted my sphincter and teleported, blind, the full extent of my range.

I would have loved to have seen Leviathan's look of surprise when I disappeared from his grasp.

"Ow ow ow ow OOF!"

"Ping ping ping ping PONG!"

I slammed against the underbelly of Level Six, then ricocheted a few times before landing on the shore not far from where I started. Painfully I dragged my bruised carcass off the ground.

"Screech!" The harpy leapt on me, her claws going straight for my eyes.

"Oh, shut up, will you!" I said grumpily and clocked her. It was not my habit to hit a lady, so I focused on her vulture aspect. She crumpled to the earth, unconscious.

"And would you let go?" I yelled at the little octopus, who was hanging on for dear life – or death – to my scrotum. I peeled him off and threw him back into the drink.

Chapter 14

"Well, that went well," I groused to no one in particular. "Still, done is done." I looked above me and spotted my perch from earlier. In a flash, I teleported back to the stone. My clothes were still there, except my skivvies, of course. I'd have to go commando style for a while.

Blasting myself with Hellfire was a good way to dry off quickly – it beat a towel any day – then I slipped back on my tunic, trousers, socks and boots. Feeling a bit more normal, I opened my secret space and took out the sandwich, which was only slightly waterlogged. I sat on the edge of the rock, my feet dangling above the water. Munching on my early lunch, I reflected that being a demon was not all about the high life. If Satan was really going to use me as his troubleshooter, there might be lots of instances where I would be placed in uncomfortable situations such as the one I'd just escaped. *No wonder he gave me teleportation powers.*

New Glasgow was being deluged by sheets of rain; the city was all but invisible and its miserable inhabitants no doubt completely soaked through. I sighed. That kind of misery was no longer mine; at least I was no longer on the receiving end of it. The thought that soon I'd be dispensing it to my former fellow damned was too depressing to contemplate.

In the palm of my hand, I crushed the Saran wrap in which my sandwich had been protected, mostly, and rolled the bit of plastic around until it was a tiny ball. A flick of my finger would send the transparent pellet tumbling into the ocean. This is what anyone else would do, whether devil, demon or human. Hell was pretty atrocious already, and litter seemed, if anything, to add to the ambience of the place, so by common consent tossing around a little trash seemed a sin that everyone indulged in. Yet, for some reason, today I found the idea unpleasant. In what seemed like an act of sedition, I put the trash back in my hidey-hole.

The rain was falling even harder now, as impossible as that seemed, so I created and maintained a little aura of Hellfire around me to stay dry. I'd already spent an hour or so being on the bottom of the ocean. I'd been wet enough for one day.

With my demon vision, I picked out an unusual skyscraper near the city center. What made it unusual was not its architectural splendor – there was precious little of that in Hell outside of New Rome, and that only because it was an intentional knock-off of the original – or its height but rather the substance with which it was made. This was a plastic skyscraper, pretty unusual, in fact probably unique for both Hell and Earth. To me, though, its only significance lay in the fact that it was right next door to a small wooden workshop in which Allan Pinkerton, one of history's great detectives, spent Eternity as the Underworld's worst cooper.

The thought of my former friend filled me with mixed emotions. We had not had a falling out. He was a former friend simply because I'd moved from the "one of us" camp to the "one of them" contingent. Except for that one time spying on Orson and Edison, I'd maintained my no contact policy toward my human associates.

But now a great longing possessed me. Being the Underworld's Superintendent for Plant Maintenance had not exactly been fun. In fact, as Hell's Super, I'd had some pretty tough times, logical enough, since it had been chosen for me as my personal form of eternal torment. And yet …

And yet, I had somehow, in the most unlikely place imaginable, made some friends, Allan Pinkerton being one of them. I had no doubt that Orson would have told everyone about what happened to me, about how I was tricked into agreeing to be a demon, how I did it only to save Flo and my other friends from a fate that I thought could have been soul-destroying, ending their existence, even in the afterlife. That was something I'd always been taught was impossible. Turns out I'd been taught correctly, but Satan did a masterful job convincing me otherwise. And so I chose to become a demon, and in the process lost almost everyone I cared about.

For while Orson's explanations would make sense to them – they'd view my actions as an honorable sacrifice – the end result still left me a demon, one of the guys in black. One of the bad guys.

"Shit. This sucks." Scrambling up from my rocky seat above the ocean, I took another glance at the plastic skyscraper. An overwhelming urge to see my friend possessed me. I just needed to make certain he didn't see me.

"Hmm," I hmmed. The skyscraper looked about three miles away. Two hops. But should I do this IFR or VFR style? In the end, I decided to travel by instinct rather than sight. Where I was going were places I knew well. I closed my eyes and jumped to the pier …

And fell into the ocean, since that portion of the dock had been destroyed by Leviathan's tsunami. I crawled out of the water, cursing so loudly that half a dozen humans ran screaming from me as if I were the Creature from the Black Lagoon. Scowling, I bathed myself in Hellfire again, drying off my clothes and skin. This scared away another crop of the damned, but by now I was in a really crappy mood so didn't much care. My tail, being covered with fur, took a little longer to dry than everything else, but soon I was ready to make the second hop. Closing my eyes again, I visualized the hay loft in the wooden building that housed Allan's workspace.

Pop.

The smell of slightly-damp hay filled my nostrils. I'd always had a bit of hay fever, so I almost sneezed, which would have been a problem, since I have no idea where I would have teleported. Fortunately, I'd been doing my Kegels regularly and practicing self-control over all those involuntary coughs, farts, hiccups, etc. When the urge to sneeze passed, I opened my eyes.

On the dirt floor beneath me, Allan was leaning over a barrel he was working on. Above him was a single, dim light bulb, the only illumination in the large, rustic workspace. It must have been hard for him to see, but he did not complain. There was no point to it, and Allan had generally been pretty stoic about his damnation. Must have been that stiff-upper-lip thing the Brits have going for them.

I had never really watched Allan at work building a barrel. He always said that the only tools he was allowed were a rubber mallet and a Swiss army knife. He had an entire wall of other tools – fine saws, rulers, compasses, adzes and heavy mallets – yet he could only look at them in longing. Allan had told me he was a terrible cooper, and his finished products were ample evidence that he wasn't lying. Yet, watching him work, I was amazed that he could do as well as he did with the few tools allowed him.

In one corner of the barn, there was a row of planks which my friend had laboriously cut from portions of oak trunks. To do that only with a knife, instead of being able to use a saw or a mallet and wedge, must have taken an incredible amount of time, but when you've got Eternity to work with, you're not exactly on a tight deadline. The planks had been meticulously whittled thinner on the ends than in the middle, so that they could be bent eventually to the shape of a barrel, wide in the middle, narrower on the ends.

Next to the wood were dozens of metal rings. These would be used to hold the planks together. There was also a pile of straw to fit between the planks and make the barrel water tight – should Allan ever get so far in the process that that was necessary. Usually, his projects fell apart long before that stage.

There was also a fire pit and a pail of water. Allan explained to me that once you got some rings on the top of the barrel-to-be, it was necessary to coat the insides of the wood with water and heat the work-in-progress from the inside out. I saw one near-barrel in this position now. There was a piece of rope – I guess Allan forgot to mention that he was allowed to use rope – tied around the bottom, and periodically he would go over and twist it tighter, using an extra plank to do the twisting, then sticking it under another piece of rope to keep it from slipping. Slowly the bottom of the barrel was assuming a shape similar to the top. Eventually, I figured he'd slap some rings on the bottom, and he'd have his barrel shape.

He also used the fire to char the insides of any barrels intended to hold, for example, wine. Hell's vineyards didn't grow the finest grapes. The stuff tasted like sour raisins that had been pulped before adding the juice to urine, but there still was an active wine industry in Hell. I know, since I'd been forced to drink these noxious vintages while I was human. Hell's Grand Cru's were used to torment the Underworld's many oenophiles.

Usually, before completed, Allan's barrels broke or flew apart, shooting with great force the metal rings that had helped maintain the shape of the thing into the air, striking Allan, punching a hole in the side of his workshop or causing other types of mayhem. The one he was working on now, though, was unusual. It was nearly finished and, astonishingly, of remarkably good workmanship. I couldn't see a crack between the staves big enough for light to pass through, and since as a demon I had twenty-one vision (humans being lucky to have twenty-twenty), there surely were no cracks.

Allan had the barrel on its side, and he was rolling it with great care against a rough stone jutting up from the dirt at his feet. He'd forgotten to mention the stone also, which I guess is okay, since a stone isn't much of a tool. In this case he was using it like sandpaper, to give the barrel a smooth finish. Occasionally, he'd use his pocket knife to remove a large splinter or an irregularity from the exterior.

And he had just finished. Allan righted the barrel, stood back and admired his handiwork, a slight smile playing around his lips.

My Go ... I mean, wow! The damn thing is just gorgeous!

I sat down on the hay with a soft thump. *What a wonder. Someone has managed to create a thing of beauty. Here. In Hell. And not just someone. Allan. My friend.*

Yes, said a voice in my brain. *It happens occasionally. Now quickly, without him seeing you, go destroy it.*

My boss had apparently been monitoring my thoughts. *But Lord Satan, it's such a nice barrel. Seems a shame to ...*

That's a direct order Minion! You are a demon now and have no free will, and don't you forget it. Now do it!

My body responded automatically. As fast as possible, I leapt from my observation point, landed with nary a sound on the dirt floor of the workshop, ran to the barrel and punched it, then raced back up to the loft. All of this happened in less than a second.

The barrel exploded, the wood shattering into tiny pieces. One of the metal hoops hit Allan full in the face, staggering him. A second one shattered the bulb above his head, plunging the room into darkness, while a companion ring crashed through a window in the back of the shop. The rain began to blow in. The remaining hoops fell at Allan's feet, tripping him.

And there was my dear friend, on his knees. No more stiff upper lip for him. In the dark loneliness of his workshop, Allan broke down, sobbing at first, then wailing, like he was keening for a dead loved one. He could not have seen me destroy his barrel. As far as he could tell, he had failed once again. Allan would never know that he had succeeded, against all odds, in making the perfect barrel. Here. In the Underworld, where success was unlawful.

It was Hell.

Good job, Minion. Now report back to me.

Taking one more sorrowful look at my devastated friend, I teleported to the docks. Before I made the last two hops to Satan's foyer, I dried my eyes. It would not do for the Lord of Hell to see that a demon had been crying.

Chapter 15

Bruce rose to stop me from entering Satan's office unannounced, but a withering look from me stopped him in his tracks.

He might as well get used to me coming and going. If I'm going to work directly for Satan, I'll be in there a lot.

My fellow demon must have figured that out for himself. "Well," he said officially, "I suppose, now that you report to him directly, unless Lord Satan tells me to the contrary, you have fairly unfettered access to his office."

"Don't worry," I said grimly. I was still upset about what had happened to Allan. What I'd done to him. "Our mutual boss always knows when I'm coming. If he doesn't want me in there, he'll let both of us know."

The doors to Satan's office opened on their own, inviting me in, silently acknowledging the accuracy of my words. Turning my back on Bruce the Bedeviled, I headed inside and took my seat before the giant rosewood desk.

The back of the La-Z-Boy was to me, and I waited patiently for Satan to turn around. There was a tap on my shoulder.

"BOO!"

I almost had a coronary. Satan stood at my side. "Bwahahahahahaha! That one never gets old."

"If you say so, sir," I said, gasping for breath.

"Oh, chill out, Minion," he said, going around to his chair, which he spun around to face me before sitting in it. "You looked like you needed a little comic relief."

"Rather not talk about it," I mumbled, looking down at my claws, which I'd unconsciously dug into my chair. I'd torn its faux leather, but apparently Satan's furniture was self-healing, for it sealed as soon as I withdrew them.

"Well, we *will* talk about it in a minute, but first I wanted to compliment you on your work with Leviathan. Bwahahahahahaha!" he said again. "Haven't seen that sorry excuse for a cuttlefish so pissed off in a thousand years."

I shrugged. "It was your memo, sir. I just read it to him."

"Yes," he said, with a grin, "but you should have seen his expression when you teleported out of his grasp. He wasn't expecting that, and he rampaged around his little waterlogged domain for a good hour after you escaped."

"Seemed like a good thing to do at the time," I opined, having recovered a little from my encounter with Allan. "Good thing you gave me teleportation powers."

Satan nodded. "I think they're really going to come in handy, with some of the jobs I intend to give you."

Great.

"It *is* great, isn't it? I now have a demon who is more powerful than most devils and smart enough to even outwit the princes of Hell. This is just perfect."

"I thought you said I was dumber that I used to be."

"Maybe," he said, scratching his chin. "Maybe not. I'm not sure how much the loss of free will is going to affect your intellect, but you seem to be doing okay for now, based on your performance with Leviathan."

"By the way, that was good work refusing to call Leviathan 'sire.' You've always been gutsy … "

"Yeah, well, if he'd squeezed me much harder, I would really have been gutsy."

"Bwahahahahahaha!" *I wish he'd quit doing that.* "Good one! Anyway, you have more than your share of courage. It has in the past gotten you in an occasional bit of trouble but should stand you in good stead, now that you're working for me."

"Swell."

"And … " he said, raising his finger to make a point, "you showed you know which side your bread is buttered on. Your loyalty is to me! Bwahahahahahaha!"

Again?

"Yes, again. This is just turning out so wonderfully. You're the perfect demon. You will be my greatest creation, and if you play your cards right, someday you will be an arch demon, Minion."

I looked up at him hopefully. "If I'm going to be your troubleshooter, factotum I think you called me, maybe I could get a better name, like Lothar or Punjab or something. Most all the other demons got new names, like Chuckles and Gomer and Maximus."

Satan frowned. "Maybe. Maybe someday. I suppose it would be undignified for an arch demon to be named 'Minion.' For now though, it's just too funny to have a minion who is actually named Minion."

Rats. That's what I thought he'd say.

Satan ignored my thoughts. He had something else he wanted to discuss. "Now, we need to examine your behavior with Allan Pinkerton. I have some concerns."

"Hey. I mean, hey, my Lord. I did what you told me."

Devil claws were tapping the rosewood desktop at preternatural speed. "Yes, but I had to tell you twice, and I had to be explicit about it being a direct order."

"Well, you'd just told me to torment one of my closest friends."

"Ex-friends. Demons and humans aren't friends. EVER."

I cringed. He was right, of course.

"Of course I'm right. I'm Satan. I'm always right."

"Yes, chief."

"Don't call me chief. I don't like it."

Just like Perry White. "May I call you boss?"

He frowned. "Sometimes, I suppose. When we're alone. Other times, call me my Lord, or sir or, even better, sire or my liege."

This was turning into a depressing conversation.

"But back to Pinkerton. True, you did what you were told to do, even though I had to say it twice, and you did it in spectacular fashion. Pinkerton was devastated."

I looked up mournfully at my boss. "Me too. That barrel was a work of art."

"Wasn't it?" Satan said, admiringly. "It's amazing to me, sometimes, what humans are capable of. They start off as such limited creatures anyway. Put them in the worst situation imaginable, play to their weaknesses rather than their strengths, even give them almost no tools with which to work, and yet sometimes, sometimes, they are capable of greatness."

"So you thought the barrel was a little bit of greatness."

He nodded. "Yes, I did, especially since Pinkerton was never any good at barrel making. That was the greatest cask he'd ever cast."

"And yet you had me destroy it," I mumbled morosely.

"Unfortunately, it was necessary. This is Hell, don't forget. People must be tormented. They're damned. Being damned isn't supposed to be a walk in the park. Hey, but don't worry about the barrel being destroyed. I took pictures!"

Satan's projection screen dropped from the black indeterminateness that served as his ceiling. A slideshow began, starting with Allan meticulously creating the planks, him using his pitiful rubber mallet to pound down the initial rings that held the top together, the soaking and firing process, the slow bending process to form the bottom of the barrel, adding rings to the bottom and across the middle, the use of the straw to close the gaps, firing the interior, and finally the slow and painful process of sanding the exterior. The last few slides showed the perfect cask on its end, the proud face of Pinkerton as he witnessed his accomplishment, then the devastation of the cask by me. I noted that Satan had some kind of super high-speed camera to capture my movement, and he managed to catch me just as my fist destroyed the barrel. Afterward, we got to witness the denouement of Allan's devastation.

I felt like hell.

"Why do you feel so guilty?" he asked me, genuinely interested. "This is Hell. Those consigned here are *supposed* to be tortured and tormented. You're a demon. If you hadn't done it, someone else would have."

What he said made sense. "I know. It's just hard for me to hurt other people."

Satan's face twisted like a corkscrew. "Well, you're just going to have to get used to it. You're a demon now, and you have a job to do. There's no going back."

I sighed. "Yes, sir. Yes, sire," I amended.

"Well, I appreciate your effort. Look, all in all, you did pretty well today. You dealt extremely well with Leviathan, and though you feel guilty about it, you effectively tormented Pinkerton. That's a good start."

"Thanks. I guess."

"Take the rest of the day off. I've already told Asmodeus to give his assistant time off as well, so go home and screw your little succubus. She's a hot one, by the way. Definitely an A plus Lilith."

"Okay. I mean, okay, my lord." I rose from my seat and trudged toward the door.

"Minion," Satan said, almost as if he had forgotten it.

"Report to Beelzebub at oh eight hundred hours tomorrow. I have another special project for you, and Beezy will show you the ropes."

"Yes sir," I said, my hand on the door knob. "Thank you, sir."

"Dismissed."

By the time I popped into Lilith's living room, she was already there mixing drinks. She poured our sloe gin fizzes into some plastic glasses, and we headed to the pool. Lilith dropped her dress on the patio – she was naked beneath – and slipped into the shallow end, placing her drink on the stone oval rim of the pool. Her breasts looked like water wings, floating before her in the limpid water. She'd never drown, that's for sure.

I'd spent enough time submerged in water for one day, but, whatever. With a shrug, I took off my uniform and joined her.

"Commando style?" she asked.

"Long story," I said, giving her a quick smooch and copping a quick feel, since I was so close. She reciprocated, the feeling part that is, though she grabbed a little lower than I did on her. "Tell you in a second. Say, why the plastic glasses?"

"Oh, you're never supposed to take a glass glass near a pool. If it broke, pieces might fall in the water, where someone could step on them."

"But … this is Hell," I said, stating the obvious.

"Safety first."

"Whatever."

As we sipped on our drinks, relaxing in the water, I felt some of the tension drain from my shoulders. I told her about my morning.

"Ooh!" she enthused, playing with a lock of my hair that had gotten wrapped around one of my horns. "You actually beat Leviathan!"

I rolled my eyes. "Let's just say that I managed to get away from him without being creamed."

"But still, he's a prince of Hell, and one of the more dangerous ones at that. Not very many demons could have pulled that off. You're so sexy when you demonstrate your puissance!"

"Well," I opined, glancing down about two feet beneath the surface, "your puissance is pretty spectacular too."

She chuckled. "Good one."

"I try."

"Then what did you do?"

It took a moment for me to respond, since Lilith had taken my hand and placed it on her puissance, which was distracting. "Well, I looked in on an old friend of mine. A human by the name of Allan Pinkerton."

"Why'd you do that?" she asked, sipping on her drink.

"Oh, I don't know. I guess all of this is a bit of an adjustment for me. Being with you is wonderful, but I miss my old friends."

"Is that all I am to you?" she said, pouting a little. "A friend?"

I kissed her again, a nice long, wet one, as wet as the pool. "You're a lot more than that, and you know it."

She smiled, satisfied. "So what did you two talk about?"

"Nothing. He didn't even know I was there. I watched him at work, making a barrel." I sighed. "It was a beautiful barrel."

"Then what did you do?"

"I destroyed it."

All Lilith did was cock an eyebrow.

"I *had* to. Satan gave me a direct order."

She pursed her lips, almost as if in disapproval. "I'm surprised that was even necessary. I would have thought you'd have known to destroy it on your own."

"Why? Why would you think that?"

Lilith took the drink from my hand and placed it and hers on the side of the pool. "Darling. You're a demon now. You're supposed to torment humans."

"I ... I know. It's just not coming very naturally to me. Besides, Allan is my friend."

"Was your friend," she corrected. "Demons aren't friends with humans. Ever."

"Well, you were my friend when I was human, and you're a demon," I said, defending myself.

"That's different. I'm a succubus. We're not the same as regular demons. I get to be friendly with everyone unless explicitly told to be otherwise. Incubi are the same way."

"Well instinctively torturing humans is not coming so naturally to me. I think it has to do with being tricked into becoming a demon."

She rolled her eyes. "Don't start that again. I don't want to fight."

"And I don't either, Lilith," I said, putting my arms around her. "I know you had no choice."

"And neither do you. No free will, remember?"

"I remember." Still, I wondered why I hesitated at all before obeying Satan's order. Something was definitely not right about my little demon brain. "That's my day. What about yours?"

"Oh, same old, same old," she said, grabbing her drink and taking another sip. "I ordered some dildos for one of the sex shops on Main, arranged for some new neon signage above Bertha's Bordello. What else? Oh yeah, I set up some appointments for Asmodeus, did the nasty with Astaroth and ..."

"What!" I said, scandalized. "You had sex with Astaroth?"

"Yeah. I was returning a favor for Asmodeus."

"But ... " I sputtered, " ... but you and I are a couple!"

"Yes," she purred, grabbing my arm, and burying it between

her breasts. "Isn't it wonderful?"

" ... and couples are true to each other!"

She looked at me in confusion. "What are you trying to say? I don't understand."

I looked around, but there was no one else to help me explain this, so I took another stab. "Couples don't sleep around on each other! We're exclusive."

Lilith set down her glass again. "Well, I'm not. I can't be. Steve, I'm a *succubus*. It's my job to have sex. It's what I was made for." She paused. "It's at the core of my being, my very nature. I could no more stop what I do than a tiger could stop hunting for food."

"Nice analogy," I grumbled. For some reason, I felt betrayed. "You said you loved me."

"Darling," she said with emotion, "I do! But I have no more free will than you. I will always have sex with other partners. What else would you expect of a succubus?"

"Nothing, I guess." I closed my eyes, thinking about all she'd said. Everything made perfect sense. What's more, my desire for an exclusive relationship with her went back to the human values engendered in me since childhood. They were pointless here; moral choices no longer had relevance.

Still, I felt disappointed. Deflated. My thoughts turned to Flo. In over two hundred and fifty years, she'd only had sex one time, and it was with me. I had a feeling she would never "do the nasty" with anyone else, because, I concluded, we had *not* done the nasty. Yes, desire was involved, but the intimate hours we'd spent together was a consequence of our mutual love.

I opened my eyes. Lilith was staring at me, not with guilt or fear, but with bemusement. She simply didn't understand. She loved me, I was sure of it, as much as she was able. That a succubus could love at all was a wonder. And in a way, I loved her too. With a gentle smile, I took her hand. "It's okay. I understand now. Thanks for being so patient with me."

Lilith moved into my embrace, her body forming little eddies in the water of the pool. "You're just tense, sweetheart, from your encounter with Leviathan. Here, let me help you relieve some of that tension."

Not all of me felt deflated, at least not anymore.

Chapter 16

The next morning, I materialized on Level Eight, just outside of Beelzebub's office. My arrival was nothing dramatic; just a few grains of sand flew into the air when my boots touched the ground. Far different from the comings and goings of the major devils.

I intended to keep it that way. There were only two demons in all Hell who could teleport, but at the end of the day, we were merely second-class citizens. Now I understood why Adramelech simply teleported, without creating some flashy special effect. That would draw too much attention to him. All the rest of demondom would be jealous, and the devils would view it as hubris. Perhaps he wasn't as dumb as he seemed.

I spun through the revolving door, putting me in Beelzebub's large rectangle of an office. The sides were made of screen; a ceiling fan spun lazily above his chair. Beezy was sitting, waiting for me, elbows on the wooden desktop before him, fingers steepled, his chin resting on them. He looked troubled when he regarded me.

"Are you okay?" I asked.

My former boss snorted. "I was about to ask you the same thing." He pointed at the vacant chair in front of his desk.

I plopped down heavily. "Well, since I now realize you can read my mind whenever you want to, you probably already know I'm not."

Beezy picked up a flyswatter and obliterated a half-dozen flies that had made the mistake of landing on his desk. He swept their remains to the floor then shook his head. "This is what comes from tricking you into becoming a demon. I told Satan it was a mistake to do it, but when he wants something, there's no denying him."

"Well, it feels like a mistake to me, but why do *you* think so?"

Beelzebub put down the flyswatter and picked up a small pencil sharpener, which he used to sharpen one of his horns. He tested the point with his finger, shook his head, sharpened the horn again. When he was satisfied, he spoke. "Minion, your situation is unique. We've never had a recruit to the Corps who did not join of his own free will."

"But I did join of my own free will … sort of." Watching Beelzebub sharpen his horn made me wonder about my own. I reached to my forehead with both hands. The one on the right felt a tad dull, and I looked at the Lord of the Flies expectantly. He tossed me the sharpener, and I went to work on the offending point.

"Yes you did, technically." He snorted. "Satan honored the letter of the law, so to speak, but he violated its spirit."

I looked around nervously, expecting at any moment for Satan to appear and thrash us both.

"Don't worry about that," Beezy said. "He won't. He knows I'm right. In fact, we spent several hours last night discussing your case."

"You mean arguing."

He smiled ruefully. "Yes, I mean arguing. At the end of the, ah, discussion, though, we both agreed that you have been correct all along. The manner of your recruitment seems to be the source of your reluctance in fully accepting your demonhood."

Beelzebub stood and walked to the side of his office. He was staring out, through the screen wall, at the bazaar that operated perpetually just outside his door. "There's nothing for it, of course. Becoming a demon is irreversible, so the best we can do is help socialize you into your new role."

He turned to face me. "Fortunately, there's hope for you. Your potential, as I'm sure you know, is enormous. Aside from your physical attributes, you have a quality of mind that could make for a great demon."

"Gee, thanks, I guess. Why do you say that?"

"Oh come on, Steve," Beezy said, a wry look on his face. "You've never been exactly a Mother Teresa. Even when you were human, you were capable of being devious, even of inflicting pain on others, and usually in very creative ways."

Satisfied with my right horn, I put the sharpener back on his desk. "Well, yeah, if they were creeps, or if I felt they deserved it. Like Edison, for example ... "

"What you can't seem to get through your head is that *all* humans down here deserve it. If they didn't, they wouldn't be here to begin with. They'd be upstairs with the rest of the goody two-shoes."

"Maybe so, though I've met some pretty good people down here. I don't relish the thought of sticking it to them."

"You don't know everything about everyone down here," Beelzebub said with a frown. "And no one in Hell, not even Satan, had a hand in their damnation."

"What about those people who sold their souls to him in their lifetimes?"

"There are very few of those," he said, pausing, "though we'll be discussing that more in a minute. My point is that Hell is part of the divine plan. The devils and demons who work down here are part of that plan. Of His plan," Beezy said, looking up meaningfully.

"Oh." Him.

He sat back at his desk and leaned forward earnestly. "We have a job to do, Steve. None of this is personal. It's business.

And every damned human down here is our charge. We torment them because we are supposed to. Get it?"

"Yes," I said hesitantly. "I understand. Don't much like it, but I understand. So, what's to be done?"

"The only thing Satan and I can think of is to keep you at the job until you get desensitized to the suffering of others."

"Will that work?"

He shrugged. "Dunno. Like I said, this is the first time we've had this situation."

"You're being awfully nice to me, Lord Beelzebub. Why?"

He grinned. "I'd tell you, but I'd have to kill you."

"Too late."

"Too true. Okay, here is one of the great secrets of Hell. We only treat the damned poorly. There's no reason to treat each other that way."

"But," I said, puzzled, "I've seen you and Satan insult each other. I've seen demons fighting each other in the streets."

"Most of that's for show. You know, Bwahahahahahaha and all that jazz. We do have our fights, like any friends or family members do. And there *are* a few devils who have really embraced evil. Satan gets off on it. So does Tink." He shrugged. "For me, it's just a job."

"And demons?"

"Well, since they actually chose to become what they are, there are many more evil demons than there are evil devils. Ironic, isn't it?"

"You said it. So what's up next?"

He stood up again and walked around his desk to my side. "Today, we go to Earth."

"Really?" I'd been told that trips to Earth were possible for demons, but I never expected to go so soon.

"Yes. Remember your comment about sold souls? Well,

we're heading up to get a signature. To be precise, I'm driving. You're to get the signature and notarize the document."

I gulped. "You mean, I'm supposed to talk someone into signing away his soul?"

"No, no! Nothing like that. No demon would ever be entrusted with that kind of work. It's very delicate, and only a handful of us ever cut the deal. Satan does most of it, and he's certainly the best. In fact, this is one he negotiated. The client has indicated he's ready to sign. You're really just a notary public in this situation." He handed me a parchment, signed at the bottom with Satan's "evil" signature, the spidery style of handwriting he used on documents of this sort. I always thought it was especially creepy, though in the old days, if he'd used this style of penmanship on his work orders, instead of his normal indecipherable script which resembled nothing so much as the handwriting on a medical prescription, I wouldn't have had to spend so much time puzzling out what he wanted.

"Oh," I said, feeling slightly better. I slipped the scroll in my hidey-hole. "That doesn't sound too bad. When do we leave?"

He stared at me critically. "Just as soon as we do something about your clothes."

"Thank you!" I said with relief. "I thought I was going to have to wear this cadet uniform forever."

"Kleider macht leute."

"I beg your pardon?"

"Clothes make the man. If you're going to be a stand-in for Satan, you need to look the part." Beelzebub waved his hand. My skin felt all tingly and my vision darkened slightly. Beezy conjured up a full-length mirror. "Take a look."

I was dressed in a black leisure suit, equally black shirt, open at the neck and with the collar overlapping the lapels of the coat, and sunglasses. I looked not dissimilar to Satan, sans tie, when he was working in his office. "Very nice tailoring. Is this Gucci?" I asked, studying the fine cut of the trousers.

"Sort of. It's really a knockoff, but I do very good work. No one would ever be able to tell the difference."

"Great, but why a leisure suit? These went out of fashion with disco."

Beezy shrugged. "What goes around, comes around. Ultimately, fashion isn't very creative, especially men's fashion."

I looked over my shoulder at the back of the coat. "Shouldn't I have a cape or something?"

Beelzebub rolled his eyes. "You're still confusing devils with Dracula."

"No, I'm sure I've seen devils in capes."

"All right, yes, occasionally. But not in recent years. Capes aren't really in fashion these days."

"Oh," I replied, slightly disappointed. "What about you? Aren't you going to change your clothes? It must be at least 2050 up there, and I doubt anyone dresses in white suits and black fezes."

"No, I'll be invisible to everyone but you. Let's go, kiddo," Beelzebub said. He put his hand on my arm and we teleported.

We appeared inside a large, domed concourse. The ceiling above was at least as big as half a grain silo, a long upward arching affair painted a rich green and dotted with the stars of a screwy zodiac, screwy in that some of the constellations were backwards. Beneath the long arch were two rows of large windows, from which glorious sunlight flowed into the space. On the far wall were three enormous windows. An information booth, topped with an old-fashioned four-faced clock, was in evidence, but the booth was empty. And everywhere there were people, hurrying to get somewhere, staring at their hands or wrists or vapidly through strange eyeglasses designed for fashion and some purpose inscrutable to me. Apparently the eyewear wasn't intended to improve vision, because the wearers kept running into other people. I decided finally that the glasses were some sort of portable computer screen.

The terminal was flooded in light. I knew it was a terminal, because I'd recognized the distinctive architecture of the building immediately. This was Grand Central Station, at the time of my death the world's largest train station. I smiled, remembering the many times I'd taken a train from the station to New Haven or Boston. I really was back on Earth.

Beelzebub swept his hand at the scene before me. "I brought you here first, because one, it usually pays to materialize on Earth in a crowded setting, but more importantly, I wanted you to see something familiar. The first time a new demon comes back to Earth, there can be a little culture shock. Or jet lag. Or something. Anyway, things have changed quite a bit in the sixty years you've been dead. Some of the old buildings have been retained, but 2055 is very different than 1995."

"Well, apparently people are still taking trains," I said, waving my hand at the crush of humanity scurrying by.

"Not really. They travel by hyperloop now."

"Hyperloop? What's that?"

"A technology that was developed thirty or forty years ago. These people travel in capsules through long, low-pressure tubes, to their destination. Takes only about twenty minutes to get to Boston by hyperloop."

I whistled.

"But enough of this. I didn't come here to lecture you on mid-Twenty-first Century modes of transportation. We're headed upstairs," he said, indicating a bank of elevators.

"Do you mean the Pan Am Building?"

"Boy, you have been out of circulation for a long time. I thought even in your lifetime, Pan Am had gone out of business."

I thought hard. "That's right. They folded a few years before I died. Some insurance company bought the building."

Beezy nodded. "MetLife. That was before the great insurance rebellion of 2030, when all American consumers, by common consent, revolted against the industry. Everyone hated insurance, sort of like they hate lawyers. Lawyers are a necessary evil. Insurance companies are not."

"What happened?" I asked, as we walked toward the elevators.

"Well, first off, people just plain got fed up with how much they were paying for insurance. Health care, long-term care, personal property, etc., etc. At its height, the insurance industry accounted for a bigger share of the American economy than healthcare, which sort of makes sense, since for a while, national healthcare was mandated, but it ran through the private insurance companies. Finally, completely fed up with the way the companies were running things, the government took over health care. By the way, the U.S. was the last country on the planet to establish a single payer system. So health insurance became obsolete. Then FEMA took over insuring houses, so there went homeowner's insurance. Computers rendered car insurance obsolete; it's impossible for ITM's to crash."

"ITM's?"

"Individual transport modules. Cars are obsolete too. Anyway, ITM's work collaboratively. They have a hive-like mentality, working together to prevent any type of collision, whether on the ground or in the air."

Interesting stuff. "What about corporate insurance?"

"The insurance companies themselves stopped that. By 2022, America had turned into such a litigious society that corporations were being sued left and right. Their tort protection policies were bankrupting the insurance industry, so it just stopped issuing them. Soon there was no insurance business to be had, and the entire industry folded."

"What's the building called now?"

"The Amazon Building."

"What's an Amazon, other than a river in South America?"

"It's the most powerful entity on the planet, even more powerful than China, which is currently the dominant economy. Amazon controls all commerce on Earth and owns most of this building, except the 59th floor, which is where we're headed."

As we walked through the concourse, I heard an occasional "oof, thump." Even though I could see Beezy, nobody else could, and they kept running into him. He'd casually knock them to the side, which sent them sprawling. Finally, Beelzebub sent a funnel of air ahead of us, gently blowing people out of our path.

Another question popped in my head. "They can't see you, but why aren't they running in terror from me and my horns?" My tail was discreetly tucked inside my slacks.

"I've hidden them. The only time they'll show is when you meet with the client."

These elevators were unlike any I'd ever seen. At least fifty long, transparent tubes ascended from the ground floor and up through the roof. "Why don't we just teleport to wherever we're going?"

"Hey, kid," Beelzebub said, pressing the call button. A panel to one of the tubes slid open. Beezy gestured for me to get in. It closed. *I'm still giving you the nickel tour,* he said in my mind.

I shot up on a column of air. The trip took only a few

seconds, and the lift's panel opened on the top floor of the building. As I stepped out, Beezy materialized next to me. We were standing next to a large, plate glass window facing north. He pointed to our left. "If you crane your neck a little, you should be able to see where Central Park is."

I did, but what I saw, instead of the huge green oasis in the center of the City, was a fortress of skyscrapers. There couldn't have been a single one less than a hundred stories high. They completed surrounded the park. "What gives?"

Beezy shrugged "Condos. Come on, we're expected. Or rather, you're expected. Oh, wait," he said, reaching into his pocket and pulling out a rubber stamp and a stamp pad. "I almost forgot to give you your notary kit and a signing pen. Remember, he signs in blood; you can use his blood to fill out the rest too. Your notary license doesn't expire, by the way, so when you're filling out the witness section, just put the infinity sign above the expiration date line, okay?"

"Sure. I can do that." I pocketed the kit.

"Now, even though you're expected, Satan likes his pigeons, I mean, his clients, to see a grand, magical entrance. Since you've never been in Lance's office before, I'll transport you. When you're done though, you can teleport yourself back to this spot, can't you?"

I looked around, memorizing details, the window, the white Berber carpet, the chrome bench beside the window. "Fine."

"Okay, here goes. Don't ham it up too much, okay?"

"Why would you think I'd ham it up?"

"I know you, that's why. Remember, you're the one who wanted a cape. Oh, your client's name is Lance Creedmore. Bye bye." The hallway by the window disappeared; I rematerialized in a spacious corner office with the same white carpeting. A man was sitting behind a massive, stainless steel desk. The room was filled with bright natural light from a dozen windows much like the one I'd just been staring out of, trying to catch a glimpse of the Park.

Lance may have been expecting me, but he was still startled at my appearance. He stood, looked me over once, and said, "Hey, you aren't Satan."

Shit. I didn't know I'd have to explain his absence. "No. I am Ste … " I paused.

"Stee? That's an odd name."

I hadn't wanted to say Steve Minion. That sounded a bit demeaning, considering I came from Hell. Besides, I didn't want a human to make a joke about a minion named Minion. Shit, I'd heard that a million times. "No. My name is … Stephan. I am a demon, serving Lord Satan, Earl of Hell."

"Oh. He's not coming himself?" Lance, a tall, handsome man in his forties, seemed offended to be handed off to an underling.

For some reason, that irritated me. I guess I wasn't impressive enough for him. I pinched the lip of his desk between my right thumb and forefinger, lifted the furniture effortlessly – it must have weighed hundreds of pounds – and put it to one side. Now there was nothing between him and me. "Sorry to disappoint you. Are you ready to sign?"

A wide-eyed Lance Creedmore nodded. I reached into my hidden compartment and drew out the contract, but I did it so fast that to Lance the paper must have seemed to appear out of the air. Casually I placed it on the desk, then pulled out the pen Beezy had given me. He reached for it, but I stopped him. "I'm afraid you have to sign in blood. Certainly Satan told you that."

He nodded and reached out his left arm, as if he were going for a blood test. Savagely, I drove the point of the pen into his palm, making him yelp. I wasn't trying to be cruel. He was just making me mad. *What a jerk. He's already rich, that's obvious. Why is he doing such an idiotic thing as selling his soul to the Devil?*

I drew his blood up into the fountain pen then handed it to him, indicating where to sign. "Do you want to read it over, first?"

He glanced quickly at the document. "No. I know I'm selling my soul to the Devil. I doubt there's a hidden clause here that would make things any worse."

Don't be too sure. Satan's very creative when it comes to damnation. Still, one can't be twice or thrice damned, so he's probably right.

Without hesitation, Creedmore signed the contract, then I took the pen from him and witnessed the document. As a last touch, I pulled out my stamp and ink pad and put my mark on the paper. With a surprise, I noted that the design was the old Plant Maintenance Department logo of a pitchfork and hard hat.

"What's this mark?"

I made a wild guess. "My sigil."

"So that's it, then, right?" Lance asked eagerly, as I picked up the contract and stashed it, my notary kit and the pen back in my pocket universe. As an added touch, I put his desk back in place. "I will get all I was promised?"

I smiled wickedly. "Certainly. Satan always honors his agreements. You'll get everything that's coming to you."

My response startled him.

"What do you me … "

I didn't hear the end of his sentence. I was already back with Beelzebub in the hallway.

Chapter 17

"What an asshole!" I hissed.

"Not here. Do you know where the zoo is in Central Park?"

"Of course."

"Meet me at the entrance and we can talk." Beelzebub disappeared. A moment later I followed.

Central Park was cast in shadow. The trees surrounding the zoo, which I'd always remembered as verdant and muscular, were dying. I looked up and saw the reason. All those condos Beezy had mentioned earlier, condos built for people who wanted beautiful views of one of the world's great urban parks, were depriving the trees and grass of sunlight. The park was slowly dying. I just shook my head, saddened by the shortsightedness of humans.

Beezy was waiting for me in front of the turnstiles at the zoo's entrance. "I've made us both invisible, so we can go into the zoo, check out the animals while we discuss things." An employee stared wide-eyed at the two turnstiles that seemed to spin on their own. "Good job, by the way. Just the right amount of drama and gravitas."

"Thanks, but why did he sign his soul over to Satan in the first place? Good grief, doesn't he already have enough money?"

"More than enough," Beezy said, grabbing a couple of bags of popcorn from a nearby concession stand and handing me one. "He's the fourth richest man on the planet."

"Then what does he want?"

Beelzebub tossed four kernels in the air and caught each of them in his mouth. "Oh, same old, same old. More money, more power, more babes. Specifically, he wants to be the richest man on Earth."

"Why should he care? It's not a competition or anything."

Beezy grinned. "It is to him."

"For some reason, I don't feel too bad about getting his signature. He deserves to go to Hell."

"Oh, he was going regardless. He's already done so much evil in the world that he's been damned for a long time."

"Huh? Then why go through this charade?"

The Lord of the Flies stopped before the snow monkey exhibit. It was a hot summer day; I could tell that by the clothing of the other tourists. Being a demon and used to Hellish temperatures, I was actually a bit chilled myself. Beezy ate another handful of popcorn. "Collateral damage."

"What do you mean?" I asked, eating some from my own bag. There was a big sign before the exhibit that said, "Don't feed the animals," but since I was a demon from Hell, I ignored it and tossed some kernels to the monkeys.

"Well, Satan figures that we'll get at least two more souls this way. Creedmore, now that he knows for certain he's damned, will feel he has nothing to lose and turn to evil with a vengeance. He'll buy corporations, dismantle them and sell off the parts, making even more money for himself, and putting tens of thousands out of work. He'll order murders, likely committing one or two personally just to experience the thrill of it. Lancey boy will also descend into debauchery. His wife, not the strongest person emotionally, will commit suicide in despair over her husband's infidelity. Suicide, as you know, is a guaranteed ticket to Hell."

"Oh no!"

"And one of his underlings will be so envious of Lance's success that said underling will eventually kill his boss. Envy and Murder. A twofer."

"And neither of these people would end up damned if Creedmore hadn't signed that piece of paper I brought him?"

"Nope."

I retched violently into a nearby trashcan. *Oh, no no no no no!*

A strong hand grabbed my shoulder. "Here," Beezy said, handing me a small phial. "Drink this."

"What's in it?" I said in misery. Nothing else was coming up, but I still had the dry heaves.

"Don't ask. Just think of it as demon Dramamine."

In a single gulp, I swallowed the contents of the phial. It burned like fire, and since I could tolerate a lot of fire, you can imagine that it was hotter than a mutant habanera. And yet, my stomach instantly calmed.

"Thanks," I said, wiping my mouth with a handkerchief he gave me. When I offered it back, he just rolled his eyes and shook his head no. I dropped it in the trashcan.

"Really, Minion, you can't be ralphing every time you have to do your job."

"I know, I know, but I just got two people who didn't deserve it damned to Hell."

"It's just business. Besides this was going to happen whether you notarized the contract or someone else did. Not the ralphing part, but the damnation, I mean."

"Great. Peachy," I said, standing up from where I'd been hunched over the trashcan for the past two minutes. "I feel bunches better."

"Ah, you must be feeling better. You're being sarcastic again." He looked at me critically. "Normally I'd slug you for it, even now that you're a demon, but sarcasm has always been your defense mechanism."

"True." I was impressed. Beelzebub had been paying

attention all these years. He knew me as well as I knew myself.

"Look," he said, patting me on the back, as we walked toward the zoo's exit. "We've got some time here, and I'd just as soon not take you back while you're a disgusting mess, okay?"

"What do you have in mind?" I asked, wiping my nose on my sleeve, noting idly that using faux Gucci to soak up demon snot was not the best use of haute couture.

Beezy rubbed his hands with relish. Then he squirted some mustard on them. (We were standing next to the concession stand again.) "Let's take in a ballgame."

"Do you mean baseball? You know how much I hate baseball!"

"Well, I like it," said the Lord of the Flies. "You get to sit there and do nothing, while nothing is happening."

"Exactly!"

"You wouldn't discount 'nothing' if you were an executive like me. Also, at a baseball game you get to drink beer, eat hotdogs, ooh, and chow down on those big pretzels!" There was a reason why Beelzebub was one of the few fat devils I knew. He loved junk food. He was also the patron devil of Gluttony. " If you're good, Minion, I'll even get you one of those styrofoam red fingers."

"Thanks, dad. So who are the Yankees playing, anyway?"

"Oh, we're not going to a Yankees game. We're going to Fenway Park."

"What??? You mean not only are you making me go to a baseball game, which is about as boring as watching dog crap cook on the concrete, but you're going to force me to watch the Red Sox?"

He shrugged. "They're my team."

"Grrr." My newly feral nature suddenly came to the fore.

"Watch it. Demons never growl at devils. It's bad form."

"Okay, I didn't know that. So who are they playing? The Cardinals or Giants or somebody else interesting?"

"No, the White Sox."

"Chicago? Aren't they the worst team in the history of the game? Why they haven't won a World Series since, what, 1917?"

"Actually, they won one in 2005. You were already dead, of course, so you wouldn't have noticed. It's been another long dry spell for them, though. They've had losing seasons for most years since."

Beezy waved his hand and transformed our clothing into something more suitable for the outing. Now we had on Red Sox jerseys, Red Sox gimmee caps, and blue jeans. Beezy also shrank down a little from his normal height. Now he was just a six foot fatso instead of a seven foot monster. Finally, he hid both of our sets of horns.

"I can't go," I grumbled, attempting a last defense. There had to be some way to get out of this.

"Why not?"

"Uh ... I can't teleport that far."

"Not to worry. I can." Then he grabbed my shoulder and transported us both to Fenway Park.

I couldn't believe it. Fenway Park in 2055 still looked much as it did when it opened in 1912. The oldest ballpark in Major League Baseball, it stood in stark contrast to the post-modernist high rises that had grown around it since my death. Despite myself, I smiled. Maybe this wouldn't be so bad after all.

Beezy got us good seats, basically by putting a spell on a couple of rich guys in a box. They wandered, bemused, up to the top bleachers and watched the game there. Then he got us a couple of beers and a few dogs (three for him, one for me).

For the next three hours, I sat next to my former boss, bored stiff with the game, but eating a lot of hot dogs and drinking a ton of beer, both of which really hit the spot. Beezy was in Hea … He was very happy, and he would periodically yell things like "You're blind! That was a strike." Or "Slide, slide!" Or "Hey, batter, batter, batter," which I never really understood but heard lots of other people yell, too, whenever a Chicago player went to the mound.

For myself, I found it hard to keep my eye on the ball, because there was another ball that mesmerized me. While Manhattan had been gray and overcast – or at least while we were at the zoo, which was the only time I was outside – Boston had been blessed with a spectacular summer day. The sky was a clear blue, and floating in the cerulean was …

The sun. Oh, glorious, glorious sun! It was warm, it was huge. I'd forgotten how big the sun was. The blindingly blissful orb baked down on me. I remembered all those childhood prohibitions against staring directly at the sun, but since I was a demon, I figured I was tough enough to take it. Wouldn't have mattered though. I hadn't seen the sun in sixty years, and I happily would have made myself blind staring at it non-stop.

Beezy elbowed me in the gut. "Pay attention. You're missing the game." Reluctantly, I turned my gaze from the sky and back to the baseball diamond.

Watching the game was so boring, so drab, yet so … normal. At the end of the three hours, I was actually enjoying myself. Privately, I hoped a miracle would occur – I'd always been one to root for the underdog – but the Red trounced the White, fifteen to three.

And Beezy really did get me a styrofoam finger, as sort of a joke I know, but I secretly treasured it. No one had given me a gift in a very long time. I put it in my secret space next to my pitchfork.

The ballpark was emptying when Beezy stood and stretched. Literally. He popped back to his full seven foot height. His horns also poked out of the skin from his forehead. I felt my own doing the same. "Well," he said, "I guess it's time we headed home."

I looked up at the sun. It was perhaps five o'clock, and while the sky was still bright, the light had dimmed somewhat as more of the atmosphere stood between us and old Sol. A few clouds had begun to form in the sky, and they partially blocked my view.

I looked to my former boss. He was in a good mood, and I wondered if he would indulge me a little more. "Before we go, do you think we could make one final stop?"

Beelzebub reached to the concrete at his feet; another Sox fan had left a beer half-finished. Beezy slammed it back in a single gulp then belched mightily, the sound echoing across the ballpark, startling a couple of pigeons that had been dozing on the scoreboard. They flew out of sight. "Maybe," he said. "Where?"

I told him.

He looked thoughtful. "Interesting choice. I go there sometimes. Great views, pretty remote."

"I've never been," I confessed, "but I always wanted to."

"Why the Hell not?" He said, grabbing my wrist. And then we were gone.

We popped back into existence some three thousand miles to the west, standing on a mountain top, perhaps ten thousand feet above sea level. Yet it was high desert. The ground was dry and white, like and yet unlike sand. Glancing to the southeast with my demon eyes, I could make out Death Valley, a bit more than a hundred miles away.

Very little grew around us; we were just about at tree line, that point where the last trees surrender to the thin air and frigid nights that come with high elevation. The few plants alive up here were gnarled and stunted. And very, very old. They were bristlecone pines, the oldest single trees in existence.

But that's not what drew me here. A lifetime ago, back when I had a life, a colleague of mine at Columbia, an astronomy professor, had told me about this spot. "The most spectacular views of the sun you'll ever get," he had said.

I looked up and caught my breath. The sun was a giant disc of yellow fire. I felt like I was in the presence of an ancient god, Ra, the Egyptian sun deity. Then I realized with a start that some of the pines around me were as old as the pyramids.

"It's the sun, isn't it?" Beelzebub asked, following my gaze, but clearly listening to the jumble of thoughts in my brain. "That's why you wanted to come here. Not the trees."

"Yes." I replied, still soaking up the light. I inhaled, enjoying the clean air also. Hades always smelled of sulfur. This smelled of fresh. "It's been a long time."

The old devil nodded. "In the old days, before the Fall, I used to revel in the glory of the stars. You think Sol is something? You should see Betelgeuse from a few million miles away. It would knock your socks off."

"I'm sure that's true," I whispered, still in awe of the blazing orb in the sky. "But this is the only sun I've ever known, and right now, it looks pretty grand to me. Like I said, it's been a long time."

Beezy smiled ruefully. "You don't know what a long time is. When Satan, I and the other contrary angels rebelled and were cast down, we were not allowed to see the sun or any other star for nearly fourteen billion years. It's only been in the last six millennia or so that we've been allowed to wander on the normal planes of existence."

I whistled. "I forget, sometimes, how old you are."

Beelzebub kicked at the dirt. "As old as old is. There's only one creature in existence older than I am."

I looked at him in shock. "You were the first being created?"

He gave me a companionable shove that almost knocked me off the mountain. "No, all the angels were created at once, right at the start of the Big Bang." He paused then said softly, "but I understand you. Whether it's been fourteen billion or only sixty years without seeing a sun, it's too long."

"Life is so short." I said, looking at the ancient pines dotting the white earth around me. "Even these creatures. They've been around for thousands of years, and yet in the scheme of the Cosmos, they have existed for only the blink of an eye. Mortal creatures must seem pretty ephemeral to you."

He shook his head. "They aren't ephemeral. Remember the law of the conservation of matter and energy. You, for example, have been around, in one form or another, for as long as I have. True, the peculiar combination of molecules that made up Steve Minion for, oh, about forty years, yeah, that's gone. But it's the combination, not the substance, that has changed. Your ashes – did you know you were cremated? – may be part of some oyster shell in the Chesapeake. Who knows? Maybe the atoms of your former physical being are making a dandy pearl right now. And while your body and brain aren't intact, there's a reasonable facsimile of them ... "

I smiled wryly. "With horns and tail added."

"With horns and tail added," he agreed, "downstairs. Your mind and your soul, they are still intact. It's one of the universe's great mysteries. In a sense, Steve, you are eternal. Doesn't that make you happy?"

"It doesn't sound so bad when you put it that way."

I still miss the Earth, though, my life here, waking up each day with hope in my heart. I sighed. "This world, this wonderful, wonderful world. There's so much to see. In life, I knew people who raced around trying to see it all. Impossible. I also knew people who went nowhere. And that was a life too. There was love of family, love of friends, love of solitude, love for the crowd. People accomplished things. Some accomplishments, like Einstein's, say, seemed so grand. Even Creedmore has done things."

"But in the end," Beelzebub said, "does any of it matter? Humans live, love, die. It seems pointless to me."

"Maybe," I said, biting my lip, "but it's also beautiful, don't you think?"

"Perhaps, yet from my perspective, the time humans have on earth, and how they spend it, seems little different from that of mayflies: busy, frenetic, desperate even, but in the end, pretty pointless."

I looked at him. "And is Hell better or worse?"

He looked thoughtful. "It's longer, anyway, though in the final analysis, about the same, I guess. Still, as long as your consciousness is firing, that's something."

Yes, that was something. I thought about Creedmore and the two others who would eventually be damned along with him. "And … and what about good and evil, and where each of us ends up?"

"Minion, you make this way too hard, as all humans do."

"But I'm not human, at least not anymore."

"No? I wonder."

That surprised me, and I glanced at him quizzically, but he would say no more on that topic.

I took a final look at one of the ancient trees, at the sun burning down from on high. "You know, every day when I lived was a sort of rebirth. There were endless possibilities, well, maybe not endless, but each day I could make new choices, change the pattern of my life, sometimes in small ways, sometimes in larger ones. Now, it's, well … "

"It's Hell. Hey, I completely get it. You're not the only one stuck down there for Eternity, you know."

I swallowed hard and nodded. *Eternity is a bitch.*

"You said it!" Beelzebub agreed, reading my thoughts. "Or thought it anyway. Are you ready now?"

"As ready as I'll ever be." *Since I really don't want to go back to … there.*

"Okay, then close your eyes, tap your heels together three times and say, 'There's no place like home.'"

I looked at him in disbelief. "You're kidding, right?"

He grinned. "Of course. Just trying to lighten the mood." He put his arm around my shoulder, and we teleported.

Chapter 18

We simply appeared in Beezy's office. This was a very discreet entrance for my former boss, but I suppose it was because of me. The thought of exploding into his office, a mushroom-shaped cloud rising from my blue jeans, was disturbing. He probably knew that.

"You'd better head down to Satan's office and deliver that signed contract," Beelzebub said, sitting back behind his desk. He slid some readers onto his nose and grabbed some paperwork that I guess required his attention.

"Okay. And sir?"

The Lord of the Flies glanced at me over the rim of his lenses. "Yes?"

"Thanks. Thank you for a wonderful day." Except for the collateral damage, of course. I could have done without that.

"You're welcome, Minion," he said, all business again.

"Any final thoughts? We discussed a lot of stuff today."

He considered the question. "Oh, I have lots of thoughts, but let me share one with you. Don't over-think this. That's your tendency, you know. Just do your job. Remember, you're not permanently hurting anyone. And try to adjust to your new status as best you can. You really don't have any other choice, so make the most of it."

I sighed, one of so many sighs today. But he was right. What was the point of struggling against my fate? It is what it is. Stupid expression, I know, but somehow it seemed to fit.

"Before I leave, could you change my clothes back to the outfit I had on when I met Creedmore?" While Beezy, upon arrival had changed his garments to his typical white suit and black fez, he'd neglected to change mine. He shrugged, waved his hand, and I stood before him in my black leisure suit. I still thought leisure suits were the stupidest fashion concept ever in men's attire, but it was black, so it looked reasonably cool. Besides, it was more dignified than a Red Sox jersey and jeans.

"Thanks." I saluted Hell's Number Two devil. He gave me a half wave and went back to his paperwork. I closed my eyes, pinched my sphincter and teleported to Satan's front office.

Bruce was there, sharpening his claws with a nail file. He looked bored. "Minion. Satan said to expect you. Nice outfit, by the way. I had one of those near the end of my life."

"Thanks for the compliment. Hey," I said, trying to be companionable. "We've known each other for a long time, and now that we're going to be working together more closely, why don't you call me by my first name?"

Bruce looked as if he'd just stepped in cow manure, that is, slightly repulsed and anxious to get the offending object off his shoe. "Demons don't have first names."

"Why, sure they do," I said. "You for example. Bruce. Remember?"

"My apologies. Demons don't have multiple names. Lord Satan has determined that for the nonce I shall continue to be called Bruce. In time, I may get a special demon name." When he said that, his face lit up with enthusiasm.

"If you did, what would it be?" I asked, interested.

"I would hope for 'Dragon,' for personal reasons."

"Makes sense," I said, considering his movie career. "I don't know what I'd want my own name to be. Nicknames have never stuck with me. They didn't as a kid, and they didn't at Beast Barracks."

"Well, for now, Lord Satan has decided that you will continue to be called Minion. So you see," he said, with mock regret, "I can't call you Steve. That's not your name anymore."

The Hell it isn't. "Fine," I said aloud. I reached in my pocket universe "Here. This is for Satan."

"Why in the Cosmos would he want a giant styrofoam hand?"

"Whoops!" I stuffed the hand back in my secret space. I was putting too much stuff in there. Pretty soon some closet cleaning would be in order. I felt around and found the contract. "I meant to give you this. It's a signed contract for Lance Creedmore's soul."

Bruce took the parchment and walked over to a large bank of filing cabinets behind him. He pulled out a drawer then leafed through it. "Cameron, Cardoman, Clooney, ah, here we are, Creedmore." He opened a fat folder and slid in the contract, then closed the drawer.

"Are these the folders for all of the people who have sold their souls to the Devil?" I asked.

"Good grief, no. We have a warehouse on Eight for most of them. These are just the active files."

"Does the boss want to see me?" I asked, pointing at Satan's closed door.

"No. Our lord and master is not even in there. He's getting a massage. However, he told me to tell you to show up tomorrow at nine." Bruce returned to his desk, snatched up his nail file and went back to work on his left index finger.

"Okay, later Bruce."

"Later, Minion," he said without looking up.

I teleported, level by level, up to Five. My chosen spot to land on my old home Level was the abandoned steel mill some blocks from my old office. With my demon vision, I could see the dilapidated trailer from there. *I wonder how Orson and Edison are getting along.*

Three more jumps would take me to Lilith's house – I still couldn't think of it as ours – but I wasn't yet ready for the cocktail hour. My thoughts were still on some of the stuff Beezy and I had been discussing. I needed to talk some more, to get some stuff out of my system, to sort out my confused mind. I needed a neutral party – no devil or demon would do – so I determined to pay a call on Charon.

My stop on Two was very short, and it was on the sidewalk outside of Lust Unlimited, the tall high rise in which Lilith worked. I figured, by now, she'd already gone home.

Charon worked on Level 0.5. He provided an alternate way into Hell than either the Escalator or the Elevator, or the Mouth of Hell, for that matter, which was only used as a last resort anyway. There was also the Stairway to Paradise, or the Stairway to Hell, depending on what end you were at, but the treads between Level One and Gates level were currently removed for security reasons. Long story.

How to proceed next? Typically, I teleported one level at a time. Two levels was at the upper limit of my teleportation range, and I'd never tried it. Yet Satan didn't like demons to go to Level One, where the Virtuous Pagans and Unbaptized babies were, for it might upset them. Of all Hell's inhabitants, they were the only ones to get kid glove treatment, so it would be best to skip that Circle of Hell entirely if possible. I figured that Level 0.5 was about a mile and a half jump, well within my range, so I closed my eyes and concentrated on Charon's boathouse.

The trip went without incident. I had comfortably jumped a level and a half. The boathouse was a foot away. I glanced around, but could not see my friend.

Level 0.5 was a large cavern of obsidian, through which a jet black river ran. While the black glass of the arching cave seemed to glow with a dull luminescence, the level was for the most part perpetually shrouded by the dark. Even my demon eyes had difficulty seeing things at a distance. At last, though, I spotted a stately gondola slicing its way through the River Styx. At its stern stood the stoic figure of Charon, ferryman of the dead, dressed in his charcoal cloak, pushing the boat along the black river with a long pole. In front of the gondola was Cerberus, the three-headed dog of Greek myth, who had been Ronnie's friend and companion for thousands of years now. The giant beastie was standing on the prow staring forward, three big grins on his face, three enormous, drooly tongues lolling to the sides of [of course] three monstrous mouths. He had seen me, and he set up a cacophony of barks. Well, not really a cacophony. He was barking out in three different pitches; I think it was a G flat chord. Pretty impressive. Anyway, the barks were not in warning, but in welcome, for Cerberus was my friend too.

With a final push of the pole, Charon sent his craft sliding smoothly onto the landing. This was no doubt aided by the nature of the River Styx, which was filled not with water but oil. That's why it was a black river, you know.

Cerberus bounded from the gondola and pounced on me. Soon I was soaked in dog slime.

A frenetic clicking came from the boat. "-... .- -.. / -.. --- --.! -.-- --- ..- / -.- -. --- .-- / -.-- --- ..- .----. .-. . / -. --- - / ... ..- .--. .--. --- ... . -.. / - --- / .--- ..- -- .--. / ..- .--. / --- -. / .--. . --- .--. .-.. .!"

What he said was, "Bad dog! You know you're not supposed to jump up on people!"

"It's all right," I said laughing. I petted the giant three heads. "Good to see you too, boy!"

He sniffed my hand, looking puzzled. Slowly, the giant mastiff crawled off me, walking around me as if performing an inspection.

I flushed. "Yeah, I know. I smell different. I'm a demon now, you know."

I swear, if a dog could shrug, Cerberus would have done it. He jumped back on me and started licking me down again. It was nice to know that the dog didn't care if I was demon or human. I was still his friend.

Hi, Steve, Ronnie said, stepping out of the boat. *What brings you to our neck of the woods?*

Crawling out from under the gargantuan and gregarious dog was no mean feat, even as a demon, but I managed it. "I just needed to talk to someone. To a friend."

Well, I'm certainly your friend, he said, giving me a companionable pat on the back. *Let's sit here on the shore. Do you want anything to eat?*

"No thanks. I'll have dinner with Lilith back ho … at her house."

Well, how about a stick of gum at least?

Ronnie always had a pack of grape chewing gum on him, and at least two or three sticks in his mouth. He passed the pack to me, and I took one.

So, what's up?

"I don't know, I … say, this stuff is really good," I said, as a squirt of intense grape flavor hit my taste buds.

Isn't it? he said with perhaps more enthusiasm than the topic warranted, but he *did* love his gum. *It's my favorite flavor!*

I started to roll my eyes but caught myself. Ronnie was my friend after all. "I know," was all I said.

Ronnie sat quietly, not pushing me to talk, but waiting patiently for me to begin. Charon was over three thousand years old, and he'd been contentedly doing the same damn thing all that time, that is, ferrying the dead across the Styx, so I suppose patience came naturally to him.

I felt as if I'd been holding my breath for three months. When I opened my mouth, all that pent-up air exploded from my lungs to form a question. "Ronnie, am I a nice person?"

That sounds softer than it came out. Really, it was probably more like, "RONNIE, AM I A NICE PERSON?!!!"

Or maybe the explosiveness of the question was just inside my head, for Charon, one of my oldest friends in the Underworld, looked at me and said in a quiet voice, *Steve, you're one of the nicest guys I've ever known.*

My eyes hurt. I didn't know why, but water was falling from them. I realized that I was crying, which was completely absurd. *A demon doesn't cry.*

"But I'm a demon now." I searched left and right for a way to escape the obvious, but there was no passage for me.

You're still Steve, he said mildly. *You are still my friend.* Cerberus chose that moment to come over and lick my hand then plopped down companionably next to me. *See? Even Cerberus knows you're still Steve.*

"Yes, but, but," I searched around desperately for words to explain what I was feeling, "but now I'm expected to hurt people."

If skeletons could smile, then Ronnie did it then. *You're just doing your job. It's just business.*

I leapt to my feet. Not knowing my own strength, I launched fifty feet into the air. "Why does everyone keep saying it's just business?" I snapped, when my boots touched the ground.

And then Ronnie, who had stood up to watch my launch into the sky, did one of the sweetest things anyone has ever done for me. He wrapped me in his ancient, bony arms and held me. For a wonder, he said nothing. Just a lot of holding.

I wept disconsolately for what seemed like an hour, but was probably only a minute or two.

Steve, he said gently. *You didn't ask to be a demon. You didn't want to be a demon. I know that. Your sacrifice for Flo and your friends was a noble gesture.*

Charon had a tragic look on his face. Of course, all skeletons look tragic, by definition, but I'd known Ronnie for sixty years, and I could tell happy bones from sad ones. These looked pretty damn morose. *Look, Steve, I don't know if it makes any difference in the scheme of things, but I believe with all of my heart, if I had a heart, which of course I don't,* he said, opening his cloak to show the blank space in his ribcage where the heart would go, *that you are a good person. It doesn't matter if you are saved or damned, human or demon. You are you, my dear, dear friend.*

We sat back down on the beach for a while. Periodically, Cerberus would come up to me, each of his heads licking me with great deliberation, trying to show me that I was loved.

Neutral parties. Both of them. Neither devil, demon nor human. And they thought I was okay.

It meant the world to me.

"Do you like your job?" I asked Charon after a while.

"It's okay, I guess. Good steady work."

"No kidding. Back and forth, back and forth, for what, three millennia?"

"Something like that."

"And you're fine with that?"

Charon shrugged, causing his cloak to fall off one shoulder, revealing a clavicle the color of ivory. *It's a job.*

"Do you ... do you ever feel bad that you're taking people to Hell?"

Not really. They were going there anyway. They just opted to go by boat instead of Escalator.

I thought about this a while, rolling Ronnie's words around

in my head as if it were a rock polisher trying to come up with some smooth nuggets of wisdom. "Beezy says that whether I torment the damned or not, they're still going to get tormented."

He's right, you know.

"I suppose so," I said reluctantly. "Still. Does that mean it shouldn't bother me?"

Ronnie shrugged. *I don't know, Steve. Does it? Does it bother you?*

"Yeah," I said at last. "It really does."

"Then that's how you feel. It is what it is."

Earlier in the day when I'd said that same expression to myself, it seemed stupid, if accurate. Hearing a three thousand year old creature say it back to me, though, was a sort of validation. Now the words seemed infinitely wise.

"Thanks, Ronnie," I said, giving him a hug, as if he were the brother I'd never had. "You're a good friend."

I try to be. Charon searched the pockets of his cloak, looking for something. His hand landed on whatever he'd been seeking, and he triumphantly pulled out a rectangle of plastic and foil. *Would you like another stick of gum?*

Chapter 19

By the time I got back to Level Two, Lilith had a wonderful meal prepared for us. We had cocktails by the pool and ate on the patio. I told her a little about my day; she reciprocated. Then we watched a Bruce Willis movie and hit the sack. We didn't sleep, of course, but spent the night screwing like rabbits, demonic ones at that, hardly taking a break, except to occasionally lie and doze in the lovely, languid aftermath of sex.

By nine a.m. I was down in Satan's office, sitting erect in my chair, waiting for my next set of orders.

"Nice outfit," he said neutrally.

"Thank you sir. I haven't had a leisure suit since the Seventies. They always looked a bit odd to me, the coats especially, like Nehru jackets that didn't have the energy to button themselves up." I flipped at the collar of the shirt, which was very wide and splayed across the top of coat's lapel. It looked like the wings of a paper airplane. "This seems a little over-the-top too, but at least the whole outfit's in black, and I don't feel like a cadet anymore."

"You know I couldn't care less, don't you?"

"Oh. Sorry sir. I'll stop talking about it then."

"Good plan." He handed me a piece of paper.

"What's this?"

"Our meeting agenda."

"We've never had one before."

"Yes, well, I'm trying to implement the practice with all my direct reports. I dictate them to Bruce – did you know he can actually take dictation? – and he types them up for me." He scratched his chin. "I could just conjure them up out of thin air, I suppose, but it gives Bruce something to do."

"Yes sir. Good thinking sir." I looked down at the paper. Item one said "inane conversation about Minion's clothing." Well, we'd covered that. The second item said "Creedmore post mortem."

"Did Creedmore die already?"

"Of course not. He just signed away his soul yesterday."

"Then why the post mortem?"

Satan pinched the bridge of his nose, as if he were getting a headache. "I wish to discuss your performance on getting his signature."

I looked nervously at my boss. "Didn't I do it right?"

"Yes, yes," he said impatiently. "I looked at the paperwork last night after my massage. All perfectly legal."

"Then what's the problem?" The Devil stared at me sharply. "I mean, what's the problem, my lord?"

He frowned. "Only about a gallon of demon vomit in a trash can at the Central Park Zoo. You know that stuff will eat through metal, don't you?"

"No. Really?"

"Yes, really. It's like battery acid. Not to mention the smell." Satan looked mildly disgusted. "Demons are not supposed to leave any evidence of their presence when they go to Earth. The zoo officials have already roped off the area and called in a HAZMAT squad."

"Oh, sorry," I said sheepishly. "I didn't know."

He strummed his desktop with his fingertips. "But that's not what has me concerned. Beezy brought me up to speed about your reaction to getting two more people damned."

"I know, it's just that ... "

"Be quiet, Minion. I know your adjustment to your new status is not going well. Beelzebub and I are in agreement. You need to start tormenting people directly, until you get used to it."

My stomach began to knot up. "Couldn't I just do things like the Leviathan job instead?"

"No. There are occasional situations like that where you can help, but not enough of them to keep you occupied."

"But," I protested meekly, "Bruce is a demon, and he doesn't have to torment people."

"That shows what you know. As a matter of fact, Bruce spends two hours every day in Slothtown, pitchforking anyone who isn't working fast enough."

"Oh."

"It's part of every demon's responsibilities to devote time to tormenting the damned. I have a worker shortage, as you well know. That's why we put so much effort into recruiting for the Corps. Note the next item on the agenda."

It said, "Torture Assignment."

"I want you to find five people today to torment. At least two acts must involve use of your pitchfork. Another must involve an acquaintance of yours, and one more must be the direct tormenting of a personal friend. Oh, and you can't combine the last two. They must be separate individuals."

"But ... "

"No buts. You're never going to be any good as a demon until you can torture the damned." He stared at me for a few moments, as if he were wrestling with a difficult problem. "Look," he said at last, "you don't have to take pleasure in this. True, many demons, most in fact, *love* inflicting pain on humans, but there is a minority of the Corps that view torment as just part of the job. They don't particularly enjoy it, but they do it, effectively, if dispassionately. If you can just get yourself to that point, and stop all this puking, I'll be satisfied."

Maybe he was right. It seemed unlikely that I'd ever enjoy

this part of my job, but if I could just treat it as an unpleasant if necessary part of my responsibilities, maybe I'd be okay. *Sort of like serving on faculty committees.* I shuddered at the thought.

"Faculty committees. Good comparison. I know how much you hated them in life, but you still did them."

Only when I couldn't duck them.

"Only when you couldn't duck them," Satan agreed. "Regardless, you still did them. And just like the occasional committee from your days in academe, you can't duck this."

"I suggest you start with three strangers, then the acquaintance and finish up with the friend. You can choose anyone you want, but it has to be a close friend, understand?"

I hung my head. "Yes sir," I said morosely.

"Good. Now, what did you think of the ball game yesterday? How about them Red Sox, eh?"

I looked up at him in surprise. He didn't strike me as a baseball fan.

"I'm not." He motioned at the paper in my hand. "Look at the agenda."

Item four: Make companionable small talk with subordinate.

"Enough of that!" he said with a yawn. "Item five?"

I read on. "Get out of here."

"Yes sir!" I said, hopping out of my chair, giving the Earl of Hell a quick salute and bolting for the door.

I made the short hop to the docks of Level Seven then sat on a nearby barrel to ponder my orders – and my predicament – at the same time idly wondering if Pinkerton had made the cask on which I'd placed my keister. Probably not, for Allan's barrels usually couldn't stand up to much weight. The thought of Allan, and that one perfect barrel of his that I'd destroyed, saddened me.

It had finally come, the moment I'd been dreading, when my eternity of tormenting the damned would begin. Hoping for some kind of loophole, I reached into my hidey-hole and pulled out my job description. Yep, there it was, first item in the list of responsibilities: "Torment the Damned." *Crap.* There was simply no getting around it. And five different people had to be my victims today.

About twenty feet away, an old tar was hopping onto a small sailboat. He reached for a line and secured it to a sail with a deftly-tied bowline. The bowline was one of the knots all Boy Scouts had to learn, and since I'd been an Eagle Scout, I of course knew it well. The sailor was preparing to raise the sail prior to heading out to sea. That was probably not by choice – no one in his right mind would sail on the ocean of the Kraken – but he was damned, so he couldn't exactly say, "Ya know, looks like rain. Think I'll stay home and read a book."

A plan formed in my brain. It would require speed and knowledge of the bowline. My demonic nature gave me the former and my status as an Eagle Scout the latter.

Fun fact: The rank of Eagle is the only one in Scouts you can retain. Upon reaching the age of eighteen, all other Scouts lose their ranks, whether they are Tenderfoot, Second Class, First Class, Star or Life. The ranks desert you, rather than you deserting them, like the carriage stranded Cinderella at midnight by reverting to pumpkin form. Not that the Scouts at that point give a crap. Those who haven't achieved Eagle Scout by about sixteen are unlikely to, because by then they have discovered girls and cars. A merit badge or two simply can't compete with burgeoning breasts and the freedom of the road.

But I, for better or worse, had made it into the highest echelon of Scoutdom, so in a way I was still an Eagle Scout. Once an Eagle, always an Eagle, we used to say. Well, actually, only I said it, I think, but still. Anyway, while people make fun of the ranks and merit badges in scouting, there's actually some pretty good knowledge that can come out of it. That's where I learned Morse code, which is what had made it possible for me to communicate with Charon and develop a friendship.

And it was going to serve me now, if I could just work up the nerve. When I had destroyed Pinkerton's barrel it had been a reflexive response to a direct order from Satan. Now, though, I was going to do my demon thing at my own initiative. I reached for the cameo of Edison at my neck, felt the raised ivory that I knew held his image press against my palm, and suddenly felt remarkably evil. At least for me.

After tying his knot, the sailor turned his back for a moment. Kicking into high speed, I ran the short distance to the boat, hopped aboard, used my Eagle Scout knowledge of the bowline to untie it and returned to the dock, hiding behind a stack of boxes due to be loaded soon onto a cargo ship. Then I waited.

The sailor turned back and saw his knot lying limply on the deck of the boat. He scratched his head in puzzlement.

You have to understand. A properly tied bowline simply can't do that. It's one of the most secure knots imaginable and is even used in rescue work. For example, if a person fell down a well, someone could take a long rope, tie a bowline with a large bow in it, and lower that end down the well. The victim could sit on the loop and be hoisted up. And the knot would never slip. Impossible.

But … this is Hell, and the sailor knew it. With a shrug, he retied the line. He glanced away briefly and I repeated my earlier mischief.

"Blast it!" he grumbled and tied the knot a third time. Holding the rope firmly in both hands, he kept his eye on it, waiting to see if it would untie itself once again. This time, though, I ran at top speed to the boat, jumped onboard, landing with a thump that must have startled him, leapt over his head and used my demon strength to break the rope. Then I blasted back to my hiding space.

I was moving so fast he couldn't have seen me. From his perspective, the rope must simply have broken. He fell backwards onto the deck, cursing.

Well done, I told myself. But something was missing. *Oh, right.* I pulled out the ivory cameo and studied Edison's silhouette. There was just something about the guy that made my blood boil. "Bwahahahahahaha!" I laughed, completing my task, then teleported to Six.

That wasn't so bad. My stomach was calm too. I'd managed to torment someone without losing my breakfast. Admittedly, it wasn't any major bit of torment, but I'd done it all on my own, and I'd even finished with the signature demonic laugh. One down, four to go.

What next, what next? I was sitting on a rock, not far from Hell's Sulfur mine. Karnaj, who was staffing the desk at the entrance, spotted me and walked over. "Hey, Minion! I haven't seen you since the day you shadowed me in the mines. Now look at you. A full-fledged demon!" He grinned, then reached out and shook my hand. "Great to have you on the team!"

"Thanks, Karnaj."

"So, what are you doing here?"

"Oh," I said, blushing slightly, "Satan has me practicing my tormenting skills, so I'm going around Hell beating up on the damned."

Karnaj rubbed his hands together enthusiastically. "Ooo, sounds like fun. Say! Why don't you come into the mine and torture some of my group? Digger wouldn't mind."

"No thanks," I said, thinking quickly. "I was just heading up to Glutton's Gap on Three."

"You sure? I happen to know that Henry Ford is right inside the entrance. I know you'd love to stick it to him!"

Henry Ford, like Tommy Edison, was one of my least favorite humans in all of Hell. I imagined poking him repeatedly with my pitchfork, soaking his white coveralls with his own blood. I could picture him having to spend the entire night rinsing out the blood, since Digger demanded that his workers show up in pristine uniforms every morning. Blood is a bitch to get out of fabric anyway, but when it's mixed with sulfur from Hell, well, you can just imagine that a little Spray N Wash wouldn't do the trick. Involuntarily, a "Bwahahahahahaha!" exploded from my lips.

"Hey, good laugh!"

"Uh, thanks," I said, privately ashamed that my demonic nature had gotten the better of me. "See you, Karnaj." With that, I teleported.

The encounter with Karnaj had troubled me, mainly because my intense dislike of Ford had triggered the cruel part of my demonic nature. Yet, in looking for an excuse not to step into the mine, I'd come up with an idea for my next act of mayhem. I made three quick hops, depositing myself on the rim of the Throat of Hell on Level Three. Another jump put me a little ways outside of Glutton's Gap, where most of Hell's Jennie Craig dropouts were spending their afterlives.

Glutton's Gap looks like a mining town from the Old West. Just outside the place an eternal barbecue is underway.

I saw the chuck wagon, with the name, "Donner Party Planners" painted on the white canvas covering the wagon. DPP was run by a group of devils and demons. The company slogan was, "Have your friends for dinner, and we'll do the cooking."

At least two hundred damned souls filled the area. Half of them were being slow-cooked in great smokers; when they were cooked to "meat falling off the bone" tenderness, the other half would eat them. Then, after the eaters were full to bursting, they would retreat to a long line of port-o-lets a hundred feet away and excrete the remains of the eaten. (There was a large banner above these outhouses, kind of like what you'd see above circus tent entrances, with the words "Donner Pass" printed on it.) These remains would reconstitute, this being Hell and all. Then the parties would switch roles. The eaters would become the eaten and vice versa. Then they'd switch again. Ad infinitum.

Donner Party Planners put on the classic barbecue meal. In addition to the, uh, meat, there was potato salad, cold slaw, beans, white bread, iced tea (both plain and sweetened), pickles and, of course, onions. The onions were my target. They lay on a dozen plates atop a picnic table near the smokers, thin sliced (the onions, not the plates or table or smokers) and ready to eat.

I got into a runner's crouch and prepared myself for a race. I was dealing with devils and demons now, as well as humans, and I needed to be extra fast to avoid detection. Pulled it off, though. The plates just seemed to disappear from the table top. I dumped the onions behind a cactus a few miles away. "Bwahahahahahaha!" I laughed in mischievous triumph, even though there was no one to hear me.

That makes two. Actually it made over two hundred, but I didn't think Satan would see it that way. I needed to perform three other demonic acts. *Now what, or rather, who should be next? Oh! I know!*

The running had felt good, so rather than teleport back to the Throat of Hell, I did a slow jog, just to get the kinks out. On my way, I stopped by the Glutton's Gap McDonalds, filching a tub of lard. When I reached the large hole in the ground that marked the Throat, I transported up one level, just outside the corporate offices of Lust Unlimited.

It was now mid-morning. Get this done, and I'd only have two more tormentations, as I began to think of them, to effect. With luck, I could be done by lunchtime. I looked at the glass doors of the high rise. On the other side of them was a circular atrium, and in its center was an elevator that led to Asmodeus's office on the top floor. The floor of the atrium was a white, highly polished marble. More than once, I'd nearly slipped on the slick stone. I was about to make it a whole lot slicker.

Other than someone who had an appointment with the Lord of Lust, very few people actually entered the building. If that person had the misfortune of being human, he or she would encounter a familiar figure, a rather ugly man with a ski-slope nose, kinky hair swept back and greased to hang close to his skull. Milhous usually lurked like a spider in an alcove, ready at any moment to rush to the elevator and slap an out-of-order sign on it. He'd never do it to a devil or demon of course, but a human, well, that was his job, to deny the damned access to the elevator. They had to use the stairs, which were normally locked.

From my secret place I extracted my pitchfork and the tub of lard. With a little concentration, I transformed my demonic weapon to a four inch paint brush. Then I rushed through the doors and rapidly painted the floor between the Dick's alcove and the elevator with the lard. Finishing quickly, I bolted from the area, being careful to stay away from my own handiwork.

All of this I accomplished in less than a second. If Milhous noticed anything at all from his nook, he might have felt a sudden but brief draft.

I transformed my paintbrush back to pitchfork form, it was a little greasy but otherwise unaffected by the use I'd put it to. I stowed it in the hidey-hole and tossed the nearly empty tub of lard over a fence. Quickly, I stuffed my tail in my trousers then lifted a hat from the head of a nearby pedestrian. It was a nice fedora, and I was sure he'd miss it, but I only needed it for a minute or so.

The fedora was a necessary part of my disguise. Milhous needed to think I was human, and my horns would have been a dead giveaway. Entering the building, and watching my step so as not to slip, I made my way to the elevator.

Milhous, dressed in his bellman's uniform, was out of his cubby hole like a shot, holding the "out of order" sign extended in front of him. But he didn't get very far. The heels of his shoes touched the lard-laced floor, and his feet went out from under him. With a loud wham, bam, thump his butt, back and head slammed against the marble. "Ouch!" he yelled, then began a long stream of invective that you never heard politicians use in public but always knew were part of their vocabulary. I whipped off my hat and turned to face him. "Bwahahahahahaha!" I laughed, in genuine glee, then zipped to the door. In my haste, I stepped in the lard and slid rather than ran out of the building.

I almost fell, which would have been very uncool for a demon. Getting tripped up by my own devious trick would have been bad form. It was a close thing, but I managed to keep my balance.

The man whom I'd deprived of his fedora was nearby, searching for his lost hat. I rushed up to him and tapped his shoulder. "Pardon," I said.

When he saw a demon addressing him, he cowered against the wall of the Lust Unlimited tower. "I believe you dropped this," I said, offering him the fedora.

"Uh, thanks?" he replied, uncertainly, as he took the hat from me. He looked inside, probably think I'd stashed a cache of rotten eggs in it, but finding it empty, he merely shrugged and put it back on his head. He turned to me again, just in time to see me disappear.

Chapter 20

I surfaced in the abandoned steel mill of Level Five. "Three down, two to go," I said to myself. But now I was at the hard part. I had to torment a friend and an acquaintance. Though I had encountered him a few times in the past, Milhous and I had exchanged fewer than a dozen words in all that time. Satan was always a stickler for having his instructions followed, so I didn't think he'd let me count Dick as an acquaintance.

Who then?

As I was pondering this, a taxi cab pulled up to the curb across the street. A young man, clean-shaven and with short, curly auburn hair, got out from behind the wheel. It was my friend Louis Braille. Louie began to run his hands over the car. I guess periodically he checked it to see if there was any damage. No cab driver in Hell had any collision insurance, and even a scratch could get him in trouble.

Having Louie there was fortuitous. It seemed a sign. He was the logical friend for me to torment. He was right here. It was too easy. And he was a close friend, one of my very best. We used to play poker together every week.

My stomach did a flip. *My next victim. Great. And it would be best if I used my pitchfork. I have to use it at least once more, and who knows if my final tormentation would allow me the opportunity?* I pulled out my weapon. Wiping the excess lard on some weeds growing against one of the factory's buildings, I tried to decide what I should do.

Hmm, I could scratch the paint on the cab. That would get Louis in a shitload of trouble, though. Is there anything else I could do?

Louis, having examined by touch the roof, main panels and

bumpers of the car, turned his attention to the tires. This gave me an idea. While he slowly worked around the vehicle, checking one tire after another, I rushed to the last wheel he would inspect. Using the tip of one tine on my pitchfork, I quickly began to bleed the air out of a tire.

Louie, who, being blind, had exceptionally acute hearing, heard the noise immediately. He hurried toward the sound, but I stepped back silently, and he never noticed me. The tire was a little low, but nothing to worry about, so he went back to the tire he'd been inspecting.

I could have just driven my pitchfork into the rubber. That would have let the air out quickly enough, but it also would have destroyed the tire, causing him a lot of grief. I needed a way to distract him. This seemed like a bad way to do it, but I couldn't think of a better idea.

A quick teleport moved me instantly and silently to the pavement half a block away. "Louie!" I yelled. "Louie!"

"Steve?" my friend said in surprise, following the sound of my voice. "Is that you?" When he got ten feet from the car, I teleported back to the tire and quickly bled off the air.

Meanwhile Louie was searching for me, running his hand along a building that butted up against the sidewalk. He started walking in a grid pattern, making certain to cover the sidewalk between where he thought my voice had come from and the car. By the time he made it back to the car, I'd completely flattened his tire and teleported back to the steel plant.

"Steve," he said softly, though my demon ears could hear him clearly. "I know it was you." Louis held up both hands, as if he were surrendering to an enemy, and went back to examining his car. He found the flat tire. "Merde!" he spat, then opened the trunk and pulled out his spare and jack.

In a little corner of the steel mill, I watched him work for a while. "Bwahahaho … crap," I said, feeling my eyes tear up. It was all I could do to keep from retching, but I managed it. I didn't know if that was a victory or a great defeat. Quietly, so as not to draw attention to myself, I watched his progress. For a blind guy, Louis was pretty good at changing a tire. He probably had lots of practice though.

He was done soon enough. Tossing the flattened tire and the jack back in the trunk, he slammed the lid closed. "I don't know why you did this to me, Steve," he whispered, "but you must have had your reasons. Wherever you are, I forgive you."

And then, curled up next to a massive steel pulley that lay rusting on the ground, I did lose my breakfast.

Louis drove off. About fifteen minutes later, having finally regained my composure, I sat up. I felt like a dead thing – well, exactly like a dead thing, since that's what I was, but more so than usual – as if there was nothing left for me to give. And yet, somehow before the day was over I had to commit one more act of demontry, another new word of mine, since I didn't feel my status in Hell's social order allowed me to call it devilry.

At least the hardest one is over. All that's left is an acquaintance. I don't even have to use my pitchfork, since it was an implement in my last two capers, and that's all Satan required of me. I stood, thinking where I might go to find someone I knew, but not too well.

The hospital was a logical place. It had more people milling around its halls, people I might know, than possibly any other place in Hell. I wouldn't be able to go there, though, without anyone spotting me. Uphir's uncanny ability to catch me whenever I entered the building would guarantee that I'd see him, but that didn't matter. What I really wanted to make sure of was that Flo didn't spot me. I would have to rely on my speed to keep that from happening.

The hospital was only a few blocks away, so I trotted over there. Taking a deep breath, I launched through the front door, covered every space of the first two floors, checking out all the stairwells as well. The elevators were irrelevant – they were always broken – so I ignored them.

She was nowhere in sight, so I slowed to a walk in the main lobby. The hospital's waiting room was as busy as Grand Central Station. There were several people there I recognized. Edward Jenner, the inventor of the smallpox vaccine, was having his blood tested by a demon. He was already being tortured enough, so I looked elsewhere. Mary Shelley was down there too, with a recently-installed set of electrical terminals in her neck, but I barely knew her and wasn't sure she'd count. Then Jimmy walked into the waiting area.

I'd known Jimmy for years, not well, but long. He was a burly man, probably a truck driver in life, who worked in the hospital as an orderly. He may have also been a homophobe, which would explain why part of his damnation was to wander the facility in a nurse's dress and high heels. As usual, he had a half-smoked cigarette behind his ear. Often when I came to the hospital, he and I would exchange pleasantries, or sarcasm – he was almost as good at sarcasm as I was. So I knew him, but we were not close. Definitely fit the acquaintance category.

But what to do? My encounter with Louis had knocked the stuffing out of me, along with some ham, eggs, rye toast and grape jelly. Oh, yeah, and coffee. Anyway, I was running on empty. I pulled my pitchfork out. *Should I use it or not? Decisions, decisions.*

Jimmy picked that moment to walk by me, carrying some new magazines in his arm to distribute around the waiting room. Well, the magazines weren't really new, unless you considered the inaugural edition of *People* to be hot off the presses. On a whim, I stuck out the shaft of my pitchfork and tripped him. Jimmy fell over, tossing the magazines in all directions.

"Oh, I'm sorry," I said, helping him up. A slightly dazed Jimmy grew even more disoriented when he saw it was a demon helping him. "Here, let me pick up those magazines for you." I zipped around the room, gathering all the loose periodicals he'd dropped.

"Uh, thanks," he said.

"Not at all. My fault entirely."

"Okay." He stared at me closely. "Steve? Is that you? It is you. I'd heard you'd become a demon, but I almost didn't believe it."

"Well, believe it," I said with some bitterness.

"What are you doing here? You don't want Flo to see you, do you?"

"No, no. Of course not." I glanced around the waiting room in paranoid fashion. She was nowhere in sight. "I'm, uh, I'm here practicing my skills tormenting the damned."

He looked at me closely. "Is that why you tripped me?"

I bit my lip. "Yeah. Sorry. Orders, you know."

"No biggie. Take care of yourself." He turned to go.

"Jimmy, wait!" I called after him.

"Yes?"

"Could I, could I do the laugh now?"

He seemed puzzled, then understanding dawned. "Sure. Knock yourself out."

"Thanks. Bwahahahahahaha!"

"Good laugh."

"Thanks. Be seeing you."

"You too. Later." Then Jimmy went back to distributing his magazines.

"What the Hell was that?" said a familiar voice from behind me.

"Hi, Uphir." I sighed.

"Do you think tripping someone counts as torment?"

"Well, he *did* have a whole pile of magazines in his hands."

Uphir snorted. "Which you picked up for him. *After* you apologized to him."

"I ... I know," I said shamefacedly. "This whole torture thing, well, it's difficult for me."

"Minion," he said earnestly, "It's your job. You've got to get a handle on this. Word is getting out about you already among the members of the Corps. They're calling you the delinquent demon."

"That's not fair! Well, not completely, anyway. For example, I've already tortured over two hundred people today, and it's not even noon. One of them was a former close friend of mine. And there was at least one individual I left in tears." I neglected to tell him the one who was crying was me.

"Oh," he said, somewhat mollified. "That sounds pretty good. Better than I'd been hearing. Just keep practicing. I'm sure you'll get there eventually. I'll tell the gang to lay off the delinquent demon crap."

"You'd do that for me?"

"Sure. I can tell you're trying. Besides, you and I go way back."

For the second time since I met him, I shook his hand, this time in genuine gratitude. "Thank you, Uphir. I really appreciate that."

"You're welcome." He put his finger to his nose. "Now you better get out of here. Flo is on her way down from Endoscopy. You wouldn't want her to see you."

"No, I wouldn't want that. Thanks again."

"Later, Minion," Uphir said, giving me a companionable pat on the back. Then he left the area.

Flo. I couldn't let her see me, but I had an irresistible urge to see her. It was all hopeless. I was a demon, she was a human, and a saved one at that. Oil and water: we couldn't mix. I had no idea how she felt about me. No doubt she was sympathetic about my plight, but, well, I just couldn't bear the thought of her spying me in demon form.

I had to see her, if only for a moment, so I counted on my speed to keep me invisible while I played Peeping Tom. I rushed to stand behind a pillar in the waiting room. And none too soon. A figure in white was coming down the main stairs.

Florence Nightingale had never been officially declared a saint, but she had all the trappings of one. And for all I knew, she was the only saved soul who came to Hell by choice in order to ease suffering.

Perhaps it was a trick of the fluorescent lights, but Flo seemed to glow as she descended the last few steps into the waiting room. I remembered art work I'd seen about the J-man and the Harrowing of Hell. He was usually glowing as he descended into the belly of the Underworld. Flo looked like she was reenacting the scene: the Harrowing of the Hospital.

Oh, my G … She was so beautiful. So pure. So strong. So kind. Her face had an ethereal beauty, yet also a sadness that seemed permanently imprinted on it. I wanted to reach out and comfort her. Hers was a soul that did not deserve to suffer.

"Steve?" she said, in surprise. "Is that you?"

Shit. I'd leaned out too far from my hiding spot. Immediately, I teleported.

Teleporting without thinking where you want to go is never a good idea. You can bounce off a mountain or find yourself submerged in water. Fortunately, or unfortunately, all of my thoughts were on Flo when I jumped, so I ended up in the one other place I most associated with her: her apartment. I was standing in her cozy living room. Light from the window — sunlight it seemed, though that was impossible — flooded the room. Flo's apartment was always an inviting space, a consequence of the FloZone effect, and today the place seemed especially cheery. There was a hand-crocheted comforter over the back of the couch. A book from her private library was sitting on a table in the small den near the entrance. She was reading a book on probability and statistics, her place marked by an emery board. I smiled; Flo had always loved math.

I wandered into her bedroom. It was sort of a violation, though I'd been there before, yet I wanted to see it once more. A light, white bedspread covered the bed, not a wrinkle in sight. Some comfy pillows were up against a modest headboard. There was a chair near the window, and a round table beside it. Atop the table was a pad of paper and a pencil. Flo had sketched something on the pad, so I picked it up to see what she had drawn.

It was me, as I had appeared in human form. The rendering was perfect; who knew that she could draw so well? Not that it should have been a surprise, for everything Flo put her hand to she seemed able to master. The drawing was smudged, slightly, and I realized with sadness that the flaws had been caused by tears.

My eyes filled with tears of their own. Being a demon, being separated from Flo, was a damnation of its own kind, and far worse than the torments I used to endure as Hell's handyman. I looked up at the ceiling, trying to stop the waterworks. When I got control of myself, I pulled out a sheet of paper from the bottom of the pad. I wrote a short note. It said,

I will always love you.

My hand nearly signed it with my new sigil, the pitchfork and the hard hat insignia that used to be the logo for my Department of Plant Maintenance. With an effort, I penned a single S at the end. Then I laid my note on top of her drawing and got the hell out of there.

Chapter 21

Satan sat at his desk, his head in his hands. "Minion, what am I going to do with you?"

I sat in the chair before his desk, swinging my legs aimlessly, like a child who had been sent to the principal for being disruptive in class. "What? I mean, what sir? I did everything you ask, and I only puked once."

"You call this stuff torture?" he said, waving his hand at a report that some weasel demon or devil had apparently compiled for him. Obviously, I'd been watched as I completed my torture assignment.

"Only I watched you, nitwit," he said, reading my mind. "These are my own notes here." He sighed. "Okay, talk me through this. First the sailor."

I patted down my pockets, looking for something, but came up empty. I looked up at my boss. "Do you happen to have a rope or a piece of string or something I could use to demonstrate?"

Satan gestured, and a rope appeared around my neck. It jerked upward abruptly, lifting me out of my seat. I dangled for a few seconds in midair, my legs kicking in a good imitation of a hanging victim, before managing to untie the noose. Yep, Satan was pretty pissed off at me. When the knot finally gave way, I fell to the floor, but landed on my feet, my demon coordination helping me in ways my human reflexes never seemed able to manage back in the old days. "Good hahh ... hangman's knot sir," giving the rope a quick jerk. It fell from wherever it had been attached above me, coiling itself neatly on the carpet.

I resumed my seat and deftly tied a bowline, showing it to him. "You see, sir, bowlines don't slip." I demonstrated. The thing held fast. "They just don't. It's just about the most dependable knot ever created."

"I get that. Big deal. Even bowlines are undependable in Hell. Murphy's Law, remember?" He wiggled his fingers, and the knot untied itself.

That's true. In Hell, if anything can go wrong, it will. "But then I broke the line, and he fell on his butt. And I did the laugh and everything," I added desperately. "It was a really good laugh, I remember."

"Woo hoo. Look, Minion. That sailor was preparing to sail out into the jaws of Leviathan. You've met our marine friend. Do you really think when the sailor fell on his butt that he was even a teensy bit distracted from his terror of drowning in the tentacles of the Kraken?"

"Oh," I said quietly. "When you put it that way, I guess not."

"You guess not. Jeez!" Satan rolled his eyes. "Having you for an employee makes me wonder why I ever went into management in the first place."

I shrugged. "Just a guess, sir, but perhaps it's because you like telling people what to do?"

Satan frowned. "Minion, I'm already pissed off at you. Keep your famous sarcasm in check, or I'll give you latrine duty in Glutton's Gap for a month."

I thought about all those outhouses near the barbecue and shuddered. Port-o-lets on Earth had nothing on their Hellish counterparts, not even the ones used at rock festivals.

"Quit daydreaming. And speaking, or thinking, of the barbecue, would you please explain to me the deal with the onions?"

"Oh, yeah," I said with some enthusiasm. "I thought that was the most clever thing I did all day."

"And why would that be? From my point of view, it was

moronic, so please enlighten me."

On my way here this morning, I'd grabbed a book from the library on the history and practice of cannibalism. It actually took me quite a while to decide which book to check out. Hell's library has a large section of its collection devoted to the subject of eating humans. Go figure. Anyway, I turned to a page I'd bookmarked.

Well, to be honest, I'd dog-eared the page. This is of course sacrilege, dog-earing a book from a library, and it can result in a whopping big fine if you're caught, but I was a demon, and evil was my stock-in-trade. I even underlined in ink the passage I wanted to show Satan. "Well, as you see here on page two hundred and thirty, human flesh is supposed to taste strongly of quinine. (I had remembered that from a book I'd read a long time ago on the Donner expedition.) I figured the onions would cut that flavor. By taking away the onions, the quinine taste wouldn't be masked, making the cannibalism that was going on at the barbecue even more noxious."

"So let me see if I've got this straight. You thought that holding the onions would intensify the torment they were already undergoing? The damned I mean, not the onions."

"Exactly! Uh, sir," I added.

"And I thought you knew something about barbecue," he said with disgust. "Anyone can tell you that you can't have a barbecue without onions. The devil in charge had to stop everything for half an hour while a demon ran to the grocery store to get some new ones. Then they had to be sliced. You actually ended up delaying the torment of two hundred souls for nearly an hour!"

"Oh. I didn't think of that."

"Still," Satan added, "it was a clever idea. You're inventive, Minion, if nothing else. I'll give you three points for creativity."

"Wait? I'm being graded on this?"

"Yes."

I looked around desperately. This didn't look good.

"By the way," Satan said casually. "The book's wrong. Humans taste a bit like veal, mild, even a bit sweet, though on the stringy side. The barbecue sauce of course would affect the flavor."

"You know what human flesh tastes like?" I asked, surprised. "So you've eaten it?"

He grinned evilly. "I'm the Devil, Minion. What do you think?"

"Oh, well, yes, of course. That would make complete sense."

The Lord of Hell waved his hand. "New topic. Making Milhous slip on the marble floor was hardly tormenting him, but at least it was funny, so I'll give you four points for that." Satan had a sense of humor, especially for anything resembling slapstick; that could work in my favor.

"But you returned the fedora to the human outside and actually begged his pardon, so I'm deducting two points." Satan pulled out a pencil and started writing all of this down.

"What should I have done?" I asked, genuinely curious.

Satan, never long on patience, looked like he was ready to blow a gasket, but he took a calming breath and answered the question. "You could have done many things, like shredding the hat, throwing it in his face, knocking him to the pavement and impaling him with your pitchfork. You know: torment!"

I pulled out a small notepad from my hidey-hole and wrote all of this down. "Right."

"Good grief, man!" The Devil shouted, slamming his hand on his desk. "Where's your sense of cruelty? You were meaner when you were human."

I chewed on my lower lip. Boy, was I in trouble. "Only to people I didn't like."

Satan's preternaturally fast finger tapping started up; soon it hit about Warp Five. Even I, with my speed and demon vision, could only see his hand as a blur. Finally, he asked, "Is there anything today that you think you did well?"

I frowned in thought, then smiled in pride. "I used my pitchfork one more time than you required."

"Yeah, right," he said, massaging his temples. "You transformed it into a paintbrush so you could spread lard on a floor, let the air out a car tire with one of the tines and tripped a man with the handle. With that last one, you actually apologized to your 'victim' before picking up the magazines he dropped! Shit!" he finished in disgust. "Did you ever think of actually sticking your pitchfork in one of your victims? That's generally how a pitchfork is used, you know."

"Yes sir. I know," I said, my head bowed in shame. "What, what did you think of my laugh?"

"Oh, your laugh was fine, except for that one time. Your 'Bwahahahahahaha!' is almost always good. So what? I have a pet gray parrot that can do the laugh as well as you. Or," he paused, "I did have, until he called me 'good master' one day and I ate him." He paused and picked up his pencil, making another note on his pad. "Still, I'll give you two points for it."

He sat back in his chair, steepling his fingers as he stared at me through his shades. "The only decent bit of torture you did all day was to Braille, and it wasn't the stupid 'letting the air out of the car tire' bit. That's about the dumbest thing I've heard of in my very long existence."

"Then what was it that you liked about that caper?"

Satan took off his sunglasses. His red eyes seemed to burn into my own. "Don't call it a caper. Shit. You make this sound like we're in a low-budget crime movie. But what you did that I liked was, you called to him. You sent him wandering blindly – which of course, is all he can do anyway – after your voice. He knew it was you who flattened his tire. That was excruciating for him."

"I know," I said simply, looking down at my lap.

"Then you ruined it all by ending up crying like a wuss. And you still puked your guts out!" The Lord of Hell looked thoroughly disgusted.

"But Louie never saw that. I … I hid. As far as he knows, I tortured him gleefully."

"Yes, that's something I suppose." Satan put the point of his pencil to his tongue, bent over his notepad and did some quick math. "Okay, I give you a nineteen on the assignment, and that's only because, in the case of Braille, you genuinely tormented someone."

"Nineteen? What's the scale?"

"One hundred."

"What? After all I did?" *After all it cost me?*

"You're just lucky I grade on a curve. Minion," he said finally, after staring at me for what seemed Eternity, "you need help. Professional help. I'm sending you to the Demon Corps shrink. Maybe he can help you self-actualize or whatever the bullshit term is that they're using these days."

"But, my lord," I said, desperately. I'd been to a therapist a couple of times in my mortal life. The first time was for panic attacks I was suffering from during the time I was up for tenure. The second was when my wife left me. Both trips seemed a whopping big waste of time. "Even if I'm not very good at tormentation, I can serve you in other ways, like I did with Leviathan."

"We've already been through this. There aren't enough

special projects to keep you busy. Besides, tormenting the damned is job one for any demon." He grabbed a copy of *Webster's Dictionary*, flipped to the demon entry and showed me.

"Demon or daemon: **\dēmən** noun. [From the Middle English *demon* and the Latin *daemon* meaning, well, demon.] 13th Century. An evil spirit who is a servant of Satan and whose primary job is to torment damned souls for all Eternity. Demons have horns and tails, oh, and faux claws made by growing their nails long and carefully manicuring them so they are extra-pointy, resembling devil claws. They also carry around really cool pitchforks. Demons have enhanced physical strength, when compared to humans, though not in the same league as devils. Demons are basically devil wannabes. Primary weaknesses generally include low IQ's and a tendency to chip their nails. (cf. devils. n.b. horns, tails, claws, faux, cool pitchforks)"

"That's an unusual definition for a dictionary." I looked at the front cover and saw the reason. It was compiled by Daniel Webster, not Noah Webster. *Hmm, I always heard that Mr. Webster, Esq., was eloquent, though I suppose a couple of centuries in Hell can degrade anyone's use of the language.* "So, there is some truth to 'The Devil and Daniel Webster' short story?"

"A little, but in the end, I got the prize I really wanted from the beginning, which was Webster's soul. The farmer was just part of the con. After I got Webster down here, I made him compile this dictionary, adjusted from standard English to accommodate some of the more arcane words and meanings we use down here."

"But never mind that," he said, rising from his chair. "I'm serious about you getting some professional help. You have an appointment in five minutes with the psychiatrist. After you're done, return here immediately. Now, begone!" He waved his hand at me, and I disappeared.

Chapter 22

When I rematerialized, I found myself in the visually sterile waiting room of some doctor. I did not recognize it. For that matter, I couldn't even tell what Circle of Hell I was on.

"The doctor will see you now, Minion," said a voice behind me. I turned. There was a demon at a small reception desk. He said nothing else, but the slight smirk on his face told me all I needed to know. My reputation had preceded me.

In trepidation, I opened the door to the doctor's office. In the center of the room was a leather couch, with brass fittings to secure the leather, and legs in the Queen Anne Style. One end of the sofa was raised, so that the occupant did not lie completely prone but with his back propped up. Unless, of course, said occupant was a moron and lay on it sideways, which would sort of drape him over the couch, but that would put his head and feet on the floor. He could also have lain on it with his feet propped up, but that would have made the blood flow to the brain and probably cause dizziness. Not wanting to buck any trends, I lay on the couch the way it was supposed to be used.

Beside me was an empty chair with a pad and pen in it. In the corner of the room was a desk made out of cardboard, with a banner display above it. The banner had a sign on it that said, "Psychiatric Help: 5 cents." The desk itself had a sign indicating that "The Doctor is OUT."

The chair behind the desk was spun around, its back facing me. Abruptly now it turned, and I saw the occupant. He was a thin man, balding. His beard and what hair he had left was all white. He wore a pair of round, black plastic glasses.

Of course. Sigh. "Dr. Freud, I presume."

"Ja, I mean, yes," he said. Freud reach to the front of his desk and flipped the "OUT" sign over to say "IN." Then he grabbed a tin can from his desk and walked over to me.

"Five cents, please."

"Not funny," I said.

"No, it isn't," he agreed, but he continued to hold out the can. With a sigh, I fished around in my pockets. The smallest bill I had was a Franklin. "I can't break that," he said.

I stuffed the bill in the can. "Keep the change."

"Sehr gut. Good." He placed the can on his desktop, walked over to the chair next to the couch, picked up his pad and pen, and seated himself. "So, did you hate your father?"

"Oh, crap!" I jumped off the couch. "Are we going to go through that? I don't have all day, you know."

Freud had a look of infinite sadness in his eyes. "Actually, you have Eternity, as do I."

"So," I said, "this is your damnation? To be a psychiatrist to demons?"

"Ja."

I settled back on the couch. "Can't be very interesting."

He shook his head. "It isn't. I almost never get something to sink my teeth into. Of course, I can't give you specific details, as that would violate doctor/patient confidentiality. Suffice it to say, though, that the biggest problems demons have are toning down their feral tendencies, a bit of confusion when they change sexually from male or female to hermaphrodite, and an obsessive concern over damaging their nails."

"Yep, that sounds pretty boring. And you've been doing this how long?"

"Since 1939, when I died. But I'm supposed to be asking the questions, not you, and since you don't seem to want to take the Freudian approach, we'll get right to the point. What's your problem?"

"You mean Satan didn't fill you in?"

Freud walked over to his inbox and pulled out a thick folder. "Unusual. Satan doesn't customarily refer someone to me directly."

"Well, I'm an unusual case." We sat there for ten minutes while Freud read through my file. This made my blood boil, being not unlike my experience with doctors back on Earth. You'd think they'd review a file in advance, so that once they entered the patient consultation room, they'd know the background.

After all, what's the point of having the chart beforehand if you aren't going to review it prior to meeting with the patient? And there's ten minutes of my hour gone already.

Finally, he looked up. "Yes, this is very unusual. Unique, in fact, in my experience. Why don't you tell me, in your own words, what your issue is?"

I leaned back against the couch and sighed. "It's hurting people. I really can't stand to do it."

He made a note on his pad. "What do you mean by not being able to stand it?"

"Well, whenever I have to torment one of the damned, I get all nauseous."

"Nauseated."

"Whatever. Sometimes I'm okay, if what I do isn't more than an inconvenience." I described the incident with the sailor and the bowline. "I was fine with that. Could even comfortably do the laugh. But the worse the torment, the more painful to my, er, client, the more reluctant I am to even try. And if I follow through, well … "

"You 'puke your guts out,'" Freud said, reading from the case file in front of him. "Fascinating."

232

"I'm glad you're entertained by my misery," I said sarcastically.

"I meant no offense. It's just that 'reluctance' isn't a word commonly associated with demons. If anything, my normal cases display an extreme enthusiasm for inflicting pain."

"I'm not saying I'm a Boy Scout, or anything. Well, actually I was, am, but that's a different story. Anyway, before I became a demon, I encountered the occasional human who pissed me off so much I didn't mind giving him a hard time." I told Freud about Edison and Ford, though my feelings toward the former had softened a little, seeing him work with Orson. "Beelzebub even gave me a cameo to wear around my neck with a silhouette of Edison's face for inspiration. It was always effective at getting me to do the old Bwahaha bit." I pulled out the amulet and showed it to the doctor then studied it. "Except now."

"You don't feel your demonic side coming out, even with this powerful trigger?"

"Nope," I said, stuffing it back down my shirt. "First time too. What a Catch-22!"

"I beg your pardon?"

"Cultural reference. After your time."

"I see. What does it mean?"

I shrugged. "No way out. Damned if you do, damned if you don't."

"Well, yes. That's fairly self-evident. Tell me, have you ever considered suicide?"

"Huh?" I said, sitting up. "I don't really think that's an option for me, do you?"

"I suppose not." He frowned and sat in silence for a minute, thinking. Then he brightened as an idea came to him. "Perhaps you should have more sex!"

233

"I don't think that's possible."

"And why do you say that?"

"My girlfriend is a succubus."

"Ach du lieber! You are right of course, you lucky fellow."

"Yes, I guess so." Ironically, the previous night had been the first time since Lilith and I had been a couple that we hadn't done it. I was so upset at seeing Flo, at spending time in her apartment, at acknowledging the extent of my love for her, that I just couldn't have sex with another woman. Lilith, for her part, didn't seem to mind at all. She enjoyed cuddling together just as much as if we'd spent the night fornicating.

But my mind was wandering. "Why would having more sex help anyway?" I asked, interested in his line of thought.

"Perhaps you are familiar with my work, *Beyond the Pleasure Principle*."

"Maybe," I said, chewing on my lip in thought. "I might have been required to read it in college."

"Possibly, though I believe *The Interpretation of Dreams* is more often assigned. *Beyond the Pleasure Principle* is one of my more controversial works."

I shrugged.

"In the latter monograph, I postulated the existence of what I called 'Todestrieb.' It translates roughly as 'death instinct,' though it more precisely means 'death drive.'"

"Death wish?" I said.

He pursed his lips then nodded. "If you prefer. The pleasure principle is, of course, Eros, or the libidinous activities we engage in. The death drive, which some people have called Thanatos, for branding reasons I think, is an urge we have to return to our earliest state, an inorganic state."

"Well, I'm already dead, so I really don't see how that applies. And I don't see how it relates to my sex life."

"Ah, yes. That is subtle. You see, when we don't get enough pleasure, or at least when mortals don't get enough pleasure, Eros is out of balance with Thanatos. Our lives, how you put it, oh yes, our lives suck, we get depressed, the drive toward death becomes an extremely powerful inner force. Some of us even kill ourselves. But when we have a full, libidinous life, the death drive is diverted, usually outward, and manifests as an instinct for destruction. So, q.e.d., a demon getting a lot of sex, will usually be even more cruel than normal."

"But I get lots of sex, and I still don't like hurting people, so that doesn't seem to explain anything. With all due respect, Dr. Freud, that theory sounds like a bunch of crap to me."

My shrink winced. "I *did* say the Todestrieb was one of my more controversial ideas."

"That's what I said. Crap."

"There's no need for you to be insulting," he said, offended. "I'm just trying to help."

We sat, glaring at each other for a while. With a huff, Freud got out of the chair and retrieved a file from his desk. "You have, perhaps heard, of the Rorschach Test?"

I rolled my eyes. "Yes. Is that what you have there?"

"Yes," he said, patting the folder. "Ten images. I want to show them to you, and you tell me what you see in the pattern."

"Fine," I grumbled, exhaling softly. "Let's get it over with."

The good doctor seemed pleased. "Wunderbar! Here's the first one."

"Bat."

"What kind? Baseball bat or … "

"Vampire bat, of course."

And this one?

"Bat."

"Bat. Bat. Bat." I said to one after another.

"Oh, come now. They can't all look like bats."

"Wanna bet? Take a look for yourself."

This seemed like a novel idea to Freud, so he flipped through the first five. "I see what you mean," he said slowly. "When they make these things, they're all kind of symmetrical, and … "

"And narrow in the middle, with big wings splaying out from there. What did you think I was going to say, ice cream cone?"

"That would have been interesting. A classic phallic symbol, but no. How about this one?"

"Well, that looks a little like a devil."

Freud looked at it. "I think so too. And these last four?"

"Bat. Bat. Bat. Bat."

He scratched his beard. "You are clearly disturbed."

"I am clearly in Hell, Dr. Freud. My best friend is a giant vampire bat. Devils and demons run the place. What am I supposed to see?"

"Fine," he huffed, putting the folder of blotches to one side. "What do you dream of? Perhaps there's something I can work with there."

"Ziggy, I'm a demon. Demons don't sleep, not unless they want to. And from what I've been told, demons don't dream when they do choose to sleep."

The doctor frowned. "That's true. What about when you were just a damned human?"

"I was an insomniac. I didn't really sleep then either. No sleep, no dreams."

"Scheiss!" he cursed, clearly running low on the tools in his tool box. "I know! Word association."

"You realize all of this is a fucking waste of time, don't you?"

He shrugged. "I have to fill the hour somehow. So here

goes. What do you think of first when I say Life?"

"Death."

"Love?"

"Flo."

"Hate?"

"Little Prick."

Freud looked at me in surprise. "You have penis envy? Only women get that. Hmm. Perhaps you are beginning to change into a hermaphrodite, as all demons do eventually, and this is but an early symptom."

"No, no," I said with impatience. "'Little Prick' is my nickname for Henry Ford. He's one of my least favorite humans in Hell."

The good doctor made another note for his files. "Oh, well then, let us continue. Hell?"

"Hell."

"No, you have to say a *different* word." He looked like a thwarted child. "It's the rules."

"Okay," I said with a quiet sigh. "Ask again."

"Hell?"

"Inferno."

"This is pointless!" Freud snapped, throwing his notebook against the wall. He glared at me.

"My dear doctor," I said mildly, "you seem to have anger issues. Tell me, did you hate your father?"

"Bite me!"

"Tempting, especially with my new fangs, but no thanks."

We spent a few more minutes glaring at each other. Then Freud turned thoughtful again. Finally he spoke. "What I can't understand is how you can resist your demonic instincts. It's not like you have any free will. Or at least, you shouldn't."

I look at him with surprise. "I would have thought you

wouldn't believe in free will, that we are all driven by subconscious wants and desires, along with the ego, id and superego working in there somehow too. You know: stimulus/response."

"Ah, yes. Determinism. That is a common misunderstanding of my theories. Actually, I believe very much in free will. Those who do not know themselves may be impelled by just those subconscious drivers you are describing, yet it is the goal of therapy to free the patient from this unconscious control. If we can't change, what would be the point of therapy in the first place?"

"All of this is very interesting, but how does it help me? You already said I don't have any free will. Shit!" I snarled, slamming my hand on the couch. "Everybody's been telling me that for months. It doesn't make me feel any better."

Freud scratched his beard. "I think, and this is just intuition talking, but I think your free will is trying to reassert itself."

"But that's impossible!" I stammered. "Isn't it?"

"I confess, I do not know. But based upon our brief time together, and what I know from over a century of studying the demonic psyche, that's my best guess." Freud pulled a stopwatch from his waistcoat. "Our time is up." He stood and handed me a bottle with a cork stopper.

"What's this?" I asked.

"Aspirin. Take two and see me in the morning."

"How will two aspirin help?"

"They won't." Freud looked embarrassed. "I just routinely say that."

"And what will you do for me in the morning?"

"Give you more aspirin. Since I usually can't help my patients, well, it just feels wrong not to give them something."

"If it's all the same to you," I said, getting off the couch, "I'll pass. Maybe I just don't respond to Freudian techniques." Though his insight about free will had been a bit of a revelation.

"Too bad," he said, with some regret. "I don't know if my guess about you is right – maybe you just have a weak stomach – but regardless, you are the most interesting demon ever to have come to me for help."

"Well, that's something, I suppose." We shook hands, and I left.

Chapter 23

I stepped out into Freud's waiting area, feeling more confused than ever. The demon receptionist, who no doubt had the esteemed doctor as his personal whipping boy, was busy rearranging some files and paid me no mind. Since I had no idea where the clinic was located, I needed to get my bearings, so I took the exit …

… and found myself in a merchant's tent. Old, moth-eaten rugs were draped over rotted cedar chests. A rack of postcards was full of different locations in Hell. "See New Rome," said one, showing a view of the golden Pantheon that was Mammon's center of power. "Swim in the Sea of Thorns, Hell's own Red Sea," said another. That was pretty accurate, for the blood of the souls being tormented there had stained the thorns a permanent scarlet. There were others: "Visit Glutton's Gap. You won't go home hungry … unless you're a glutton," and "What happens in Lustland, stays in Lustland."

I remarked to myself how much of Hell I had seen in my sixty year sojourn here. Probably far more than most of the inmates, who generally were consigned to one place for Eternity.

"May I help you, sahib?" Said an Irishman who was apparently the proprietor. He was dressed in desert garb, a little the worse for wear. He made an unconvincing Arab.

At that moment, I saw a meager display of herbal remedies, including a generous supply of snake oil. "Would you like some aspirin to add to your collection?" I tossed him the bottle Freud gave it to me.

He looked at them suspiciously. "Do they work?" The question was legitimate. Most pain killers in Hell were ineffective.

"I have no idea. Keep them or toss them," I said, and headed toward a portion of tent that had an "EXIT" sign above it. As I pulled back the flap, I noticed the Irish Arab placing the bottle next to the snake oil.

I was standing in the middle of the perpetual bazaar that operated near Beelzebub's office on Level Eight. Having my bearings, I immediately teleported back to Satan's office, per instructions.

Bruce was pacing nervously as I appeared. "Go on in," he said quietly. "He's expecting you."

"How's his mood?" I whispered.

"You don't want to know, though you'll find out soon enough." For the first time Bruce regarded me with sympathy. "Good luck, Steve. I think you're going to need it."

I walked toward the closed doors of Satan's office. They swung open silently. Swallowing hard, I stepped inside.

The Earl of Hell was at his desk, reading intently. His face was flushed, and his mouth formed a cruel downward arc. He did not have on his happy face.

"This is an outrage!" he screamed, taking a folder I recognized and throwing it into the black emptiness behind him. "That quack! That charlatan! If he weren't already in Hell, I'd put him there."

Quietly, I slid into the chair before my boss. I just hoped Satan didn't start shooting Hellfire in all directions, a habit of his when he was peeved. He looked at me, and the frown turned into a scowl. "Did you get anything out of that bunch of psychological mumbo jumbo?

"Not much, my lord. Hey, was that my folder?"

"Yes. So what?"

"So," I began hesitantly, "so what about doctor/patient

confidentiality?"

"What do you think I am, an HMO? Shit! I'm the Devil, you putz! You have no right of privacy in my domain."

"Oh. Of course not, sire." Still, I was disappointed. There ought to be things you can count on, on Earth or in Hell.

"I was hoping that he could figure out what was wrong with you." Satan waved his hand, and the folder floated back from wherever he had thrown it. "All that's here is some horseshit about your free will trying to reassert itself. Hah! Ridiculous." He threw the folder back into the void.

Interesting filing system. I wish I could have done that in life. Never could find anything once it was filed away. "Do you think there could be any truth to it?"

"Does horseshit imply 'promising diagnosis' to you, idiot? Your free will *can't* reassert itself. You forfeited it when you became a demon!" He summoned the folder one last time, made it float ten feet in the air above his head and blasted it with Hellfire.

This was so confusing. Satan was my master, and his grip on my mind and soul should have been absolute. Yet what Freud had said seemed so logical to me; it seemed to explain why I was unable to adjust to my demon state. I knew for certain that I wasn't just the victim of a weak stomach. Never had been. Stress always got me in the chest.

And ... I almost felt that, if I tried, I could say no to the Devil.

Satan had taken off his sunglasses and was studying me carefully. "You're even worse than before," he concluded. "Your mind is such a jumble that I can't even read it right now." He stood abruptly, and the red La-Z-Boy rocketed backward, out of sight. "This was a mistake. I should never have made you a demon."

I looked at him in shock. In all my years in Hell, never once had I heard Satan admit to making a mistake. "Maybe you should just change me back," I said, then clamped my hands on my mouth, as if I could catch the words before he heard them.

The Lord of Hell looked at me with the coal black version of his eyes. He looked as frustrated and defeated as I felt. "I can't change you back, even if I wanted to."

"That's what I thought." *This is me. I'm a demon. Get used to it.*

The Earl of Hell cocked his head, as if listening to a voice far away. "What was that?"

"I said, 'that's what I thought.'"

"No, what were you thinking about? Blast it! Something Freud said to you must have fucked with your mind. All I'm getting are random words and static. It's like trying to tune in to a weak radio signal."

I don't think I'd ever seen him look so frustrated. This wasn't his fault — well, it was — but he hadn't been trying to make my lot in death any worse. Becoming a demon was considered a great honor down here, and he'd done his level best to make me the greatest demon ever. Now he couldn't even read my mind. For some reason, I actually felt sorry for the old Devil. "I was just thinking that being a demon is what I am now, and somehow I need to get used to it."

He looked at me in surprise, not expecting such a cooperative attitude.

Finally, I laid my cards on the table. "Look, my lord Satan, I never really wanted to be a demon — you and I both know that — but I am one now. And I'm *your* demon. I work for you. Somehow I have to be able to make this adjustment. I can't stay in limbo forever."

"This isn't Limbo," he muttered. "That's up on One." Then he spoke with more conviction. "But I understand what you're saying, and you're right, by damn! We'll make this work."

Satan got up from his chair and began to pace back and forth, arms crossed at the wrists behind his back. "There's only one thing I can think to do with you, and that's to keep throwing you into situations where you will be compelled by my direct command to torment the damned. Eventually, you'll adjust. You'll have to, or simply go insane, which in the case of being a demon, is just about the same thing."

"Right." I closed my eyes. This was pure Hell, far worse than anything from when I was Hell's Handyman.

"Steve." I opened my eyes to see a look of sympathy on Satan's face. It was only for an instant, and then it was gone. But Satan put a hand to his mouth, as if he'd revealed a huge secret to me. He shuddered.

The moment passed. "Minion," he said briskly, slipping back on his sunglasses. "I'm going to give you a baptism of fire. Listen very carefully. I order you to proceed directly to Level Five. Take your pitchfork. Take a pie. I command you to torment Orson. You may warm up with Edison if you wish, but I expect you to really stick it to your best friend. And just to be clear, by 'stick it,' I mean to repeatedly gouge Welles with your pitchfork until he faints from the pain."

"Orson?" I said in shock. "But … "

"No buts. This is a direct order from the Earl of Hell. Now, Go!" He waved his hand at me and I was gone. Satan had been uncharacteristically flustered, though, and his aim was off. I found myself flung all the way to Level Four.

"Nice day," said a voice behind me.

I turned to find an old vagabond, all alone, bloodied and snarled in the Sea of Thorns.

"Not really," I said softly.

The old man sighed. "No, I suppose not. Looks like rain."

I glanced up. A dark cloud was forming above us. Any second now, acid rain would fall, making the gashes on his skin sting like all get-out. I looked around for something with which to cover him, but there was nothing. At another time, I might have turned my pitchfork into an umbrella and loaned it to him; unfortunately, though, I was going to need my weapon in a second. I looked apologetically at him. "Sorry about that."

He shrugged, undoubtedly a painful gesture, with all those thorns digging into his body. "So it goes. Have a good one."

"Right. Thanks. Uh, you too." I teleported to the steel mill on Five.

Down the street was the trailer. Orson and Edison might be off trying to close a work order, but somehow I doubted it. My gut told me they were inside. I took my pitchfork out of its hidey-hole.

On the sidewalk in front of the abandoned mill, a crazy old man was standing on a wooden crate. He was dressed in a black duster, torn in many places. His hair was white, and he reminded me of the aged fellow I'd just left on Four. In life, I'd seen his kind many times. They haunted the walkways along Broadway, near 116th Street, outside the university gates that, when closed, could turn Columbia into a fortress.

This was a street preacher, though what he had done to land himself in Hell was beyond me. From his mouth, a stream of incoherent ramblings flowed. Then abruptly he stared at me, as if all along he'd known I was watching him from the grounds of the mill. His words became clear, as if a lens had suddenly been focused: " ... he turned, and said unto Peter, Get thee behind me, Satan: thou art an offense unto me: for thou savourest not the things that be of G ... "

At that moment, four demons ran around the corner at top speed. The pummeled him with baseball bats; they stabbed him with pitchforks. Yet he didn't utter a sound of protest.

I walked by the scene, wide-eyed. The demons were too busy to take notice of me, but the old man gazed at me unflinchingly. I crossed the street, just as the demons hauled him off. I trembled, thinking what they were about to do to him. Quoting scripture down here was considered blasphemy.

I stood on the sidewalk before the trailer. It looked much the same as it always had: dilapidated, forlorn, a place that was little more than a rectangular box housing two inmates who occasionally were paroled to the wider realms of Hell, where they did work that was meaningless, if compulsory. That was punishment enough, to work in pointless perpetuity, but my job was to somehow make it worse, if I could.

There could be no more delay. My fingers were clinching my pitchfork so hard that my knuckles were white. *Now or never. Now and ever*, I amended. Taking a deep breath, I rushed forward.

My body, running at speed, slammed into the door, shattering it. Inside the trailer, Orson and Edison were hunched over a pile of work orders, performing triage, that is, pulling out the handful of jobs they thought they could manage from the hundreds that they couldn't. The sound of crashing wood and glass made them jump. "Steve?" Orson said, staring at the familiar-looking demon breathing heavily in the door jamb. "Is that you? I ... "

With a roar, I launched myself at the two of them and, using a single swipe of my hand, swatted both to the floor.

Now what? Not having any bright ideas at the moment, I brandished my pitchfork and yelled out a bloodcurdling, "Boogaboogabooga!"

It wasn't textbook, but unlike the end of a tormentation, when you had the signature "Bwaha, etc.," there wasn't a set phrase for the beginning. "Boogaboogabooga!" seemed as good a start as any.

Certainly it was effective. There, curled up in the fetal position, in absolute terror, was Edison, still perhaps my least favorite human in all of Hell. Even Orson looked nervous.

I couldn't think about Orson – not yet – so I focused on the Wizard of Menlo Park. I'd start with him; that would be easier. But, rearing back to strike, I looked down at my intended victim. Here was just another old man, a damned soul, as I once had been. He was crying, shaking in terror. He knew how much I had always disliked him; no doubt he was expecting soon to be hanging from the tines of my pitchfork.

"No, Steve," said Orson from the side. "Don't do this. Please."

"You!" I hissed, conjuring a lemon cream pie – Orson's least favorite, his pie of punishment – out of thin air. "Shut up!" Like a pitcher at a major league game, I went into my windup and prepared to launch the pie. My friend just stared at me, a great sadness in his eyes.

A feral scream erupted from my throat. And then another that turned into a sob. "No!" I shouted and hurled the pie at the office time clock. There was a boing, as if the clock's spring broke. "I won't. I won't do it!" I reached to my neck and drew out the cameo with Edison's face on it, crushing the amulet to powder. Then I drove my pitchfork so hard into the linoleum that it plunged through the floor and embedded itself in the earth beneath the trailer. King Arthur himself couldn't have extracted it. I fell to my knees, sobbing.

To my surprise, both men helped me to my feet. Edison was still shaking, but Orson was a rock. "What just happened, Steve?" he said softly.

"I said no." The thought shocked me. "I denied my demon

instincts. I refused to follow a direct order from Satan."

"I thought that was impossible!"

"It should be."

At that moment, I heard something in the back of my brain. It was Satan, trying to communicate with me, but it was all garbled. All I got was, *Minion, what are you ... skrz ... snap ... crackle ... pop..*" Then there was silence.

"Tom," I said to Edison, gently. "I'm really sorry I frightened you. For that matter, I'm sorry for all the things I've done to you over the years."

"Oh, well," he huffed, trying to seem like nothing particularly special had just happened, that he hadn't nearly been demon fodder. "That's okay, I guess. Forget about it." And in what was the most gracious gesture I'd ever seen him make, he offered me his hand. I shook it gratefully.

"Do you think you could give Orson and me a few minutes alone?"

He nodded. "Orson, I'll be getting some parts from Dora. See you, Minion, er, Steve." He walked through the space where the door used to be and was soon out of earshot.

"Sorry about the door, Orson," I said, sitting on the edge of the desk.

"Skip it. Steve, did you really say no to Satan? Did you really exercise free will?"

I grinned. "Yes, I did. I'll probably be thrown in with the gang of traitors in the Ninth Level of Hell for it, but I did."

"So, you're no longer a demon. If you have free will, you can't be." He looked me up and down. "You sure as hell look like a demon, though."

I shrugged. "Once a demon, always a demon, or at least so I've been told. But I'm definitely a fucked-up one. And I certainly have free will. I'm convinced of that now."

Orson settled heavily into his chair. "What a marvel!"

"Yes. I don't know what the future holds for me, but I am no longer in thrall to the Lord of Hell." A great weight seemed to lift from my chest, and I felt happier than I had in a very long time.

"What are you going to do now?"

"Dunno. Maybe I'll be like Zorro, righting wrongs and all that jazz."

"You'll need a mask," he said with a smirk.

"There's that." With my demon ears I heard the pounding of twenty demon feet on the pavement outside. "I've got to get out of here. They're coming for me."

Orson grabbed my arm. "Where will you go, Steve?"

"I don't know." I smiled then hugged him. "Take care, my friend."

Ten demons crowded through the door. Each held a pitchfork, and they roared when they spotted me.

"Get thee behind me, Satan," I intoned softly. And then I teleported.

Chapter 24

My instincts had told me immediately that they would come for me. A demon gone rogue could not be tolerated in Hell, and Satan would want me collared pretty quickly. At the same time, my very existence would be an embarrassment to him. Perhaps he'd want it done on the q.t. Well, if you consider the ten demons who had just tried to catch me at the office as being on the q.t. Still, I didn't know how wide the alarm had gone out.

Satan, if he chose, should have been able to spot and grab me in an instant, though whatever had happened to release my free will from its bondage seemed to have disrupted our mental link. Also, he seldom wanted to do his own dirty work. He was a manager and preferred to delegate. This combination of factors – the need for discretion, my apparent invisibility on the telepathic radar and Satan's disinclination to deal with his own laundry – could work in my favor, at least for a while. Perhaps, just perhaps Murphy's Law might not kick in immediately.

Oh, I knew they'd catch me eventually. Satan would try to do this on the sly for a while, but if necessary, he'd send the Hordes of Hell after me. *So be it.* In the meantime, I intended to give them a run for their money.

Usually when I teleported, it was between circles, one at a time, since two would push the limits of my range. In the interest of precision and efficiency, I generally traveled to the same locations. By now, my patterns had likely been noticed by someone, probably by Big Red himself, so this time, I decided to mix things up. Instead of going up or down, I went sideways, materializing in front of the greeting stand at Red Square, one of the major nightclubs on Level Five. Red Square was primarily a hangout for the damned, but an occasional demon came to the place, usually just to cause some mischief, so I didn't think I'd stand out if I showed up there.

The maître d'evil was at the stand, reviewing his reservation book. Behind him, the table area and the large bandstand were dark. He looked up at me. "Minion? I heard you'd become a demon. Nice horns, by the way."

Excellent. He doesn't seem to know I'm on the lam.

"Thanks." I'd finally gotten used to the horns and generally forgot I sported them, except when I was shampooing, when I'd occasionally gouge myself on one of the points. Don't know why my horns mattered at this point, but it was good to know that, as demons went, I cut a dashing figure. "Not as nice as yours, of course, but mine grew in okay, I guess." It didn't hurt to suck up a little, especially now, when the last thing I needed was any additional conflict.

He nodded, accepting the compliment. "I didn't see you come in. Are you here for a table? It's a little early yet."

"No. I was just wondering. Could I use your bathroom?"

The devil grinned mischievously. "You bet. I haven't had a chance to send anyone in there to trash it before the humans show." There was nothing like a demon or devil to really get a john into a disgusting state.

"Well, I'll do my best. Might be in there a while."

"No problem," he said, knowing that a good restroom desecration required thought and effort. "Take your time." Then he went back to studying his book.

I slipped into the Men's room. The first thing I did was pee on the floor, leaving a bright yellow puddle below the urinal. Then I pulled out a bunch of paper hand towels, wadded them up and threw them on the checkerboard tiled floor. Next, grabbing a roll of toilet paper, I stuffed it in one of the crappers and flushed, which got the thing overflowing, covering the floor with water and soaking the paper towels. Finally I hunched over and released an enormous fart, which filled the Men's Room with an odor that made rotten eggs smell like Chanel No. 5 by comparison. My favor to the devil accomplished, I concentrated, tightened my sphincter and jumped all the way to Seven.

I wanted to see if I could teleport two levels. If yes, my movements would be less predictable, or so I reasoned. Teleporting downward seemed to make the most sense, at least for my first time. If I came up short, I'd just fall a few hundred feet, which was nothing for a demon. If I erred going up, though, I could slam into the underside of a circle or displace some rock as I inadvertently materialized underground. Neither situation would cause serious hardship, but I suspected both would give me a headache.

And me without my bottle of aspirin.

My target was the stone outcropping on Seven that I'd used to watch for Leviathan. My aim was good, if a little short; I materialize twenty feet above it.

"Screech!" the harpy chirped desperately, just before I did a bellyflop on top of the creature. *Oops. Forgot about her.* I crawled off the avian mess, which at the moment was not unlike a lumpy old feathered mattress. The harpy was out cold. *Good. She probably didn't have time to recognize me.*

Okay. I think with a little more concentration and an extra hard squeeze, I can manage a full two miles. Another weapon for my arsenal. Next, I hopped to Six, along the drive leading between Hell's sulfur mine and Slothville, where Belphegor oversaw Eternal punishment for the incorrigibly lazy. The cracked and rutted pavement looked as if it had not had attention in fifty years. On the other hand, the asphalt could have been brand new, then thoughtfully textured by construction workers to make trips along it an unpleasant experience for the damned.

The landscape along the road consists primarily of boojum trees, very popular for landscaping purposes in Hell, primarily because devils like to say the word "boojum." Boojums look more like cacti than trees, and they usually grow in the desert, but whenever Satan wants a place to look particularly desolate, he'll make sure and plant a grove of the things. These were blackened, though, as if someone had taken a flamethrower and carefully charred each one. The trees offered me little cover, but on the flip side, I could see many leagues in all directions.

I'd chosen this spot on purpose. The road was usually devoid of traffic. Those in Slothville didn't have a moment to spare for a joyride in the country, and the workers at the mine rarely bothered to make a trip to town. This time was no different. For miles around me, not a creature stirred. I appeared to be completely off the radar, at least for the nonce.

These hops were not accidental. I wanted to know how many people were looking for me, and if a devil on Five was unaware of the situation, I judged that Satan's employees on the other levels didn't know about my situation and status yet. I also wanted to know the limits of my teleportation abilities. Two miles, maybe a bit more, seemed manageable, with effort.

My next destination was also with a purpose. There was someone I really needed to see. I hopped to Four for a nanosecond, then concentrating on a certain piece of furniture in a certain office, I teleported, landing right next to Lilith's desk.

"Steve!" she said, looking up from some paperwork. "What a nice surprise! Do you want some coffee?"

I smiled fondly at my demonic paramour. She was gorgeous that day, as always, dressed in a tight black business suit and white collared top, with just enough buttons open to display her at her bosomy best. Her long auburn hair framed her fair, freckled face with glorious curls, accentuating her startling blue eyes, and her full lips were painted with a rich, come-hither lipstick. It was impossible to look at her without an astonished gasp, even after all the time I had spent with her.

"Thanks, but no. Don't really have time. I just wanted to come by and tell you something."

She smiled, coming around the desk to give me a hug. "What's up? Will you be late for dinner tonight?"

"Very late," I said nodding. "In fact, I'll be a no-show."

Lilith made that adorable little moue of hers. "Oh, and I was going to make a soufflé and everything. What's going on?"

I took her by the hand and led her over to one of the large, plate glass windows that overlooked Lustland. Though the day had barely started, the city was shrouded in darkness – it always was, mainly to show off the profusion of gaudy neon signs that identified the brothels, seedy motels and sex shops. What went on in Lustland stayed in Lustland, as the postcard I saw in the bazaar had advertised, and the perpetual dark of the metropolis reinforced that it was a place of secrets, secret lust, secret longings, secret disappointments.

Lilith and I stood close together, looking out the window at the cityscape. I embraced her, stroked her hair. I wanted to soak Lilith in, the look of her, the smell of her, for I didn't know when we would see each other again. Or if we ever would. "Sweet one," I said finally, "these past few months with you have been wonderful."

Lilith was purring under my caress. She took my hand, kissing its palm. "Yes, they have, darling, but that isn't what you've come to say, is it?" The succubus looked at me with the wisdom of millennia in her gaze. She may have only looked about twenty-two, but she'd been around for a very long time.

"No," I said, smiling ruefully. "I just wanted you to know, to always know, that in our time together, I've come to love you very much."

She brightened. "You ... you love me? You do? You really do?"

"Yes, but ... " I didn't know how to say the rest without hurting her, "but I can't have sex with you anymore."

Her response wasn't quite what I expected. "Oh? Okay." Then she kissed me on the lips.

I was stunned. "You're fine with that?"

She burrow her head in my shoulder. "Sure. No more sex with you? Phht. Steve, I have sex all the time. It's great, especially with you. I enjoy sex but, heck, it's my job. One sexual partner more or less isn't a big deal, not compared to this."

"This?" I said, still surprised by her calm reaction. "This what?"

"Love," she said, beaming. "All I've ever wanted was to be loved. No one has ever told me he loved me before. Not and meant it, anyway," she said with a grin. "Plenty of lust, of course, and sometimes guys get the two confused, but love. Wow."

I thought about Lilith's long existence. The child of the original Lilith and the archangel Samael, she'd always been a daddy's girl, a daddy she loved to distraction but got to spend almost no time with, seeing as how the two of them were on opposite sides of the celestial fence. As a child in a very large family (666 sisters and half-sisters, all sired by the good guys' bad guy), she must have gotten forgotten frequently – middle child syndrome. In all her centuries of life, for her not to feel loved, well, it was just a terrible thought.

I held her long, kissed the top of her head. "Well, I mean it."

"I know you do. That's what makes you saying it so special. And I love you too," she said, looking up at my face tenderly. "Flo is part of this, at least the no-more-sex part, isn't she? I know you still have feelings for her."

"Yes, she's part of it." I didn't want to tell Lilith that Flo was all of it, really. Seeing her yesterday had convinced me that she was really the only woman for me, even if I could never be with her again. Flo was my true love, and yet when I told Lilith I loved her, that was true as well.

"That's okay." Lilith smiled. "You have a big heart. There's room in there for more than one love."

I smiled back. *There's love, and then there's love.* But I didn't say that. Instead I said, with a sorrowful smile, "I'm a demon. I didn't think I was supposed to have a heart at all."

"Silly!" she said, poking me in the ribs. "Of course you have a heart. The biggest one I know."

"Lilith, I may not be able to see you for a while." Like all Eternity, I suspected, if Satan got his way. "In fact, I can't stay much longer, because … "

The door to the inner office opened, and Asmodeus stepped out. "Minion! What hubris to come to my stronghold, considering your current status!" He reached out his hand, and an invisible force grabbed me, pulling me away from the window and from Lilith's grasp.

It made sense that Satan would tell the princes of Hell about my defection. They, more than any, would understand the dangers of a rogue demon on the loose. Other than the princes and a few other powerful devils, few in the Underworld would individually be able to stand against me. Satan had built his superdemon a little too well.

Smiling a little sheepishly at Lilith, I finished my thought. "I'm also in a little bit of trouble right now." I tried to teleport, but my special ability was now common knowledge across the Netherworld, and Asmodeus must have compensated for my skill. His hold on me was secure. I couldn't move.

"A little bit?" said the Lord of Lust. "You disobey Satan, and you call that a little bit of trouble? That's putting it mildly."

Again, I struggled in the invisible grasp. A faint sheen of perspiration formed on the devil's brow, but his grasp remained firm. "Satan was right about you. You're very strong, probably stronger than most devils, and that makes you way too strong to remain at large. Fortunately, you are no match for a prince of Hell."

I squirmed harder in his grasp. *So you say, but I see your arm shaking.* Yet he was right. He was stronger than me. A little.

He frowned. Having a mere demon give him this much trouble was making him mad. Without taking his eyes off me, he spoke to his assistant. "Say goodbye to your lover boy, Lilith. Where he's going, I don't think they allow conjugal visits."

Lilith's face flashed her dismay, but she quickly suppressed it, and Asmodeus, still focusing all his attention on me, missed the expression. She said, "That's good, boss. I was getting tired of him anyway. And now that he's out of the picture, you'll get Nightingale in the sack in no time."

"Nightingale?" Asmodeus said with a start. He had always had a hard-on for Flo. In that moment, his eyes glazed over with lust, his attention on me wavering as he probably began fantasizing about bedding the one woman who'd escaped his grasp.

Speaking of grasps, the invisible grip on me relaxed slightly. I took my chance and teleported. Just before I disappeared, though, Lilith winked at me.

Chapter 25

I did a two mile hop to Level Four, teleporting to the side of Old Dependable, an active volcano that erupted constantly. No one in his right mind spent any time around the mountain, for its lava was one of the hotter substances in all Hell. It could give even the most hardened demon a major owie.

Fortunately for me, I remembered a cave I'd seen there once. The lava tended to just flow over the entrance to the cavern, almost but not quite sealing it. It was this entrance to the cave that I shot for, and I landed right on its lip then darted inside before any lava could fall on me.

My entire body ached. The grip Asmodeus had on me practically crushed my skeleton, and it was but a minor consolation that he had maintained it only with some effort. My body was covered in bruises, something I wouldn't have thought possible anymore, since I'd departed the ranks of damned humanity and joined the Demon Corps. Demons are tough, but I guess even a demon is not proof against a major devil. *I probably couldn't even take TNK-el, that little shrimp, though it would be fun to try.* I'd always wanted to kick him like a football, just to see how far he'd fly.

The space in the mountain was larger than I was expecting. The stone ceiling was a good forty feet above me; the breadth of the cavern was easily double that. I sat down heavily on a rock inside the cave. My bruises were already fading, but I was tired, spent emotionally as well as physically.

It wasn't going to take Management very long to corner me. I knew now to stay away from major devils, which probably meant, since Satan had surely mobilized all of the princes in the demon-hunt for me, I would have to keep on the move. That meant teleporting constantly, because I didn't think running would do the trick. Teleportation didn't take much out of me, though doing it repeatedly made my sphincter sore. I'd never done more than about twenty hops in rapid succession. How long could I keep it up before I got a cramp or something?

I had to face facts that sooner or later, they'd catch me. There was really nowhere for me to run. A prince of Hell was on every level except One, Three and Five. I'd be spotted on One immediately. The virtuous pagans didn't like demons and would turn me in on sight. Three was the realm of Gluttony, Beezy's responsibility, and while my former boss spent most of his time on Eight, he kept close watch over both circles. Five had more damned humans on it than any other Level – it was practically one giant city – and Satan himself monitored it. Five was also where I knew the most people, human, demon or devil, so I'd be spotted in moments there. All I could think to do was to keep jumping, go down swinging, until someone finally got me.

I sighed, shifting uncomfortably on my rock. There was no telling what Satan would do to me, once caught. It wouldn't be pleasant, that's for sure. In fact, I couldn't think of any other place for him to put me except down on Nine, in one of the Traitor's Cells. It would be appropriate. I had betrayed him.

He could, of course, cast me out into Chaos, like I'd seen him do with a fire giant once. I shuddered at the thought.

But, no matter what, I wasn't going to turn myself in. Satan would show me no mercy, regardless. If I was going to defy him, I'd be defiant to the end. In the meantime, this cave seemed as good a place to hide as any.

I opened up my secret space and took out my sack lunch. Normally I made my own, but today Lilith had wanted to do it. She'd made me a roast beef sandwich. To go with it, she'd slipped in a large bag of Fritos. Despite my predicament, I smiled. Fritos were my favorite. She'd even packed a Dr. Pepper, not my favorite, but it was better without the two types of schnapps she'd put in it to make a crackhead slammer. I didn't really need to eat, no demon did, but it was a pleasure to do something so mundane, so I tore open the Fritos, took the sandwich out of the Ziploc bag, and started to eat.

A black shadow cast the cavern in darkness. There was a rush of wings. Suddenly the cavern was a lot less spacious.

"Hi, BOOH," I said. "Did you spot me when I landed outside?"

"Skree."

"Are you here to take me to Satan?"

My batty friend shifted uncomfortably on his feet. "Skree."

"Hey, it's okay. He's your boss. It's your job. Want a Frito?" I asked, holding up the bag.

"Urm." The only thing BOOH liked better than Fritos was blood. He was, after all, a vampire bat, though a colossal one. I kept a few Fritos for myself and tossed him the bag, which he caught with one of the small hands attached to his wings. He finished the bag, while I finished my sandwich. "Want some Dr. Pepper?"

"Skree."

"Didn't think so. You don't know what you're missing, though," I chugged down the soft drink.

We sat quietly together for a few minutes. Neither one of us wanted to mention the elephant in the room, that I was now a fugitive and we were on opposite sides for the first time since we'd known each other. Probably I could have teleported before he grabbed me. Probably, though BOOH was almost as fast as Beezy. Perhaps even if he grabbed me, I could teleport, though BOOH had a grip of iron. He might be the equal of a strong devil. I just didn't know, and I had little stomach to find

260

out by setting the two of us in conflict. I made a decision. I would do nothing that would get BOOH in trouble with Satan. "BOOH, I'll come without a fight, if that's what you want. You're my friend, and if someone has to catch me, I guess I'd want it to be you, but could we talk a while first?"

BOOH sighed softly, clearly relieved that I wasn't going to put him in a difficult situation. "Urm."

"Thanks. This has all been kind of difficult for me. I talked with Ronnie a little about it, but well, I need to tell you my story. You're one of my best friends too, and I want you to know what's been going on."

I got off the rock – it was pretty damn uncomfortable – and sat cross-legged on the flat surface of the cave. BOOH, having quickly dispatched the Fritos, including the bag, leaned back against a wall.

"Mind if I smoke?" I asked him.

"Urm."

"Thanks." A small plume floated from the top of my head and soon blended in with the smoke of the volcano. Ever since I'd become a demon, I periodically needed to release a little bit of heat. Maybe my new status had given me extra fire in my belly, but whatever the reason, whenever I was a little tense, smoking relaxed me. But just a little. I wasn't a chain smoker or anything. More of a social smoker.

I sighed. "BOOH, this has been very hard for me. I don't know if you've heard the whole story behind me becoming a demon. Probably not, since I know you don't go in for gossip."

"Skree."

"I didn't think so. Well, you see, it all started with Flo." I told my friend about how I'd been tricked into believing that she had been kidnapped and that her soul would be destroyed forever if I didn't agree to become a demon.

BOOH was visibly upset. "Skree!"

"Yes, I know. It was a dirty trick, but in Satan's defense, he *is* the Prince of Lies. And regardless, he followed the letter of the law, mostly, if not its spirit."

"So, anyway, to save Flo, and at the time I also thought to save Orson, Allan, Nicky and Louie, I agreed to become a demon."

I held my hands out to him. He sniffed them, as if he could learn something by doing that. "I've always believed this is the crux of my problem, why tormenting damned humans is difficult to the point of abhorrence to me. Because while I agreed to be a demon, it wasn't entirely of my own free will."

"Skree."

"Yeah, it really *is* a bitch. And then there's this whole free will thing. Supposedly, when I agreed to become a demon, I forfeited my free will, but from the very beginning, there were certainly commands that I resisted."

"Skree?"

"Oh, mostly the ones that involved hurting people, but there were even times when I questioned Satan's judgment, to his face even."

My batty friend blew a hair off his nose. "Ur-Urm."

"You said it. Just asking for trouble. But there it is. I'm just not somebody's toady."

"Skree?"

"Oh, a toady is like a 'yes man.' Funny word, isn't it? Anyway, things finally came to a head today, when Satan ordered me to torment Orson."

BOOH didn't say a word, but the shock on his face was clear.

"Satan figured the only way to get me comfortable with hurting people was, as he called it, a baptism of fire. If I could hurt one of my best friends, I could hurt anyone."

I buried my face in my hands. "But I just couldn't do it. I refused. Yes, I know, that should have been impossible, but I did it. And so now it appears I'm a demon who has free will. Which is why you've been sent to catch me."

BOOH wouldn't make eye contact with me. He leaned back against the wall and began etching farm animals on the stone with one of his claws.

I patted his leg. "This whole situation sucks, but you had nothing to do with it. I know you have to take me in. In fact, if you're thinking about not doing it, just stop right now. I won't let you get in trouble over me."

The great Bat out of Hell, my close friend, looked at me finally. His eyes were moist, blood-moist, but moist. I got up and we hugged each other.

"There's no place for me now anyway. I'm not really a demon anymore. And I'm not human. Satan will probably just find some place where no one will ever find me, lock me up and throw away the key."

He looked worried. "Skree! Skree!"

"I've thought of that. Satan may feel it necessary to hurl me out there. If I don't fit into the scheme of things, in Heaven or Hell ... " BOOH looked horrified, and I clamped my hand over my mouth. "Well, what do you know about that? I can say the Heaven word and not get creamed for it. God, Yahweh, Jehovah, Jesus, Christ, Holy Spirit, Holy Ghost, Trinity." I tested each of the words on the censored list, and I could say them all. "Hmm. Well, anyway, yes, being thrown into Chaos is a definite possibility."

I got to my feet. "Well, now you know the whole story. We might as well go."

BOOH scrambled off the dirt then hunched down for me to get on his back. This gave me an idea. "No, my friend," I said. "I don't think it would do for me to ride triumphantly on your back. You should carry me like carrion in your claws, just like you used to in the old days, when we first met."

"Skree?"

"Yeah, I'm sure. It's okay. This will be better for you, I promise, and it won't hurt me any."

BOOH hung his head in despair but nodded. This was going to be very difficult for him. Fortunately, I intended to lessen his guilt soon enough.

Since the cave was a little tight for a good liftoff, we walked to the entrance. BOOH splayed his wings, and the hot lava fell down upon them. He seemed completely unaffected. "Skree?"

"Yes, I'm ready." I put my back to him, he launched into the air and grabbed me by the shoulder blades.

I knew something about BOOH that probably no one else did. He had a ticklish spot. I'd discovered it quite by accident in the early months of our relationship when, while flying from one circle of Hell to another, I'd killed a little time by scraping some dried offal off his legs. I was counting on that place to be his Achilles' Heel.

Patting my friend companionably, I reached up to the spot, which was just a little above his left set of claws. While BOOH flew, I started to tickle his secret place.

It didn't take long. Soon he was quivering all over, his shoulders going up and down rapidly, which is what he always did whenever he laughed or giggled. This destabilized his flying. Finally, he couldn't take it anymore, and his grip on me loosened.

I dropped like a stone. "See you, pal!" I yelled to the wide-eyed bat then disappeared.

Chapter 26

I rematerialized in the very cave we'd just left.

That went well.

When BOOH showed, I fully intended to let him take me in. I didn't want him to get in trouble. But, in this situation, there was no good outcome for my blood-sucking friend. If he had let me go, even if he were capable of disobeying a direct command from his master, he would have gotten an incredible amount of grief. Satan loved BOOH above all creatures in the Cosmos, so the bat probably wouldn't have gotten too much shit from letting me escape, but it would definitely have hurt their relationship. Yet, I was also BOOH's friend; he would likely have done his duty, carting me to Satan and the fate awaiting me, but the bat would have felt terrible about it forever.

This way, he had done his level best to do his duty. *It's not his fault he's ticklish.* I'd secured my own escape, fair and square. BOOH had done nothing wrong and would not be blamed.

I did not intend to stay long in the cave, but for now thought it safe harbor. Who would expect me to return to the very place we'd just left? Probably BOOH would, eventually. He knew me well and was quite smart.

So I had only a little time to plan my next course of action. I needed to stay on the move, so I mentally plotted out ten destinations, designed to be random and make me difficult to track. I did some leg stretches and a few Kegels, which I hoped would loosen up the old sphincter. There was a noise outside. Figuring it was BOOH, I hopped.

First I landed back on Six, along the same road I'd visited earlier. Now, though, the stretch was populated with devils and demons, standing like centurions on both sides of the pavement. A second after I appeared, Belphegor, of all devils, materialized. I felt sorry for the lazy bum; the effort he must have made was incredible – for him anyway. Still, after my experience with Asmodeus, I didn't dare give another prince of Hell a chance to get his metaphysical mitts on me. Almost as soon as I had arrived, I jumped again, this time to Five.

I knew Level Five like the back of my hand; it was where I'd spent most of my afterlife. Five being the most urbanized of Hell's circles, there were few deserted places here. Those that were, like the steel mill, had been intentionally abandoned. I skipped my regular landing spot there and plopped instead on top of the library. As soon as I did, though, the two dragons that guarded the entrance sensed me and began to roar. With a high-pitched pop, TNK-el, his signature Slurpee in hand, appeared. The little creep was fast, grabbing me with an invisible hand nearly as strong as that of Asmodeus. Satan hadn't been kidding; TNK-el was a very powerful devil, despite being vertically disenfranchised. "Minion," he said, a nasty edge to his voice. "I was hoping I'd be the one to catch you. Satan told me it was you who played that little trick on me in the cafeteria. I'll get you for that. Bwahahahahahaha!"

Yes, Tink was very strong, but I could still move, just a little. Perhaps if I distracted him for a moment, the way Lilith had distracted Asmodeus, I could get away. "Oh no! Your Slurpee!"

"What about my Slurpee?" He looked down momentarily at his drink. With an effort, I broke his grip and jumped again.

Now I was on Three. I arrived next to what looked like a deserted grain silo a ways outside of Glutton's Gap. In reality, it was a carefully camouflaged piece of Hell's HVAC system. I chose this spot because I'd visited here once before and found the area pretty desolate. Also, knowing exactly where it was, I could teleport there from memory. But again, I found the place crawling with Hell's minions. Right after I arrived, Adramelech appeared. This time, though, I didn't try to run. I'd been itching to see if I was as strong as he was. I'd managed to take Digger, early in my training, and since then, I'd only gotten stronger. The only demon in Hell, other than myself, who was more powerful than the head of the sulfur mine was his boss, the so-called King of Fire.

Adramelech bellowed and charged me, and I braced for impact. Turns out I was as strong as he: exactly as strong. We wrestled for a while, threw fire at each other. Each time we engaged resulted in a stalemate. Adramelech was bigger than I, so his reach was longer, but I was faster. The two advantages cancelled each other out. Again, stalemate.

The other demons, seeing how evenly matched Adramelech and I were, began to close in. No one ever said demons had to fight fair, and while I believe that in time I would have beaten Adramelech, that wasn't going to happen if all those demons decided to play dog pile on the Minion. Time to hop. Problem was that I didn't have time to concentrate on teleporting while the King of Fire was distracting me. I just needed a second, though, and fortunately, since Adramelech couldn't outthink a pet rock, buying a second was pretty easy.

"Hey, fire fuck!" I yelled, hoping to make him mad. I did, judging from the Hellfire he threw at me. "Don't trip on your shoelaces!"

"Trip on *what*?" he roared, looking down.

Jeez. He really *was* stupid. He wasn't even wearing shoes. "On nothing, you dumb ass!" I teleported again.

On Four, I stayed as far away from New Rome as possible. A fleet of harpies in the air spotted me. They screeched, and Mammon, all twenty-five feet of him appeared. To my knowledge, this was the first time in well over a hundred years that he had physically left his center of power, but he did it. He didn't look very happy over the necessity of coming after me. If he got anywhere near me, he'd likely pound me back to invertebrate status before turning my gelatinous remains over to Satan. That didn't sound like much fun, so I jumped immediately.

Everywhere my experience was much the same. An all-points bulletin had apparently been put out for me, and every creature in Hell, or at least the non-human ones, was gunning for me now. From Four, I hopped multiple times, just as fast as I could, sometimes transporting or occasionally running at top speed across a level. Sometimes I'd hop one, sometimes two circles at once. Once I even jumped down two and a half, materializing in midair. As I fell, I saw a host of demons swarming, like ants, beneath me, so I hopped again. I'd go up; I'd go down. I'd go forward; I'd go back. Someone was always waiting for me.

I teleported to Tae Bayan, Shit Town, on Level Seven. I almost never came to Hell's Pacific Rim equivalent, which I hoped would lend me some anonymity. Perhaps I could lose myself in the crowd of what was perhaps the most densely-populated area in Hell. No such luck. A devil on the street spotted me immediately and raised the alarm. I jumped. The last thing I needed was Leviathan showing up. He was already pissed off at me.

Level Nine was unthinkable, and Level Eight not much better, but I was running out of options. I was also running out of steam. I chose Eight, but stayed far away from Beezy's office, materializing instead on one of the high mesas many miles away from the bazaar.

For a wonder, there was no one in sight. I breathed a sigh of relief.

Just as a giant foot drove me into the ground.

"GIVE IT UP, STEVE! YOU KNOW YOU CAN'T WIN!" It was Beelzebub, of course, in one of his giant incarnations. He must have been at least a hundred feet high; he could have even been five hundred for all I knew. It was kind of hard to tell, because there was just a whole lot of foot covering the hole I'd made in the dirt, where he'd driven me like a nail.

I was disoriented from the force of the blow, which was undoubtedly Beezy's intent, but I wasn't immobilized. Not yet. I didn't know if he needed to physically lay his eyes on me in order to deliver the magic whammy, or if he thought I was too discombobulated from the smooshing I'd just received to do much of anything. If the latter, he was mistaken. A trapped animal can do amazing things. Blindly I hopped.

Oh, shit! I was standing on white carpet, staring at a wide-eyed Bruce. In an instant, with all my remaining strength, I jumped back to Eight, then up the circles, one after the other, one at a time. I didn't feel strong enough to find deserted places to land, so I used my regular landing spots in a hope that no one would think I was stupid enough to return to familiar haunts. And I wasn't; I was just too tired to concentrate on anyplace new. Nor did I attempt any two-circle jumps. Flashing for but an instant on each of the levels before teleporting again, I moved upward rapidly: Eight, Seven, Six, Five, Four, Three, Two, and then to One.

I hopped to the pro shop, near where Homer rented out golf carts to the virtuous pagans who played the game. (Limbo had been converted into a gated golfing community a few years earlier.) Since Homer was blind, I figured that, even though I was a demon, I'd be able to hide there for a while. But it was no good. He may have been blind, but he had a good nose.

"Αυτό που είναι εκείνη η φρικτή μυρωδιά?" which meant, "What is that horrible smell?"

Rats.

Homer commenced to hollering, and the entire pro shop emptied to see what was going on. There was Socrates, my least favorite Greek gadfly, along with Aeneas, Cicero and about fifteen others. I could have taken them all, but they put up such a ruckus that I knew soon someone, probably Satan himself, in Lucifer guise, since he always tried to put on his best face with these characters, would show. "Hey, guys. I don't want any trouble," I said, backing away from them.

I backed and I backed and I backed, but they kept coming forward, holding their noses and hurling insults at me, mostly in Greek or Latin. Keeping my eyes on what was rapidly turning into a mob, I backed blindly. And so it came to pass that I fell into the hole of the Par One course, which was the opening of the Throat of Hell on this level.

Crap.

Long I fell, or at least I would have, if about halfway down to Level Two, I decided to try for Mount Erebus. The mile-high frozen stalactite that hung from the underbelly of Level One was inhabited by only one creature, Ymir, a frost giant, and he was at its far end. My sphincter was so sore, I thought I'd ruptured it, but I tried to teleport to the base of the mountain.

I was unsuccessful. Erebus is contained within its own pocket universe, not dissimilar from my demon hidey-hole, and it repelled my attempt to transport to its surface. I jumped, got bumped back to where I started then tried again. Same result, so I decided to teleport to the maintenance scaffold that ran along the bottom of Two to the base of the mountain. From there I could easily use my demon strength to reach the giant spike of ice.

"Damn it!" I yelled in frustration. There, waiting for me, were two fallen seraphim, their bright blades glowing with fire.

I was desperate, hanging from a rung of the scaffold, and so exhausted I was ready to drop the entire mile to the Second Circle. *Where to go? Where to go?* I thought briefly about Gates Level, but I was damned, and Peter would not stand between Satan and one of his own.

In a final act of desperation, I jumped to the one place I had left. As my feet touched the sandy shore near Charon's boathouse on Level 0.5, I screamed out, "Sanctuary! Sanctuary!"

Why, sure, Steve, Ronnie clacked out in Morse Code, as he and Cerberus stepped out of the boathouse. *What's up?*

Chapter 27

"Oh, God, Ronnie," I gasped, not even aware at the time that I'd used one of the no no words. Charon didn't seem to notice. "I'm so glad to see you."

Cerberus, always glad to see me too, leapt on top of me and licked me to within an inch of my death. Ronnie looked at me with concern.

Talk to me, Steve. What's wrong?

And so I told him as we sat on the ash-covered shore by the River Styx. I told him about recovering my free will, defying Satan and becoming a fugitive.

"I'm so tired, Ronnie," I said at last, sniffling a little bit, I'm not afraid to admit. "So damn tired. And I don't know where to go, or what I'll do."

My friend, my oldest friend in Hell actually, gave me a hug. *Why, you'll stay here with me and Cerberus. For as long as you wish. Satan may eventually figure out you're here, but he can't read my mind, you know.*

This was true. Satan had allowed a large number of magical and mythological creatures into Hell. He considered figures like Prometheus, Sisyphus and even Charon as iconic, wonderfully emblematic of the grim afterlife of Hell. But for some reason, he could not read their minds. Nor could he read mine, not any longer, I reflected with surprise.

"Still," I said slowly, "it's only a matter of time before they come to claim me."

They can't, he said, simply.

"Why not?" I asked, wiping my nose on my sleeve.

No one can come here without my leave. It's in my contract.

"Contract," I said derisively. "And when did Satan ever

honor a contract?"

Steve, Satan is many things, but he is not a welsher. Charon looked thoughtful. One thing I liked about Ronnie was that he was completely devoid of prejudice. He probably hated the derogatory expression, "welsher," but really, there's not a better alternative out there, so he shrugged and continued. *My contract says that no one can enter this level without my permission.*

"So why are you so confident that he won't find some loophole to exploit?"

He huffed. *Really, Steve, I know Satan is older than I am, but I'm no spring chicken. While I may work for him, I'm not afraid of him. For one thing, I'm not a Christian, Jew or Muslim. He has no power over me in that regard. Also, I've been around for thousands of years. You know, I read things pretty carefully before I sign.* Ronnie shrugged. *Of course, he'll find a way around our agreement in time, but he'll have to fight the union too.*

"Beg pardon?"

The Satan's Employees Infernal Union. I'm president, you know.

"Really?" I'd been on SEIU contract negotiating teams before, but suddenly I realized I'd never known who our president was. "So how long have you been president?"

He smiled. *Oh, two or three thousand years. I'm also the chief steward. Anyway, while I'm sure Satan will eventually come charging in here, once he figures out where you are and can get past all the union legal hurdles, I figure you have months before that happens.*

Months. A long time, yet nothing in the scheme of Eternity.

I also have friends in high places, he said significantly.

"What do you mean?"

Well, I never like to trade on my connections, but Death is my big brother, after all.

This was true. Mortimer carried a lot of weight in the Cosmos. Satan would tread carefully around Charon. So I had a little time.

I don't have a place to put you up, he said with regret. *I work the Styx without rest, as you know, and I don't have a room of my own.*

"Maybe I could stay in the boathouse?"

No, it leaks, I'm afraid. There's really only one fit place for you to stay. He looked at me with amusement. *Can you guess where?*

"Ronnie, I'm completely exhausted. Don't make me play Twenty Questions. Just tell me where."

The ancient ferryman for the dead gave Cerberus a brisk pat down. *Why, in the dog house, of course.*

The irony of the suggestion was exquisite. I'd built that dog house personally, my first big job after being consigned to Handyman Hell.

It may be a little crooked, but Cerberus assures me it's water-tight. And it's pretty big for a dog house. You and he should be just fine in there.

Despite everything that had happened that day, despite my exhaustion, I laughed. "That sounds great. Thanks, Ronnie. Thanks, Cerberus," I added, patting my host's three heads.

And so it was settled. I moved in with the guard dog of Hades. We actually made pretty good roommates, except he never brushed his teeth, so he always had dog breath.

I did what I could in the days ahead to earn my keep, but truth be told, Ronnie didn't need my assistance. The handful of recently-dead who required a ferry ride across the Styx was minimal. Back in the day, when he performed the same role for

Hades, the Greek god of the Underworld, his client base was much larger. These days, most people consigned to Hell simply rode down on the Escalator, and only those few of a more romantic bent traveled by ferry into the land of the damned. Charon could handle his current case load in his sleep, and there was little I could do to help, except entertain Cerberus with the more-than-occasional Frisbee toss.

It wasn't a life; it wasn't an afterlife. I was simply marking time. Still, the panic I'd felt during the demonhunt across Hell faded, and I fell for a while into a thankfully mindless day-to-day existence, if an afterlife as *demona non grata* counted as an existence at all.

A day came when Charon said he needed to run an errand. *There aren't any scheduled appointments today, but if you could pole my gondola along the Styx a couple of times, I'd appreciate it. You never know when someone will be shooting a promotional video.*

"Sure thing, pal," I said, taking the pole – and charcoal cloak – he offered me. "Where are you off to?"

My business, he said, then headed up the path toward Gates Level.

Cerberus and I plowed the water of the Styx several times that day. We even had an unscheduled client, a former professor at a midwestern college who had taught Dante and insisted upon traveling by Charon's ferry into the land of the Dead. Wearing my borrowed cloak, I kept my mouth shut, and did my best to take him across to the other side, where he would hop aboard the Escalator to take him the rest of the way.

"You're not very good at this, are you?" he said, after I slipped for my third time in the stern of the boat. Cerberus growled at him, and he shut up.

At the end of the day, the Hound of Hell and I crawled into

the dog house. I had no idea how hard work it was to ferry people across the Styx. My shoulders were killing me. (Funny how even a super-strong demon had muscles – like the ones for rowing – that he didn't use every day.) Even though I didn't really need to sleep, after my shift in the gondola I gratefully lay down next to Cerberus in the dog house.

"Steve?" said a familiar voice.

Slowly, I crawled outside. Standing before me, in this land of gray and shadow, was a glowing figure in white. It had been so long since I'd seen such brightness that my eyes stung. "Flo? Is that you?"

"Yes," she said softly, helping me to my feet.

"But, but how did you get here?"

I brought her, Charon clacked.

Flo hugged me, wrinkling her nose. "You stink."

I winced. "Demons stink, I guess."

"No, you smell of dog. This must be Cerberus," she said, as the great, three-headed hound followed me out of the dog house. She held out her hand for him to sniff, which he did. Satisfied, he gave it a gentle, almost reverent lick. Then, tail wagging, he went back inside the dog house, returning with his battered Frisbee.

"Don't let him sucker you into a game of fetch," I advised. "He'll never want to stop."

She patted one of the animal's heads then looked up at me. "I've been looking for you for months. Why didn't you come see me?"

"Oh, well, you know," I said, shuffling my feet in embarrassment. "I didn't think you'd want to be seen with a demon."

"And did you not think I knew how it happened, why it happened, that you became a demon in the first place? Oh,

Steve, Orson told me everything!" Then, in tears, she hugged me again, not letting go.

I brushed her chestnut hair, snagging a claw in one of her tresses. "Does it matter? However, I got this way, I'm a demon. Humans tend not to like demons."

"Well, I like this one," she said fiercely. "I never stopped loving you, darling."

"You didn't?"

"Of course not! I gave my heart to you, and all of Satan's machinations cannot reverse that."

I sat down on the beach. "Gee, I wish I'd known that. It might not have changed the outcome, but it would have made things a little easier on me."

Charon cleared his throat. Actually, it was more a series of clacking sounds, since he didn't really have a throat to clear, but his meaning was crystalline. *I think I'll leave you two alone for a while. Come on Cerberus. I'll play catch with you.* And off they went.

"You know, of course," I said to my love, "that I'm totally screwed."

"If you mean that you are a fugitive," she said primly, "yes of course."

"It's not just that, though I don't relish Satan getting his hands on me. I'm not a human anymore. I'm a demon, and a failed one at that. A demon without portfolio." In retrospect, that sounded way better than totally screwed.

"Darling," she said, nestled up against me, "you are the most remarkable man I've ever met."

I looked at her in surprise. "Why do you say that?"

"Satan exerted all of his will to shape you as a tool for his hand. Those months of brainwashing in Beast Barracks, stripping you of your free will, or at least so he thought: you stood up to all of that, throwing off the shackles he placed upon you. And then you managed to avoid everything and everyone he threw at you: devils, demons, the princes of Hell, even BOOH."

I grimaced. "Just barely. You should have seen me when I arrived here. I was half-dead. Well, I was all dead, but you know what I mean."

"Yes, of course."

"Flo," I said, looking into her eyes, "what am I going to do? I can't stay here forever. Sooner or later, Satan will figure out a way to reach me, even in Charon's protected realm, and that will be the end of me. The Devil can't have a demon with free will running around. It sets a terrible precedent for his operation. I'll be imprisoned forever or thrown into Chaos. And even if I managed to stay free, once a demon, always a demon. The transformation is irreversible."

She frowned. "I'm not so sure about that. I have an idea." Flo got off the ground and brushed the back of her dress. There wasn't a speck of dirt on her, like she'd been Scotchguarded or something. "Come with me."

"Where are we going?" I asked, getting off the ground.

"To see St. Peter," she said, taking my hand and heading toward the Pearly Gates side of the Cosmos.

I stopped abruptly. "We'll get caught. Surely Satan has been keeping an eye on you, and by now, he must know you're here."

"Certainly, but he doesn't know what I'm thinking. He's no more able to read my mind than he can Charon's."

"Hmm. I don't think he can read mine anymore either. When my free will broke out, it sort of short-circuited our telepathic link."

"That does not surprise me. The mind of a demon with free will must be completely incomprehensible to him."

I frowned. "That won't stop him from waylaying us on the way."

"He can't," she said simply.

"Oh, he's the Earl of Hell. He can do almost anything."

Flo frowned. "I don't pretend to understand all the arcane jurisdictions that exist in Heaven and Hell, but apparently, this end of the River Styx," she said, indicating the shore and the beach house, "is officially part of Gates Level. Charon and I have convinced St. Peter to grant us free passage to his desk."

"What? How did you manage that?"

"I asked him."

"Oh."

We headed up the sloping path that led toward the Pearly Gates. "How did you get here anyway?"

"We took the Elevator to Gates Level and walked down."

"But … but you have to have a key to do that."

"Charon has one. We used his." She reached to her neck and pulled out a chain with a key. "I have one too."

"How come?" I asked, as we trudged along the path.

"I'm saved and can come and go between Heaven and Hell as I like. Peter gave me the key so I wouldn't get any guff from that horrid demon … no offense … "

"None taken."

" … who runs the Elevator."

From around a bend ahead, I could hear the sounds of catcalls and obscenities. "Are you sure we'll be able to make it to Peter's desk?" I asked nervously. "Sounds like we're getting ready to be ambushed."

Flo narrowed her eyes. "Satan and his minions won't dare touch us, but that doesn't mean they won't try to intimidate you."

"Great."

We made the bend and found the path lined on both sides with devils and demons. "Minion, you traitor!" Karnaj shouted. "Give yourself up. You don't have a chance."

"Yeah!" Digger shouted, shaking one of his shovel sized hands at me threateningly.

"Minion," said a smooth voice from the side. It was Asmodeus. "I never liked you. You will pay for your insolence."

Even Maximus was lining the path. He shook his pitchfork fiercely, but he refused to make eye contact. And he kept quiet. *At least they're not all against me.*

"What a coward!" yelled Uphir. "Needing a girl to protect him."

Up until then, I'd just tried to keep moving forward, keeping my head down, but Uphir could always make my blood boil. "I don't need her to protect me from you. You know I'd dismantle you!" My hands had clenched into fists.

"Then come and try!" he taunted. "Come on. I dare you. No. I *double* dare you!"

I started to move toward him. This guy would go down with one good punch. But Flo put her hand on my chest. "No, Steve."

"But he double dared me!" I said, as if that would justify any action I took.

"St. Peter said that if you caused any violence in the Gates Area, his protection would cease. You just have to put up with the taunting a little longer. See?" She pointed out a thin cirrus cloud that was only a few dozen yards ahead.

I ground my teeth and kept walking. The taunts and threats increased, so that I couldn't even hear myself think. Now we were pulling even with the path that led to the Well of [Damned] Souls, the vast lake that held most of the good in a damned person's soul. Somewhere in there was a portion of my own being. It still maintained a connection to me, but it was not allowed to go to Hell.

For over sixty years, I had traversed the Circles of Hell with little more than half my soul source, a fact I'd learned only a few months ago. Now, only the bad in me and that good which was inextricably bound up with some bad remained.

As we walked past the path leading to the Well, Hell's hecklers began to thin. By the time we reached St. Peter's desk, there were none.

There was a crowd of souls waiting their turn with Heaven's Concierge, but they parted when Flo and I approached his workstation. Guess he'd been expecting us. "Well, Miss Nightingale, I did as you asked and granted Minion safe passage, but I don't know what you expect me to do now."

"St. Peter," she said with great deference, "Steve told me the story of his damnation. Is it true you decided it by a coin toss?"

Peter blushed slightly but nodded. "Sometimes the scales are so evenly balanced, there's no other way."

"I would like you to give him a do-over."

"What? Why that's unheard of!"

"But you know all the good Steve has done since he went to Hell! You know he's refused to torment the damned, despite his demon status."

The saint frowned. "Yes, I know, but that's irrelevant when you're making your decisions based on the Book of Life." He thumped the great tome on his desk with his hand. "Good deeds done after death can't be considered."

"Well, I don't see why not," she huffed. "Especially since Steve is in this fix in part because of you."

"What do you mean?"

"You know exactly what I mean!" she said in high dudgeon. (Only people born in the Victorian Era can be in high dudgeon, but Flo was, and so she was.) "If you hadn't mislead him about the nature of Azazel, Satan never would have been able to trick him into become a demon."

As if on cue, Satan materialized on Gates Level, followed in short order by Beelzebub. "What is going on here? I have come to claim my own." He reached forward an invisible hand, and I felt myself being draw toward him.

"Stop it, Nick," Peter said. He made a short cutting motion with his own hand, and as if a rope had been severed, the pulling on me stopped. "You may be able to take me in a fight, but up here I am the final authority."

"If you're the final authority," Flo persisted, "then give Steve a do-over."

"Yeah, double or nothing?"

Peter rolled his eyes. "You realize, of course, that that makes no sense at all. Twice damned is only an expression."

"Oh, right," I said, chewing on my lower lip. "Well, how about best two out of three?"

"What are you talking about?" Satan said, clearly peeved.

Peter nodded toward Flo and me. "They're trying to talk me into doing the coin toss again, giving Minion a second chance at Heaven."

"What! Outrageous! I forbid it!" Satan grew to giant size. I noticed though, that Beezy was keeping quiet. He looked interested in the pissing contest between the two.

"Now, listen, Nick!" Peter said heatedly. "You may be top dog down there in the cellar, but I don't answer to you. I can do whatever I like." He turned to me. "Okay, Minion. Best two out of three, but we count the first one."

I nodded, swallowing hard. Down by one already.

The saint reached in his pocket and pulled out a quarter. "Call it, Minion," he said, flipping the coin in the air.

"Heads!"

Peter let the coin fall to the surface of Gates Level, so there would be no accusations of the toss being rigged. As the coin landed, the clouds parted, giving everyone a clear view. "Heads it is. Next toss determines it." He reached down and picked up the coin.

"Stop this!" Satan bellowed, shrinking back down to normal size.

"Can't now," Peter said blithely. "Minion's soul hangs in balance. Call it, Steve." He flipped the coin in a high arch.

I was paralyzed. My tongue seemed stuck to the roof of my mouth. I looked over at Satan, who was grinning.

"Hurry!" Flo yelled, giving me a shove.

"T … tails! Tails!" I stuttered.

The coin landed.

Chapter 28

Now, I've heard about this happening. Even saw a 'Twilight Zone' episode that was built around it, but never did I expect to really see it. The coin landed on its edge, perfectly balanced.

"Well, I never," St. Peter said.

"Will you look at that," said a man standing behind us.

The coin began to wobble. I looked toward Satan, who was concentrating intensely on the coin, his lips pursed. "Hey, no fair!" I yelled.

From the direction of the Pearly Gates, a breeze began to blow. It tossed the coin on its head.

"Tails it is," Peter smiled as he looked toward the entrance to Heaven. "I think that's definitive."

At that moment, a nimbus of light surrounded me. When my blindness went away, I knew what had happened. The good part of my soul had returned to me from the Well of [Damned] Souls.

A loud string of expletives emitted from Satan. He stared first at me and then at the Gates with loathing. With a final curse, he disappeared in a puff of black smoke.

Beelzebub had remained impassive through it all, but now he caught my eye. There was a slight smile, and a little salute, then he too was gone.

"Ow!" I yelled. My horns had just fallen on my feet. I reached in my trousers and pulled out my tail. It wasn't attached to me either anymore. I looked questioningly at St. Peter.

"What did you expect?" he said, grinning. "We can't have a demon in Hell. Sorry about the hair though."

I turned to Flo. "What does he mean?"

Florence ran her fingers over my forehead. I could feel her fingers touch skin that moments before had been covered with thick locks of hair. "Now you look like you did when I first fell in love with you. You know, I always liked you best this way."

I took her hand and smiled. "Then, it's perfect. Now what, St. Peter?"

Peter had gone back to work, processing the fellow behind me. Turns out that he had won the jackpot and was headed toward the Pearly Gates. "Now you follow him into Heaven."

"Let's go, Steve," Flo said, taking my arm.

"What?" I was a bit disoriented. Everything in my afterlife had reversed so quickly.

"You're going to Heaven, and I'm going with you. We're never going to be parted again."

"But, but what about your work down in Hell?"

"I'll miss helping down there," she said, with some regret, "but we're a couple now, and if it takes going to Heaven to stay together, well, so be it."

"If it takes … " St. Peter shook his head. "Florence, you are one of a kind."

"Come on, Steve," she said gently, and led me toward the Gates.

The man who preceded me had just reached the steps, when a black chute opened at his feet to one side of him. A load of coal seemed to fall from his body. He looked idly at what had happened, shrugged, and continued on to Heaven.

I stopped short. "Hey, Pete," I said, with uncharacteristic familiarity. His head popped up from the Book of Life. "What just happened to that man?"

"Oh, the chute? Well, it's not unlike what happens at the moment of Damnation. Unalloyed evil is not allowed into Hell, and so it leaves the bodies of the Saved before they enter the

Gates."

I turned to Flo. "You've been to Heaven before. Has this happened to you?"

"No," she said simply. "Apparently, and I say this without false modesty, what little evil exists in my soul is inseparable from the good."

"I doubt I can say the same." I looked over at Peter, who shook his head emphatically no.

"Hmmm." Ever since the flash of light, I'd felt like myself. During my sixty years of damnation, I'd always felt a bit dumbed down, as if I'd lost a portion of my being, which of course I had. For the first time in a long while, I felt whole. I looked at the chute, still open, as if it was waiting to gobble up a portion of me.

I was good. I was bad. I was a mix of both, but I was me now. I felt whole, integrated. "Flo," I said slowly.

"What, darling?" She seemed to understand I was wrestling with something, and she was prepared to give me the time I needed to sort it out.

"If you had not met me, if you weren't in love with me, what would you do? Would you go to Heaven now? Are you ready?"

"In all honesty, no," she said demurely. "My thoughts on this really haven't changed. I can do more good in Hell than in Heaven."

I beamed in pride at my love. "Then, let's make it a partnership."

"What?" she said.

"What?" said St. Peter, coming up to us. "Oh, no. Not again!"

"Florence, Peter, if I'm damned, I lose a portion of myself. If I'm saved, I still lose a portion of myself. Maybe it's a bad portion, but it's part of what makes me who I am."

"That's what I thought," Peter huffed, then went over to his desk. He opened a drawer and drew out a key, tossing it to me. "For the Elevator. You're still saved, you know. Always will be. If you ever change your mind, this will make sure you're able to get back up here."

"Thank you, St. Peter," I said, pocketing the key. "For everything. Come on Flo, let's go back to Hell and do some good."

Grinning, Flo turned toward the Elevator.

I stopped her. "Why don't we take the scenic route? We can visit a bit with Ronnie and Cerberus."

Flo embraced me, wiped a tear from her eye and nodded.

Arm in arm, we headed back to the River Styx.

Made in the USA
Middletown, DE
18 March 2017